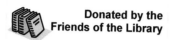

**Donated by the
Friends of the Library**

Murder of a Creped Suzette

**Center Point
Large Print**

Also by Denise Swanson and available from Center Point Large Print:

Murder of a Royal Pain
Murder of a Wedding Belle
Murder of a Bookstore Babe

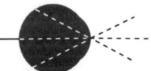

**This Large Print Book carries the
Seal of Approval of N.A.V.H.**

Murder of a Creped Suzette

Denise Swanson

CENTER POINT LARGE PRINT
THORNDIKE, MAINE

This Center Point Large Print edition is published in the year 2012 by arrangement with NAL Signet, a member of Penguin Group (USA) Inc.

PUBLISHER'S NOTE: This is a work of fiction. Names, characters, places, and incidents either are the product of the author's imagination or are used fictitiously, and any resemblance to actual persons, living or dead, business establishments, events, or locales is entirely coincidental.

The text of this Large Print edition is unabridged.
In other aspects, this book may
vary from the original edition.
Printed in the United States of America
on permanent paper.
Set in 16-point Times New Roman type.

ISBN: 978-1-61173-306-8

Library of Congress Cataloging-in-Publication Data

Swanson, Denise.
  Murder of a creped suzette : a Scumble river mystery / Denise
Swanson. — Large print ed.
    p. cm. — (Center Point large print edition)
  ISBN 978-1-61173-306-8 (library binding : alk. paper)
  1. Denison, Skye (Fictitious character)—Fiction.
    2. Murder—Investigation—Fiction.
    3. School psychologists—Fiction.
    4. Women psychologists—Fiction. 5. Large type books. I. Title.
PS3619.W36M84 2012
813′.6—dc23
                                                    2011041788

To my good friend, and trivia team member extraordinaire, Beverlee (Angel) Porter. Thank you for nearly single-handedly spreading the word about my books throughout Canada.

Acknowledgments

A big thank-you to Donna Sears for telling me about a music promoter trying to turn her town into the "Branson of the West."

Author's Note

In July of 2000, when the first book in my Scumble River series, *Murder of a Small-Town Honey*, was published, it was written in "real time." It was the year 2000 in Skye's life as well as mine, but after several books in a series, time becomes a problem. It takes me from seven months to a year to write a book, and then it is usually another year from the time I turn that book in to my editor until the reader sees it on a bookstore shelf. This can make the timeline confusing. Different authors handle this matter in different ways. After a great deal of deliberation, I decided that Skye and her friends and family would age more slowly than those of us who don't live in Scumble River. So to catch everyone up, the following is when the books take place:

Murder of a Small-Town Honey—August 2000
Murder of a Sweet Old Lady—March 2001
Murder of a Sleeping Beauty—April 2002
Murder of a Snake in the Grass—August 2002
Murder of a Barbie and Ken—November 2002
Murder of a Pink Elephant—February 2003
Murder of a Smart Cookie—June 2003

And this is when the Scumble River short story and novella take place:

• • •

Chapter 1

"WALKING THE FLOOR OVER YOU"

Skye Denison had to admit that Flint James was hot. Neither the engagement ring on her finger nor her utter aversion to sports of any kind altered the fact that the pro quarterback turned country singer looked like a Greek statue—if statues wore cowboy hats, had smoky whiskey-colored eyes, and sported really good tans.

Flint leaned on the side railing of Scumble River Park's newly constructed grandstand, gazing at the early evening sky. The rising star appeared unconcerned about whatever was transpiring at the back of the stage, where a cluster of guys wearing jeans, T-shirts, and baseball caps surrounded a man dressed in an expensive country-western-style suit.

To Skye, the group of men looked like the featured critters in a Whac-A-Mole game—first one head would pop up, scan the audience, and duck back down; then another and another, before starting the process all over again. It was obvious that something was wrong, but what? While the others appeared merely irritated, Mr. Suit looked apoplectic.

According to the liberally distributed flyers, the program was supposed to start at six thirty. It was already a quarter to seven, and although the park was ablaze with lights and there were amplifiers scattered around the stage's perimeter, nothing was happening.

Perhaps the out-of-towners didn't understand how much the good citizens of Scumble River valued punctuality, but Skye knew that if something didn't happen soon, people would begin to leave. Small-town Illinoisans considered arriving fifteen minutes early as the equivalent of being on time, the stated hour as barely acceptable, and anything afterward as intolerably late.

The only thing that might persuade everyone to hang around was the complimentary refreshments. An open bar tended to keep most Scumble Riverites happy for quite a while.

Skye fanned herself with the old grocery list she had found in the pocket of her khaki capris and watched for her fiancé, Wally Boyd. As chief of police, he was on duty tonight.

Usually he wouldn't be working on a Saturday night, but the entire Scumble River police force—six full-time officers and two part-timers—was patrolling this event. An affair like this one needed all the crowd control available. It wasn't often that a celebrity like Flint James performed anywhere near Scumble River, let alone at a free concert.

Which brought up a good question. Why? Why would Flint James agree to come to the middle of nowhere and sing, especially without charging for tickets?

As Skye slapped at a gnat buzzing around her ear, she caught sight of her uncle, the mayor. Dante Leofanti was seated front and center on something resembling a red canvas throne. It had a canopy, a table attached to the arm, and even a footrest. His wife, Olive, sat by his side in a smaller version of the same elaborate chair, although hers was baby blue.

Skye narrowed her eyes. Nothing happened in the mayor's town without his knowledge and permission. Dante must have approved the use of the park, the permit to build the grandstand, and the authorization to serve alcohol. He would certainly know why Flint James was singing here, but did Skye care enough to go over there and ask him? No. Dante treated information like a commodity, and she didn't want to be in his debt.

More to the point, she really didn't *need* to know. There was an extremely fine line between concerned and nosy, and because Skye suffered from curiosity overdrive she usually erred on the wrong side of that line. But not this time.

She wasn't on duty as either the town's school psychologist or the police department's psychological consultant. She was just at the concert to hear some good music and have fun with her friends. Whatever was going on was not her problem. For once she would mind her own business.

Speaking of friends, where was Trixie? Skye's BFF, Trixie Frayne, and Trixie's husband, Owen, were supposed to have shown up half an hour ago. Skye checked her cell phone. It was on—she often forgot to power it up—but she didn't have any messages, so her friend hadn't tried to reach her.

Skye attempted to call Trixie, but got her voice mail. After leaving a message asking Trixie and Owen to meet her by the refreshment stand, Skye threaded her way through the crowd looking for them.

While she walked, Skye dug through her purse for a barrette, desperate to get her humidity-frizzed chestnut curls out of her face. The freshly ironed white sleeveless blouse she had put on just before leaving home was now wrinkled and limp, clinging to her ample curves like a damp shower curtain. Autumn had begun three weeks earlier, but the unusually high temperature made it feel like it was still the dog days of summer.

Skye considered giving up on Trixie and Owen and going home. She could relax in the air-conditioning, watch a movie, and spend some quality time with her cat. Although she liked country music, without Wally or her friends the concert wouldn't be much fun.

Besides, she wasn't fond of outdoor events

unless the weather was perfect—a circumstance rarely found in the Midwest, where it was often necessary to switch from the heat to the A/C and vice versa on the same day.

Still, when you lived in the same small town where you grew up, worked in public education, and were engaged to the police chief, it was a good idea to show your face at social gatherings. And Skye had finally admitted that she did want to be a part of the community. It had taken her a while, but after five years she recognized that moving back to Scumble River, despite its rigid sense of right and wrong, had been a good decision.

Given the choice, she would stay in her hometown for the rest of her life. Too bad this evening was beginning to feel like it would last at least that long.

Skye had reached the edge of the lawn-chair-and-blanket-seated audience without spotting her friends. Where in the heck were they? She ground her teeth. *Shoot!* Not only was there no sign of Trixie and Owen, but now she needed to find a bathroom—fast.

Unfortunately, both Port-a-Potties had lengthy lines and Skye was fairly sure she couldn't wait for her turn. On to plan B. There were bathrooms in the picnic area located behind the grandstand at the far end of the park. With any luck, no one would have thought of them.

Skye took off at a brisk trot, but a few steps from

her goal, she was stopped by a red plastic ribbon strung between several sawhorses. A large white sign with black lettering read:

Employees of Country Roads Tour only.
Trespassers will be prosecuted.

Crap! There was no time to come up with a plan C. If she didn't get to a toilet soon, she would embarrass herself big-time. Skye looked around. A silver Airstream with COUNTRY ROADS TOUR painted on its side was pulled in front of the bathroom, but there wasn't anyone in sight. She stopped and listened. It was completely quiet. Excellent. She'd be in and out with no one the wiser.

Skye ducked under the ribbon, paused for a nanosecond, then darted toward her objective. Arriving a little out of breath, she found that the trailer was parked so close to the building she could barely get the screen door halfway open. She squeezed through the gap and sighed with relief when she saw the empty stalls.

A few minutes later, Skye was washing her hands when she heard angry voices coming from inside the RV. *Yikes!* She had to get out of there before she was discovered and arrested. Wouldn't that be a delightful headline: Chief's Fiancée Arrested for Using Forbidden Bathroom.

Skye plastered herself against the wall, willing

herself to become invisible, which was a stretch considering her opulent figure. She snuck a quick look through the doorway. A large open window was situated directly across from the bathroom's entrance. Why in the heck didn't they have the air-conditioning on and their windows closed like normal people?

While waiting for her hair appointment last week, she had read in *Entertainment Weekly* that some singers disliked A/C because they thought it was bad for their vocal cords, but this was ridiculous. It was close to ninety degrees and muggy; surely those conditions couldn't be good for anyone, even a star's delicate throat.

Skye shook her head. Why didn't matter. The window was open, and if she tried to leave now, the suit-wearing guy from the stage who was talking heatedly to Flint James would see her and call the police.

Taking another peek, Skye noted that Flint's usually handsome face was an ugly scarlet mask, his broad shoulders were rigid, and his hands were fisted. His previous air of indifference was gone, and it looked as if he was itching to punch the other man in the face.

The ex-quarterback had a good five inches and fifty pounds of muscle on Mr. Suit, and could easily cause some real damage to the other guy. Flint might even kill him if the blow landed in exactly the right spot.

Should she call Wally? Make her presence known? Skye wavered. Maybe it was a guy thing, and she would just get herself in trouble if she interfered. A good time to keep your mouth shut was when you were in deep water, and she'd promised herself she would stop rushing in to help people who hadn't asked for her assistance. Then again, she didn't want anyone to get hurt.

Before she could decide, Mr. Suit's booming voice brought her attention back to the two men. "We have no choice. Suzette isn't here and we can't reach her. We have to get this show on the road."

"That's not my problem, Rex." Flint jabbed Mr. Suit, aka Rex, in the chest. "The star does not go on first. And I'm the star."

Obviously the opening act was MIA. Skye wrinkled her brow, trying to remember what she had heard about Suzette Neal. All she knew about the girl singer was her age—twenty-two—and that she had lived in the area as a child, although no one Skye had spoken to had recognized Suzette's name or claimed her as kin.

"It's more than half an hour since we were supposed to start the program." Rex grabbed Flint's shoulder. "I order you to get your ass onstage and sing."

"No." Flint shook off Rex's hand as if it were an annoying insect. "Check my contract. You can't force me to perform out of order."

"Do it this one time and I'll make it worth your while." Rex's tone turned cajoling. "This concert is no big deal. Just a freebie to get the locals on our side. I promise it will be good for us both."

"That's what Suzette wants. You already gave her one of my best songs—one I wanted to sing myself—and you forced me to do a duet with her." Flint crossed his arms. "Don't think I'm not onto her schemes."

"You're not the only one who's onto her." A blonde dressed in skintight jeans, a red sequined tank top, and crimson stilettos pushed her way between Flint and Rex.

Skye shrank back against the wall. She hadn't realized there was anyone else in the Airstream.

Cocking her thumb at Rex, the woman said, "I warned him about that girl. I told him I didn't trust her as far as I could run in high heels."

"Kallista, sweetheart." Rex sandwiched the blonde's fingers between both of his palms. "I'm sure something terrible must have happened to keep Suzette away. You know she was dying to sing for her hometown and show everyone how far she's come."

"She probably isn't even really from this place." Kallista blew an irritated breath through heavily glossed lips. "She only said she was after you told her you'd decided to open the new country music theater here."

Skye blinked. A country music theater in

17

Scumble River? How would people react to that? They generally didn't like change, but a theater smacked of money and glamour, so maybe they'd be tempted.

"Now, baby girl, how about you do your big daddy an itty-bitty favor and go back in the bedroom and try calling Suzette again? Then later tonight your big daddy will do you just how you like." Rex turned Kallista around and patted her on the rear until she started walking.

Ew, ew, ew. That was just icky. Why did men talk like that to grown women?

Skye squirmed, but focused back on the action when Rex said to Flint, "You have to help me out here. I thought you were a team player."

"Right. And what did that get me last time? A blown knee and a ruined career." Flint shook his head. "Now I'm looking out for number one."

"With that attitude, I don't know how you fool all your fans into thinking you're such a nice guy."

"Really?" Flint let out a scornful huff. "You're the one who taught me that sincerity is everything, and once you can fake that, you've got it made."

Rex ignored Flint's jab. "You seem to be forgetting that you're my creation." Rex snapped off each word as if they were bites of peanut brittle. "Without me you'd still be singing at a honky-tonk, living in your truck, and depending on the tips from a pickled-egg jar to eat."

"Don't give me that crap. We both know you

18

didn't do me any favors." Flint spat out the words contemptuously. "If I hadn't been a damn good singer and songwriter, you wouldn't have raised a finger to help me."

"There's more to success in this business than talent," Rex retaliated, his voice rising.

"Bullshit!" Flint leaned down until he was nose to nose with the smaller man. "Now find that little whore and get her out onstage before I really get mad." He grasped Rex's lapels and lifted him off his feet. "I'm not letting you or her ruin my career."

Yikes! Skye whipped out her cell phone. It was time to call the cops.

Chapter 2

"SEVEN-YEAR ACHE"

Before Skye had finished dialing Wally's number, a dusty black pickup pulled perpendicular to the Airstream. She craned her neck around the doorway and watched a young woman dressed in a ruffled denim miniskirt, a pink stretch-lace, off-the-shoulder top, and pink cowboy boots bolt out of the truck before it had completely stopped moving.

The woman ran around the front of the RV, disappeared from Skye's view for a second, then reappeared in the trailer's window as she flung herself at Rex's feet, sobbing. "I'm so sorry. My cousin insisted on taking me to meet his friends in Joliet and I-55 was a parking lot and the battery on my cell phone is dead and—"

"We'll talk about it later, Suzette." Rex hauled the girl off the floor. "Right now you need to perform."

"But my hair and makeup—" Suzette touched her waist-length black mane.

"There's no time for that." Rex propelled her backward. "You look fine."

"But my costume," Suzette wailed. "My beautiful sparkly dress."

"Next time."

As Rex and Suzette disappeared from sight, Flint called after them, "Don't forget to tell that new bass player that a diminished fifth is not an empty bottle of Jack Daniel's."

Rex grunted before screaming at the band to get onstage. A few seconds later Skye could hear him yelling, "Get your rear in gear, Suzette, while we still have some audience left."

Skye turned her attention to the pickup. It was still idling by the side of the trailer, but from her angle she couldn't make out the driver. Who was Suzette's cousin? Black pickups were as common as cornfields in Scumble River, so that was no clue.

As if sensing Skye's interest, the driver backed up and screeched away in a cloud of dust; a soccer ball tow-hitch cover and a metallic oval bumper sticker sparkled in the taillights. She glanced toward the Airstream, but the window was now closed. The shades had been pulled down and there was nothing left to see.

This was her chance to escape unnoticed. Skye slipped out of the bathroom, sprinted across the grass, and zipped around the sawhorses.

Once she was past the barrier, she could hear instruments tuning up, and she took off running toward the grandstand. It looked like the concert would finally start, and after all she'd been through, no way would she miss a minute of it.

Skye spotted Trixie at the very rear of the audience, sitting on a blanket spread under an enormous tree. There was a good view of the grandstand and the oak's trunk provided a backrest. Trust Trixie to get a good spot, even when she was among the last to arrive.

Waving, Skye headed in her friend's direction. Trixie wore cutoffs, a tight hot-pink tank top, and fuchsia sandals that laced up her calves. Not exactly the look most small towns expected from their high school librarians. But with her short cap of smooth brown hair and big brown eyes, Trixie looked cute in the outfit rather than trashy.

As Skye sat down, Trixie handed her a blue plastic cup and demanded, "Where have you been?"

"Where have *I* been?" Skye took a sip and coughed. Trixie had added rum to the Diet Coke. Quite a bit of rum. *Uh-oh.* Trixie generally drank only when she was upset. "I was here on time. Where were you? And where's Owen? Is one of the animals sick?"

Owen was a farmer, and the livestock's well-being was his number one priority. A while back he had sold off all the cattle and pigs, but a few days ago he'd bought a herd of exotic animals, having decided to try his luck with emus and llamas.

Trixie hadn't been pleased with her husband's purchase, but the farmer's daughter in Skye had been sympathetic. It was only a couple of weeks into the harvest, and already everyone knew that this year's searing drought would cause yields to be at least twenty percent below average. Farming had such a thin profit margin, Owen probably felt the need to try something drastic to get into the black.

"I have no idea where Owen is." Trixie took a gulp of her drink. "And those stupid animals are fine. They live better than I do."

"He isn't at home?" Skye raised a brow. Except for business, Owen rarely set foot off his acreage. And she doubted he was buying seed at seven o'clock on a Saturday night.

"No. He left around two thirty." Trixie wrinkled her forehead. "He told me he had to talk to some guy, but he never answered me when I asked who. I assumed he'd be back by five for supper, but he didn't show up."

"Is that unusual?"

"Very." Trixie bobbed her head. "He never misses dinner."

"Hmm." Skye wasn't sure what to say. "That is strange. Maybe he had trouble with his pickup. You said the engine's been cutting out."

"If he had a cell phone like everyone else in the known universe, I could have called him." She grimaced. "Now I don't know if he's dead, drunk, or joined the Foreign Legion."

"Does he usually let you know where he's going and when he'll be home?" Skye wasn't sure if Trixie was worried or angry or both.

"Most of the time." Trixie tore a paper napkin in to shreds, not meeting Skye's eyes. "But we've been fighting, and he might be mad at me."

"I could ask Wally if there've been any accidents in the area," Skye offered, not asking the reason for the couple's quarrel.

"Maybe later." Trixie pushed out her bottom lip. "I left Owen a note. If he doesn't show up or phone before the end of the concert, we can involve Wally."

"Okay." Skye hugged her friend, and as she sat back she remembered attempting to reach Trixie earlier. "You know, when you were late, I tried your cell and it went straight to voice mail. Have you checked it lately? Maybe Owen tried calling, couldn't reach you, and left a message like I did."

"Shoot!" Trixie dug her phone from her purse and flipped it open. "I turned it off when I was at the library and forgot to switch it back on." She pressed a button, then scrolled through the in-box.

"Anything?" Skye asked.

"Just you." Trixie sagged against the tree trunk. "Nothing from Owen."

"Darn."

"Never mind." Trixie pasted a smile on her face and handed Skye a bag of chips. "Let's enjoy the music and worry about my missing husband later."

Suzette had a good voice. Skye wasn't sure if it was a great voice or if the girl had star quality, but Suzette was pretty and the crowd was well lubricated, so when she finished, the audience hooted, whistled, and applauded enthusiastically.

While Flint James was being introduced and taking his place, Trixie said to Skye, "So, you never did tell me where you were when I got here."

Skye explained about her pressing bathroom mission and the scene she had witnessed, then added, "I haven't heard anything about a country music theater going up in Scumble River. Have you?"

Trixie drained her cup and stood. "One of the

24

kids mentioned that his father's construction company had been hired to work at the old Hutton dairy farm, renovating the barn and outbuildings."

"The property near the I-55 exit?"

"I think so." Trixie wrinkled her forehead. "I'm surprised there haven't had to be town meetings about zoning issues and other stuff regarding the theater."

"I'm not." Skye crossed her arms. "If this Rex guy approached Dante with a plan to bring tourist dollars into town, and the mayor liked what he heard, Dante would call a closed meeting of the town council and get whatever approvals he needed that way."

"Yeah. The whole council is full of good ol' boys your uncle can control." Trixie pointed to Skye's cup. "Want another one?"

Skye shook her head. "I'm good." There had been enough rum in her first drink to last her all evening. Besides, alcohol made the heat feel worse.

While Skye watched Trixie join the line at the bar, Flint began his first song. His sexy baritone sent a shiver up her spine. He sang about shooting to the top, falling to the bottom, and starting all over again. A journey to which Skye could relate.

She was lost in the music when someone touched her shoulder. She swallowed a startled yelp and looked up. Owen had arrived.

"Hey." He smoothed his straight black hair off his forehead.

"Hi." Skye noted that his hair was wet. He must have come straight from a shower.

"Trixie around?"

"Yep." Skye jerked her chin toward the bar. "She's getting a drink."

"Okay." Owen fingered his silver belt buckle. "Thanks."

When he turned away, it struck Skye that she rarely saw him wearing anything but work clothes. Tonight he had on navy dress slacks, a blue-and-yellow-plaid pearl-snapped shirt, and snakeskin Tony Lamas. She eyed him thoughtfully. Owen was attractive in a sinewy, ascetic way. Not her type, but she could see the appeal.

Skye watched as he intercepted Trixie on her way back to the blanket. He took his wife's arm and they moved several feet from the performance area. Skye was glad they had opted for privacy. She didn't want to be present for a conversation that was bound to be unpleasant. Besides, Trixie would tell her all she wanted Skye to know, and that would be best for both of them.

Flint sang two more songs before Trixie returned, alone. She sat silently until the concert ended an hour later, with Flint and Suzette singing a duet.

Once the clapping died down, Mr. Suit took the stage and announced, "Hello. My name is Rex Taylor." He had a compact build, tightly curled sandy-colored hair, and an air of commanding

26

self-confidence. "I'm a music promoter from Nashville and I have a vision. A vision of prosperity for all. A vision of Scumble River as the next Branson, Missouri."

Skye narrowed her eyes. Rex didn't look like a psychic, and she'd bet his vision had less than a fifty-fifty chance of coming true.

He had paused, no doubt expecting applause, but the audience was unusually hushed, as if waiting for the next cowboy boot to drop.

Skye scanned the crowd, noting a mixture of smiles, frowns, and puzzled expressions. Clearly, her fellow Scumble Riverites were as wary as she was.

Finally, after the silence built to an uncomfortable intensity, Rex cleared his throat and went on. "I put on this free concert tonight so you could see what the future can be like. See that if you help my dream come true, you can share in the rewards."

Was this some pyramid scheme? Skye wondered. Now people were buzzing with anticipation. She bit the inside of her mouth, worried they were about to be taken in by a con man.

Rex allowed the excitement to build, then said, "This project will mean an influx of jobs for the community, not to mention tourist dollars."

Trixie elbowed Skye. "This guy's awfully slick. The town better be mighty careful."

"I wonder how deep Uncle Dante is already into this scheme."

Before Trixie could answer, Rex's voice rang out, "Right now, we'll be hiring mostly construction workers, but once the first venue is ready, we'll need employees for various types of positions."

Skye and Trixie looked at each other. All the small towns in the area had been hard-hit by factory closings and crop failures. People would definitely want to buy the goods this guy was selling.

Rex finished his speech with, "And since I want all of my new friends to have a good time, the bar is staying open until ten."

A rousing cheer went up, followed by a mad dash toward the free drinks.

Skye got to her feet, saying to Trixie, "Want to come with me and talk to the mayor?"

"No, thanks." Trixie started packing up. "I'd better head home."

"Okay." Skye hoped everything would be all right between Trixie and Owen. "Good luck."

As Skye walked toward the grandstand, the straw that had been spread over the ground in an attempt to make the area look like the inside of a barn clung to her bare legs. She frowned. It was a good thing Rex hadn't brought in cows and pigs for an even more authentic ambiance, or the sandals she was wearing would really have been a fashion mistake.

While Skye made her way through the crowd,

she overheard the owner of the real estate agency saying to the people seated around him, "This could be exactly what Scumble River—heck, all of Stanley County—needs. We've been trying for years to get tourists off the highway and into our town to spend their money."

A couple of steps later, Skye came upon Dr. Wraige, the school district superintendent, making a speech to several parents clustered in front of him. "Our school budgets are so far in the red they look like a Valentine's Day card. Taylor's plan will bring in businesses that will provide a tax base of which we are sorely in need. And as I always say to our students, if opportunity isn't knocking, it's time to build a door."

The last group Skye passed before reaching her uncle was a bunch of eighteen- to twenty-year-olds. Several of them looked familiar, especially the girl leading the discussion. Xenia Craughwell wore the righteousness of youth and the irreverence of black nail polish.

Skye was well acquainted with Xenia, a high-IQ rebel who had barely made it through Scumble River High and now attended film school in Chicago. Xenia had raised an arm and was outlining a plan of attack to persuade Rex Taylor to include other types of music in addition to country, and to build a movie theater as well.

Skye pursed her lips. All three factions had good

points, but she was still worried. She'd seen too many get-rich-quick schemes come and go. And she didn't want her town or its citizens to be bamboozled.

Chapter 3

"FAMILY TRADITION"

When Skye finally made it through the crowd and reached the grandstand, she saw the mayor hurrying away with Rex Taylor. She started to follow the two men, but stopped after only a few steps. Maybe it would be better to talk to her uncle another time—alone. The mayor tended to bluster a tiny bit less, and tell the truth a tiny bit more, when he wasn't playing to the balcony. For Dante, all the world was a stage, and he didn't care where the audience sat.

As Skye hesitated, a soft voice near her hip asked, "Did you need to speak to your uncle, dear?"

"Not really." Skye leaned down and kissed her aunt's paper-soft cheek. Olive smelled of old-fashioned face powder and attar of roses.

"He'll be right back." Olive sat rigidly, as if she had a metal rod for a spine. Her short ash blond hair was sprayed into a helmet so hard that NASA could use it for the next moonwalk. Her pale yellow shoes precisely matched the stripes in her dress and the purse leaning against her leg. Pearls adorned her ears, throat, and wrist.

"That's okay, Aunt Olive." Skye patted her aunt's arm. "It wasn't anything important. I was just a little curious about Mr. Taylor's plans."

Skye tried to back away, but her aunt gripped her hand. "Don't go." Olive had moved to Scumble River from Chicago as an eighteen-year-old bride, and nearly forty-five years later she still seemed ill at ease if she was left alone among the natives for too long. "Really, Dante won't be a minute." She peered anxiously over her shoulder.

"Do you need something, Aunt Olive?" Skye felt sorry for the fragile woman.

"No." Olive pulled Skye down into Dante's abandoned throne next to her own seat. "We never seem to get a chance to chat. I haven't seen you since the Fourth of July picnic, and we hardly got to say more than a few words to each other there."

"Family parties are a little overwhelming." Skye yanked the footrest's handle upward but returned it to its original locked position when she nearly tipped herself out of the chair. "How have you and Uncle Dante been?"

"Good." Olive nodded at her own word as if trying to convince herself. "Everything's fine with us. How are your brother and his new wife?"

Vince had shocked everyone by eloping to Las Vegas with Skye's Alpha Sigma Alpha sorority sister Loretta Steiner. Skye knew that was her aunt's real reason for their tête-à-tête. Even after a month, their marriage was a hot topic among the town's gossips.

"Excellent." Skye was happy to talk about her brother's nuptials, especially if it kept the conversation away from her own stalled wedding plans. She and Wally were in limbo until his annulment came through.

Skye peeked at her watch and saw it was nearly nine thirty. She was supposed to meet Wally in a few minutes, but with the free booze still flowing, she doubted he'd be able to leave anytime soon. The number of officers required to keep the peace was directly proportional to the amount of beer consumed.

"Your mother said they're planning to live in town and Loretta will commute to the city." Olive's expression was doubtful. "Can that be right? I mean, it's a good hour and a half one way."

"Yes, Mom's right." Skye gazed intently into her aunt's eyes, not wanting Olive to stir up the family. "They've already started looking at houses."

"That's what May said, but I wondered if it was just a pipe dream on her part."

"Not at all. Since Loretta is a criminal defense

attorney, she doesn't need to be in her office every day. She can telecommute a lot of the time."

"How modern." Olive sounded slightly wistful as she added, "Though I think Vince might have enjoyed living in the city."

"I guess." Skye wrinkled her nose. "Then again, I think Vince enjoys himself wherever he is."

"Well, it will certainly be interesting when we *finally* get to meet her for ourselves."

Skye had cautioned her brother that eloping would open up a can of worms. It didn't take much bait for their relatives to start gossiping. "Mom is planning a party for them around Christmas."

"That'll be nice. Although the holidays are such a busy time of year." Olive leaned down and picked up her handbag. "And since we're all eager to have a chance to get to know Loretta and her family, sooner would be better." She unsnapped the gold clasp and rummaged inside. "We were certainly astonished when we heard that Vince was married."

"I can understand that." Skye chuckled. "No one thought he would ever settle down, since he was having such fun playing the field."

"True." Olive pulled a yellow lace-edged handkerchief from the depths of her pocketbook and dabbed her brow. "But we were more surprised by his choice of brides than by his tying the knot."

"Oh?" Skye's stomach tightened.

"Yes." Olive replaced her hanky and took out a gold tube. "Loretta certainly wasn't what we were expecting for Vince's wife."

"Why is that?" Skye's voice had an edge to it. Loretta was African-American and Skye had been afraid some of the family might object to an interracial marriage. "She's beautiful and intelligent."

"I'm sure she is, dear." Olive applied a fresh coat of dusty rose lipstick. "But perhaps a tad too sophisticated for Vince?"

"Huh?" Skye was relieved her aunt wasn't referring to the color of Loretta's skin, but had Olive just called Vince a hick?

"What she means," an impatient male voice said, breaking into their conversation, "is that Vince likes them young, pretty, dumb, and agreeable, not mature, elegant, smart, and with a mind of their own."

Dante had materialized in front of them like a malevolent poltergeist. He was short and stout, wearing a disgruntled expression and a black denim leisure suit that had gone out of style forty years ago.

Skye forced a pleasant smile and said, "Vince has changed—grown up."

"Right." Dante snorted. "They'll be in divorce court before the new year."

"You're wrong, Uncle Dante." Skye refused to

let his statement stand. Others could kowtow to the mayor, but she wasn't about to—not on this issue. "Why would you even say that? Vince and Loretta are in love and that's all that matters."

"Love is a myth women made up to keep men in line." Dante folded his arms. "It's certainly not a good reason to get married."

"Then why did you get married?" Skye blurted out, then wished she hadn't when she saw her aunt's stricken expression.

"To produce an heir." Dante waddled closer to the women, looking a lot like a pissed-off penguin. "Now, if you two are through gossiping and Skye will get her butt out of my seat, I'd like to get out of here before the parking lot becomes a madhouse."

Skye jumped up and gestured to Dante's canvas throne. "Be my guest." She tilted her head. "You must have had very important business with Mr. Taylor to stick around this long."

Dante didn't respond to Skye's probe. Instead he jerked his chin at his wife and said, "Olive, are you going to sit there all night?"

"No, Dante." Olive leaped to her feet, nearly saluting. "Sorry."

Dante ignored her, folded both the chairs, shoved them into their carrying bags, heaved the straps over his shoulders, and picked up the cooler, then marched off without a backward glance.

"Bye, dear." Olive waved to Skye, then hastily tottered after her husband, but not before Skye noticed the tears on her cheeks.

"Shit!" Skye stomped her foot. She had failed to learn anything about Rex Taylor's scheme, and she'd hurt her aunt. "Shit! Shit! Shit!"

"Do you kiss your fiancé with that mouth?" Wally's amused baritone enveloped Skye.

She turned to find him directly behind her. "Only if he's lucky."

Chief Walter Boyd was an extremely attractive man who superbly filled out his crisply starched police uniform. He had eyes the color of Godiva chocolate, curly black hair with just a touch of silver at the temples, and a year-round tan. But it wasn't his handsome face or sexy body that made Skye love him; it was his sense of humor and his compassionate nature.

"My horoscope said something great would occur today." Wally's dazzling white smile was rueful. "And thus far nothing even close to good has happened to me, so you must be it."

Skye flung herself into his embrace, reveling in feeling his muscular arms around her and his solid chest beneath her cheek. "You can tell me all about it on the way home." She gave him a lingering kiss, then took his hand and tried to lead him toward the parking lot.

Wally didn't budge. "That's why I was looking for you. It'll be quite a while until I can leave."

"Darn." Skye's smile was teasing. "And here I was planning to make you forget all about your troubles. Is there a problem?"

"Too many to list." Wally winced as the sound of shouting interrupted them. "Let's just say I sure hope they run out of beer soon."

"Gee, and I thought the open bar would bring out the best in everyone," Skye mocked.

A cherry bomb exploded somewhere behind them. "Sorry about tonight," Wally said over his shoulder as he took off running. "I'll take you somewhere nice for brunch after church tomorrow."

"No problem." Skye waved. "Go do your duty and keep Scumble River safe."

On the way to her car, Skye paused to watch a brawny man in his early thirties tip over one of the Port-a-Potties. Once it was on its side, the man yanked open the door and pulled out the occupant. He plucked a plastic six-pack holder off the guy's head and plopped it on his own skull. A tussle ensued between the two men, with the victor bloodying the nose of his foe and reclaiming his crown.

Clutching a bottle of Budweiser, the winner climbed on top of the downed outhouse and screamed, "I'm the king of the world."

Skye shook her head. Testosterone really should be declared a controlled substance.

Not far from the monarch's throne, a dozen or so spectators circled two women who were stripping off their clothes to the song "Boot Scootin' Boogie," which was blaring from a boom box nearby. Once the exhibitionists were down to their bras and panties, the bystanders cheering them on tossed each lady a can of Aqua Net—apparently the only weapons available. Once they had drenched each other with the hairspray, the women squirted the onlookers until the canisters were empty.

Immediately two gentlemen from the audience handed each woman a pillow. They turned back-to-back, paced off ten steps, turned, and ran at each other. A few smacks and the pillows began to tear. Soon feathers filled the air and Skye quickly moved away before she started sneezing.

She was walking near the riverbank when she spotted several guys, some clad in boxer shorts and others in tighty whities, attempting to jump into the river but being kept at bay by most of the Scumble River police force. It looked like an adult version of the game Red Rover, Red Rover. As one of the wannabe swimmers ran at the line of cops and was driven back into the group, another of the aspiring skinny-dippers would try to break through the wall of officers and leap into the water.

The would-be bathers were either drunk past the point of all survival instincts or not from Scumble River, because the locals all knew that the dam caused dangerous currents, and attempting to swim off the park's shore was a good way to commit suicide.

Sending up a heartfelt prayer that none of the revelers would manage to slip past the cops, Skye continued toward her car. She knew that tomorrow they would all be as hungover as a sheet on the clothesline, but better a raging headache than a trip to the morgue.

Scumble River Park was a small finger of land that extended into the river for a half mile or so. It was usually accessible by car from Maryland Street, but that entrance had been blocked for the concert and people had been directed to leave their vehicles next door at the Up A Lazy River Motor Court.

The last stretch of her hike to the motor court's parking lot was deserted, and Skye thankfully crossed the footbridge and climbed into her trusty aqua and white '57 Bel Air convertible.

Even though she lived north of the city limits along the west branch of the Scumble River, the drive home took less than ten minutes. Then again, most trips around Scumble River and its environs took less than ten minutes. With a population only a shade over three thousand, the town didn't cover many miles.

A couple of years ago Skye had inherited the Griggs house, as the old two-story white edifice would always be called, and she had been renovating it ever since. Tonight, as she steered her car through the twin redbrick columns at the end of the driveway, she admired the newly restored wrought-iron gates. When she had first moved into the house, the gates had lain rusting in the weeds. The ornate double *G*s entwined in the center were a gloomy reminder that the previous owner, Alma Griggs, had begun her married life there as an affluent wife and died a poverty-stricken widow. By refurbishing the property, Skye felt she was giving Mrs. Griggs the memorial she deserved.

At the end of the long driveway, Skye first turned the Bel Air to the right, then spun the wheel around and pulled into the left side of the detached two-car garage. She had finally sold the ancient Lincoln Continental that had occupied the other half for over a year. Skye had found the car, like a lot of Mrs. Griggs's possessions, hard to relinquish. She wasn't sure why she felt such an attachment to the old woman's belongings, but she did.

Once Skye was out on the sidewalk, the halogen pole lamp she'd had installed near the driveway provided a circle of illumination that extended all the way to her front door. It made the short trip from her car to her house feel safer, and having helped the police solve several murders, Skye was usually more alert to her surroundings than the average Scumble Riverite.

Tonight, however, her mind was on Rex

Taylor's announcement and Skye was lost in thought as she mounted the porch steps. On autopilot, she approached the front door and inserted the key in the lock. But before she could turn it, a loud squeak followed by footsteps penetrated her reverie. She whirled around, staring into the darkness until a slight figure stepped into the pool of light.

"Oh, my God!" Skye gasped. "You scared the life out of me. What are you doing here?"

Chapter 4

"BEHIND CLOSED DOORS"

"I'm so sorry." Skye's uninvited guest clasped her hands to her chest, putting her breasts in danger of breaking free of her tank top's plunging neckline. "I'm Suzette Neal. One of the singers with the Country Roads Tour."

"I know." Skye noted that the petite woman had changed into nylon shorts and sneakers. "I was at the concert and enjoyed your performance very much."

"Oh. Thank you." Suzette's cheeks turned a pretty pink. "I forgot that people might recognize me now."

"Did you run out of gas or break down?" Skye

asked, looking around. There was no sign of any vehicle in the driveway. There weren't any other buildings along this section of Brook Lane, a barely paved, narrow, twisting farm road. The only explanation Skye could think of for Suzette's presence on her front porch was a combination of car trouble and a dead cell phone.

"No." Suzette nibbled on a ragged cuticle. "Actually, I jogged out here."

"Oh." Skye wrinkled her brow. "Are you staying in the RV at the park? That has to be at least five miles from here."

"No." Suzette shook her head. "Most of us are at the motor court. Only Rex and Mrs. Taylor are using the RV."

"I see." Suzette's answer solved the how of her arrival, but not the why. "So you ran out here for exercise?" When Suzette didn't answer, Skye added, "I try to swim three or four times a week, but I don't always make time. You must be pretty dedicated to jog after a demanding performance."

"Can we go inside?" Suzette twisted her head, as if checking for spies. "We're pretty exposed out here and I really don't want anyone to know I'm talking to you."

Exposed? Skye blinked. It was after ten at night and the only hot-blooded creature that might see them had four legs and fur. What was Suzette up to?

"Please." The singer's voice cracked.

42

Skye mentally shrugged. Letting a stranger into her home wasn't a good idea, but Suzette was, at most, five feet tall and a hundred pounds. Skye topped the young woman by seven inches and more pounds than she cared to admit. Surely she could take Suzette down if she had to.

"Of course." Skye stepped back and allowed Suzette to precede her.

"Thanks." Suzette darted over the threshold into the foyer, the rubber soles of her shoes thumping on the hardwood floor. "I'm sorry it's so late, but it's hard to go anywhere without everyone knowing about it."

"That's fine." Skye followed her, flipping on the light before closing the door. She wondered how Suzette had slipped away earlier that day, and why she felt the need for secrecy. "I imagine when you're touring and living in close quarters, privacy is at a premium."

"Yes." Suzette grimaced. "I had some important personal business in Joliet today, and because I had to sneak away, I was late getting back for the concert. If Mrs. Taylor didn't watch me like a hawk, I could have gone earlier and been back in plenty of time."

"Why does Mrs. Taylor monitor your movements?" Skye pointed down the hall with its recently painted mocha walls and past the freshly varnished curving staircase. "Let's sit in the kitchen."

"Mrs. T doesn't like me. I've always been nice to her"—Suzette's brown eyes were shiny with tears that she quickly blinked away—"but she keeps trying to convince Rex to get rid of me."

"Hmm." Skye could think of several motives for Kallista Taylor's animosity. "Maybe she's jealous of you. After all, you're a little younger, a little thinner, and a little more beautiful than she is."

"Rex flirts with all the gals." Suzette shrugged off Skye's compliments, but she bit her lip and looked away. "I've never given him any encouragement and Mrs. T knows it."

"Is she a singer, too?" Skye noticed Suzette's discomfort at the mention of Rex's attentions and offered the young woman another motive for Kallista's behavior. "Maybe she's envious of your talent."

"Mrs. Taylor used to sing, but something happened to her vocal cords." Suzette knelt on the newly tiled floor and called, "Here, kitty, kitty."

Bingo, Skye's black cat, sat next to his empty dish and stared. Clearly he wasn't budging until he'd been fed. When Skye didn't immediately pop open a can of Fancy Feast, he nudged the bowl in her direction.

"Eat your dry food." Skye shook her finger at the feline. "You know the vet said only one container of the mushy stuff per day."

"Mew."

Skye ignored Bingo's attempt to sound like he was starving and asked Suzette, "Can I get you something to drink? How about some of my mom's famous chocolate chip cookies?" The twenty-pound cat was in no danger of fainting from hunger or expiring from malnourishment, but the tiny singer looked like she might be.

"Coffee would be great." Suzette perched on a kitchen chair, her feet not quite reaching the floor. "I can't have anything to eat, though. I wish I could, but I can't afford to gain a pound or my costumes won't fit and Rex will call me a fat cow."

Skye bit her tongue. A cow? Except for her boobs, which had to have been surgically enhanced, Suzette was the size of a ten-year-old.

"I imagine you and Mr. James will be leaving Scumble River tomorrow." Skye pasted on her best hostess smile. "Where's your next engagement?"

"Nowhere for a while." Suzette gaze flicked around the kitchen, resting briefly on the granite counters, then the stainless-steel fridge, and finally the cherry cupboards. "This is real nice."

"Thank you." Skye smiled proudly. "I just had it remodeled. They only finished last month," she explained, then tried to focus on the matter at hand—whatever that was. "You don't have another gig lined up?"

"No." Suzette cleared her throat. "Actually, this

was my first big concert and I almost missed it." Her shoulders drooped. "I didn't get to wear my costume or curl my hair or anything."

"But you sang really well," Skye assured her.

"Well, my aunt always said that when you stumble, you should make it part of the dance." Suzette shrugged. "And Rex *is* grooming me to be his next breakout star, even if right now I make my living as his administrative assistant." Her expression brightened. "Rex promised that as soon as the Country Roads Theater opens, I'll be singing full-time."

"That sounds wonderful." Skye turned toward the coffee machine and filled it with water, then measured out the grounds. She was dying to find out why Suzette was there, but she knew from her experience as a school psychologist that it was best to let people tell their stories at their own pace.

"Anyway, we'll all be in the area for the next week." Suzette's tone was cheerful. "Rex is meeting with prominent Scumble Riverites, overseeing the beginning of the theater remodel project, and interviewing people for various jobs."

"And of course Mrs. Taylor will be here. I can't imagine her leaving her husband alone," Skye muttered half to herself as she took mugs off the shelf. "But surely Mr. James has another concert scheduled."

"Flint is staying a couple of days to do meet and greets." At Skye's puzzlement, Suzette clarified. "You know, be charming and butter up sponsors and investors and so on. He's really good at that. Everyone always likes him."

"Right." Skye was surprised at how sweet and down-to-earth Suzette was; except for the boob job, she was not at all what Skye would have expected after overhearing Flint and Kallista's unflattering comments about the young woman.

"So," Suzette said as Skye turned her back to reach into a drawer for spoons, "I guess you're wondering what I'm doing here."

"Yep." Skye moved toward the table but kept her gaze on the tray she was carrying. The singer seemed to be able to talk more freely when she didn't have to maintain eye contact. "I am."

"Someone told me you're good at solving mysteries." Suzette studied her chewed fingernails. "That you figure things out when the cops get stuck."

"I've helped out the police a few times," Skye answered carefully.

"I heard you're the small-town Nancy Drew." Suzette tilted her head. "I didn't know who she was, but I Googled her after the concert and Wikipedia said she was a girl detective in some old-timey books."

Skye mentally *tsk*ed. How could someone not have heard of one of the best girl series ever written? Suzette had probably never read Trixie Belden mysteries or Cherry Ames novels, either.

Granted they weren't modern, but then neither was Shakespeare.

"Who told you I was the small-town Nancy Drew?" Skye hoped the *Star* hadn't run another story about her. The local newspaper tended to exaggerate her part in solving crimes. She'd been relieved that her name hadn't been mentioned in connection with Scumble River's past few murder investigations, especially the last one. As far as she knew, there hadn't been any articles lately; someone, aka her mother, would definitely have mentioned them.

"He . . . she . . . the person asked me not to say." Suzette took a sip from the cup Skye had placed in front of her.

Skye waited for the singer to continue, and when she didn't, asked, "So what do you need a detective for?"

"Before we get to that, I need for you to promise you won't tell anyone anything I say." Suzette stared imploringly at Skye.

"I'll keep the information confidential." Skye sat opposite the young woman. "Except from my fiancé, who's the chief of police and very discreet." Once Suzette nodded, Skye added, "And if there comes a time when I think that not revealing the information will cause someone physical harm. Then I'll have no choice but to break confidentiality, because I won't let some-one get hurt."

"I guess I can live with that." Suzette bit her thumbnail. "I need for you to help me look into the circumstances surrounding a death that occurred in Scumble River twenty-seven years ago."

"Why are you interested in something that happened before you were born?"

"Well, that's one of the most crucial secrets." Suzette licked her lips. "I'm actually not twenty-two. I'm nearly thirty." She took a breath. "Which is why I had to slip away this afternoon. There was someone I needed to talk to about this death, but I can't let Rex know I'm interested or he'll figure out how old I am."

"Oh." Skye didn't have to ask why the singer was lying about her age. Youth was an important currency in the entertainment business. "Still, what connection to the deceased do you have?"

"The woman was my mother."

"I'm so sorry." Skye patted Suzette's hand. The sadness in the singer's voice brought a lump to Skye's throat. "How did she die?"

"The official report says she slipped in the bathtub and hit her head."

"But you don't believe that." Skye studied the young woman. She was deeply touched by Suzette's air of vulnerability.

"No, I don't." Suzette's puppylike brown eyes hardened. "I was there when it happened, playing in my bedroom. And I have this vague memory of a lot of screaming and then a door slamming."

49

"I take it no one believed you?" Skye could just picture the adults discounting a three-year-old's account of events.

"My dad always said I was too young to remember anything."

"Does he still feel that way?" Skye wondered if perhaps Suzette's dad had been the one she heard screaming at her mom, and that's why he had tried to convince his daughter it was all in her imagination.

"He was killed in a car crash a couple of years ago." Suzette swallowed hard, then continued. "After Mom died, he quit his job and joined the army. He was completely overwhelmed by the idea of taking care of me. I was raised by his aunt in California and I rarely saw or heard from my father." Suzette's voice was low. "My aunt said that Dad seemed to feel as if he didn't deserve to have any love or happiness in his life."

"Your aunt sounds like a special lady."

"She was." Suzette smiled tearfully. "In every way that mattered, she was both a father and mother to me. She passed away when I was in college."

"You've had a lot of losses in your life, two of them from accidents." Skye paused to form her next question carefully. "Do you think that might be why you want to believe your mom's death wasn't some random occurrence? That there was meaning to it? Someone besides God to blame?"

"No." Suzette shook her head so vigorously that her hair, which she had piled on top of her head, slipped free from the large tortoiseshell clip securing it. "I know what I heard. Someone else was at the house that day, and I want to find out if that's who murdered my mom."

Chapter 5

"SUNDAY MORNING COMING DOWN"

As Skye got ready for church the next morning, she thought about Suzette's plea for help. The singer had seemed so alone in the world. It wouldn't be that difficult for Skye to read over the police file and chat with a few of the locals who might remember Mr. and Mrs. Neal, especially Mrs. Neal's fatal accident. But, for once, Skye would seriously consider getting involved before she rushed to someone's assistance.

If she agreed to help Suzette, she didn't want to regret that decision. And truth be told, Skye didn't hold high hopes that anyone would recall much about the couple. They had lived in Scumble River for less than a year, a long time ago. However, Skye knew good and well that if the townsfolk *did* have any knowledge of the incident, they would talk to her a lot more easily than they would to a stranger.

Skye had agreed to consider looking into Mrs. Neal's death, and promised Suzette an answer by Monday afternoon. The singer had suggested Skye pick her up at the barn-to-theater remodel site, where Rex had set up a mobile office, as Suzette would be spending most of her time there.

After Mass, Skye sat in the parking lot and pressed the various buttons required to listen to the message on her cell phone.

Finally, she heard Wally's voice say, "Hi, darlin'. With all the drunk and disorderly arrests last night, I need to do a heap of paperwork this morning, so instead of coming to the house, meet me at the police station after Mass. We'll go to brunch from there."

She smiled. Wally was such a hard worker. Scumble River was lucky to have him. He could easily get a job in a bigger, better-paying, and more prestigious department. Thank goodness, money clearly wasn't his number one priority or he'd be in Texas working for his father, the owner of a multimillion-dollar oil company.

When Skye arrived at the police station shortly after eleven a.m., she was surprised to find the parking lot nearly full. Scumble River's PD occupied one side of a two-story redbrick edifice.

A tiny lobby, the dispatcher's work space, an interrogation room, and a couple of cubicles equipped with built-in desks, computers, and phones were located on the main level, a rarely used holding cell occupied part of the basement, and Wally's office was on the second floor. The other half of the building held the city hall, town library, and mayor's office.

There was no one behind the counter when Skye pushed through the frosted-glass door. The Scumble River police, fire, and emergency departments shared a common dispatcher who covered the phones and radios and handled paperwork for the officers. During the week, three women, including Skye's mother, May, worked thirty hours each, rotating between the afternoon and midnight shifts. A fourth woman worked straight days. Two additional younger women worked the weekend shifts, but Skye could never remember their names. They were part-timers in a position where people rarely lasted more than a year before finding a better-paying, less stressful job.

Skye used her key to let herself into the back of the station. Where was everyone? She walked down a narrow hall toward the combination coffee-interrogation room and peered through the window. The dispatcher was sitting with a female suspect as an officer interviewed the woman. *Ah.* That explained the deserted reception counter.

53

Figuring that Wally was probably in his office, Skye mounted the steep steps to the second floor. As she neared the top, she heard voices. She'd paused, not wanting to interrupt Wally if he was with someone, when a round of clapping rang out. *Hmm.* The police chief seldom received applause.

Skye tilted her head, listening. *Ah.* The sound was coming from the mayor's new office, not Wally's. A couple of weeks ago, Dante had had an opening cut between the city hall and the police department, taking a part of the library in order to construct a larger office for himself. Her uncle must be holding a meeting, which was why there were so many cars in the parking lot.

Curious, Skye stepped into the city hall's half of the upstairs and walked quietly to the open door. When she peeked inside, she saw Rex Taylor in front of Dante's desk facing a semicircle of chairs occupied by some of Scumble River's most influential citizens. These people were not the sort to give up their Sunday morning lightly. They'd be present only if there were momentous issues to discuss or serious money to be made.

As Skye watched, Suzette, wearing denim short shorts and a sleeveless pink gingham blouse with the shirttails tied between her breasts, poured champagne for the bigwigs. The singer filled Rex's flute last, and he put his arm around her. She shifted her shoulders and shrugged off his embrace.

Rex smiled benevolently, as if dealing with a temperamental child, and allowed her to move away. As he raised his flute, his expression was instantly transformed. Now he radiated warmth and sincerity. "Sit back, ladies and gentlemen, sip your bubbly, and behold the future of Scumble River."

Right on cue, a screen behind Rex descended from the ceiling. Dante hit the light switch and moved to a projector set up on a tripod in the rear. He fumbled for a moment; then blurry gray snow appeared.

Rex hit a few keys on his laptop and a computer-enhanced image of Scumble River materialized. The recorded voice of Flint James said, "Welcome to the Branson of Illinois. Thousands of tourists attracted to the Country Roads Theater will flock to the area, spending their money and turning this sleepy town into a thriving metropolis."

Skye stared in appalled silence. From the Elvis Encounter Wax Museum and Haunted House, to the Scumble River Dinner Cruise aboard a coal barge, to the Hoedown Saloon Review with barely dressed girls performing a dance routine, each highlighted attraction was tackier than the last. The pièce de résistance was Rex's vision for the surrounding farms. He wanted to turn them into "farmcation" resorts, where the guests could experience a taste of farm life—without any of the unpleasant chores or odors, of course.

By the time the promotional presentation ended, Skye's head was throbbing and she leaned weakly against the wall. If Rex Taylor had his way, Scumble River would become nothing more than a hokey tourist trap with vacationers clogging the streets and crowding the stores. The laid-back small-town feeling that she had come to appreciate would be gone forever, and in its place would be her idea of a nightmare.

Skye glanced around the room, gauging the reaction of the attendees. They seemed to be split into two factions—some frowning, shaking their heads, and whispering furiously to their neighbors, and the others smiling and taking notes. She prayed fervently that the negative group would be the more influential.

Rex rose from the seat he had taken during the program. "You have probably been wondering why you were invited here today. What do I want from you? Nothing. I'm here to give you something. The once-in-a-lifetime chance to make a fortune." He pointed to Dante. "Your mayor and city council took the first step in guiding this town to financial security when they approved the country music theater complex I'm building. Now it's up to you to follow their lead and invest in Scumble River's future."

Dante beamed and folded his hands over his considerable stomach.

"This is your opportunity to cash in on all the

tourists I'll be bringing into the area with my theater," Rex continued. "I've already arranged for several country music stars to perform here, and for numerous travel companies to schedule their buses to stop here during the summer vacation season."

Skye flinched. *Oh, oh!* Now even some of the frowners looked interested.

"I'll be making appointments to talk to each and every one of you privately in order to advise you about the types of businesses you might want to open that would attract sightseers." Rex made eye contact with everyone present before saying, "The first ones on the gravy train will make the most money. Make sure you're not one of the people who only catches the caboose."

All around the room, voices were raised and arguments erupted. Two men were already on their feet, fists clenched. Skye started to go into the office, but stopped in her tracks. There was nothing she could do or say to influence anyone's opinion. Her uncle was obviously in full cahoots with Rex. The outcome of the music promoter's plans was completely out of her hands. Skye's only hope was that the people in the room who hadn't drunk Rex's Kool-Aid would continue to abstain.

Discouraged, she went to find Wally. The brunch he had in mind had better offer some-thing stronger than champagne.

• • •

For once, I-55 wasn't under construction, and it was a pleasant drive north to the restaurant Wally had chosen. He entertained Skye with stories about some of the funnier arrests from the previous night's drunken revelries, and she, in turn, filled him in on the scenes she had witnessed on the way to the parking lot.

When they reached I-355 and the more intense traffic, Wally grew quiet, fully focused on the highway. He handled his car, a sky blue Thunderbird convertible that had been a fortieth-birthday gift from his wealthy father, with calm confidence.

Skye gazed at Wally's handsome profile, lost in her own thoughts. She needed to talk to him about Suzette and the meeting she had witnessed in Dante's office, but didn't want to distract Wally from the road, so she remained quiet until they arrived at the restaurant.

The Clubhouse was located next to Oak Brook Mall, a fashionable shopping area on the outskirts of Chicago. The two-story redbrick building sported a bright green roof and black-and-beige-striped awnings.

As Wally pulled up to the valet stand and turned over his keys, he said to Skye, "I hope you're hungry. I hear they have a spectacular brunch here."

"Great. I'm starving." Skye waited until he

came around to open her door, then took his arm. "I slept in this morning, and didn't have time to eat anything before church."

"Did Bingo shut off the alarm again?" Wally asked as they strolled into the restaurant.

"No. I just got to bed so late last night that I couldn't wake up." Skye noticed the hostess waiting for Wally to claim their reservation. "Let's get our table; then I'll tell you all about it."

The woman led them up a dramatic sweeping staircase, over a beautiful floor of dark and light wood in a checkerboard design, and to a half-moon area one step up from the rest of the room. On their way they passed several massive buffet tables loaded with everything from eggs Benedict to petits fours.

The hostess showed them to a secluded table covered in a pristine white tablecloth and laid with intricately folded napkins, gleaming silver, and sparkling crystal. She waited until they were seated side by side on the leather banquette, then handed Wally the wine list and gestured to their server, who was standing nearby.

Once their drink orders were taken, Wally turned to Skye. "What kept you up past your bedtime?"

"Not what, who. Suzette Neal."

"The girl singer from the concert." Wally wrinkled his forehead. "What did she want?"

"Me to solve a murder."

"What?" Wally cocked a dark brow. "Someone was killed and no one told me?"

"Yeah, right." Skye chuckled. "No, this happened before you joined the police force."

"Well, that's a load off my mind." Wally pretended to slump in relief. "A cold case."

They were silent as the server put their drinks in front of them and told them about the brunch.

After he left, Skye said, "Let's get our first course; then I'll tell you the rest."

"Okay." Wally grinned. "I know a hungry fiancée is a cranky fiancée."

"You always say that, and it's always not funny." Skye slid from the booth and marched toward the seafood bar.

Moments later they were back at the table with heaping plates full of spicy shrimp, boiled crab claws, and smoked salmon on toast points spread with cream cheese and topped with capers.

Before digging in, Wally asked, "Why did Suzette come to you?"

Between bites, Skye explained about the mysterious person who had told Suzette that Skye was the Scumble River Nancy Drew, ending with, "Of course, anyone who reads the paper could be the one who called me that."

"Yep." Wally licked a bit of cocktail sauce from his finger. "So tell me about the murder."

Skye took a swallow of her mimosa, then told him about Suzette's mother. When she finished, she narrowed her eyes and said, "Tell me the truth. You probably think I shouldn't agree to do it."

"I don't see any reason not to take the case. If it seemed like a plausible accident, there wouldn't have been an autopsy or much investigation." He reached over and squeezed her hand. "And I knew when we started dating that you weren't the kind of person who could turn down a request for help."

"You are so sweet." Skye couldn't stop herself from comparing Wally to her ex-boyfriend Simon Reid, who would have blown a gasket if she had told him she was going to nose around in something that wasn't any of her business. "Have I told you lately how much I love and appreciate you?"

"Not today." Wally gave her a one-armed hug and kiss that promised more when they were alone.

Chapter 6

"HARPER VALLEY PTA"

Mmm. Skye sighed contentedly and snuggled between the smooth cotton sheets. Struggling not to wake up, she kept her eyes closed and reveled in the touch of Wally's strong fingers on her body. She felt a twinge of disappointment when his hands withdrew, then shivered when she felt the warmth of his breath on her ear.

Wally's lips brushed hers, a teasing promise that finally forced Skye fully awake. His brown eyes sizzled with heat that burned through her core, and she moaned. Immediately his mouth covered hers and he pulled her hard against him.

After they made love, they fell back asleep, and the next thing Skye knew, sunlight was pouring through the gap in the drapes. She checked the clock on the nightstand. *Crap!* It was ten after seven. She had exactly twenty minutes to get dressed, drive to school, and sign in before she was officially late.

She nudged Wally awake, leaped from the bed, and sprinted into the bathroom, shouting over her shoulder, "I thought you said you set the alarm."

Her shriek as she stepped into the cold shower drowned out his reply. Five minutes later, when she rushed back into the bedroom, Wally had disappeared. Grateful that she now kept some clothes at Wally's house, she pulled on an aqua blouse and a black twill pantsuit, then shoved her feet into black loafers. With a quick glance in the mirror, she twisted her damp hair into a knot on the top of her head. There was no time to do her face or have breakfast, and the enticing aroma of brewing coffee nearly made her whimper with frustration.

Dashing through the kitchen, Skye thrust her hand into her tote bag, searching for her keys.

Thank goodness they had picked up her car and parked it at Wally's house after returning from Oak Brook.

Wally tried to hand her a commuter cup as she ran by, but she was moving too fast to grab it. He called after her, "Sorry about the alarm. Maybe I turned it off in my sleep."

"Whatever," Skye muttered. She had other things to worry about right now. Like the three principals evaluating her performance. And at the moment, she couldn't remember if she was supposed to be at the grade school or high school first. Luckily the two buildings were close.

While she drove in their general direction, she flipped through her calendar and discovered she was due at the elementary. She breathed a sigh of relief when she saw her first appointment wasn't until eight.

Skye squealed into the parking lot at seven twenty-seven, took the first available spot, bolted out of the Chevy, and jogged to the entrance. Using her key, she let herself in and made a beeline for the office. As she signed the attendance book, she checked the clock. Seven thirty on the dot.

Phew! That was close. Caroline Greer was the nicest of the three principals Skye worked for, but she would definitely be upset if there was a problem she needed the school psychologist for and Skye wasn't available.

Though Caroline was the nicest principal, she had provided the worst office space for Skye. It had started out as a storage room for the dairy refrigerator and other cafeteria supplies, and still smelled like sour milk.

After unlocking the door, Skye squeezed past the pair of folding chairs occupying two-thirds of the floor space, edged behind her desk, and settled into her seat. She rummaged in her tote bag until she found her makeup case, then hastily applied a dusting of bronzer, a couple coats of mascara, and pale peach lip gloss.

Checking her watch, she saw she didn't have time to get a cup of coffee before her consultation with the PE teacher, so she tucked her purse into the drawer and pulled out the teacher's file. Skye's body cried out for caffeine. She sighed. The day hadn't even started and she already felt stressed. Which was exactly why she hated running late.

Considering that the gym teacher didn't like Skye, and didn't agree with the educational philosophy she was urging him to follow, the discussion went well. They were just finishing up when there was a knock on the door.

Skye frowned but called out, "Yes?" She had the DO NOT DISTURB sign on the knob—not that it ever stopped anyone from interrupting her.

Fern Otte, the school secretary, poked her head inside. The tiny wrenlike woman's feathers were visibly ruffled and she twittered, "Ms. Denison, Mrs. Greer needs you at the PTO meeting immediately."

"Okay." Skye rose from her seat, said good-bye to the PE teacher, and asked Fern where the meeting was being held.

"The gym." Fern turned to go, saying over her shoulder, "Hurry."

Passing a row of windows on her way to the gymnasium, Skye glanced outside. The sun was already beating off the asphalt. More unusually high temperatures were predicted for that afternoon along with a thunderstorm, and she was thankful she was scheduled to spend the afternoon in the air-conditioned high school.

Caroline Greer greeted her at the door of the gym. "An unusual situation, I'm afraid."

Skye heard two arguing female voices as she eased inside. She surveyed the assemblage. A dozen or so women in their late twenties and early thirties sat around a couple of long tables in a T formation. Several of them gave the impression they were about to make a run for freedom.

At the center of the T, two women stood toe-to-toe yelling at another. The tiny blonde was Skye's cousin Ginger Leofanti, president of the PTO. The brunette facing off with Ginger was Theresa Dugan, one of the teachers. What in the world had set Theresa off? She was generally calm and good-natured.

Skye had been trying to figure out why the principal had summoned her. Caroline preferred to handle most matters by herself, usually calling on Skye only if she needed specific special education information. Now she knew. Caroline couldn't afford to offend the PTO president, but she also didn't want to take sides against her own employee. She was undoubtedly hoping Skye could either resolve the situation peacefully or shoulder the blame.

"What's going on?" Skye whispered to Caroline. It was hard to tell what the disagreement was about since the women were currently stuck in a round of *Did too*s and *Uh-huh*s.

"Branson of Illinois," Caroline answered, then edged toward the exit. As she hurried from the room, she said, "I'm sure you can smooth things over. Let me know when you've got this under control."

"Wait!" Skye called after the principal, but the door had already clicked shut.

Suddenly the shouting behind Skye increased in volume, and she whirled around. The remaining women had left their seats and chosen sides.

"Everyone"—Theresa put up her hand, palm toward Ginger, and said—"calm down."

"Have you ever noticed," Ginger said, playing to the crowd, "that the person who tells you to calm down is the one who riled you up to start with?"

Several of the women nodded and someone shouted, "Yeah, it's always the ones who think they're better than everyone else."

"Ladies, that isn't the case at all," Theresa appealed to her faction. "You all know I'm not like that."

"Well, if you didn't have such a cushy job with a guaranteed salary and benefits, you'd see how wonderful Mr. Taylor's plans are." Ginger poked the teacher in the middle of her chest with a stubby fuchsia fingernail. "As long as people keep popping out kids, you don't have to worry about unemployment."

Cushy job? Teaching? Skye always suspected her cousin wasn't the sharpest eyebrow pencil in the makeup case, but now she had proof. Ginger wouldn't last a day in front of a classroom.

"And if you weren't such a selfish, greedy fool, you'd admit what his scheme would do to our town." Theresa fluffed her short curls. "That awful man is going to turn Scumble River into a cheap tourist trap with traffic jams, tattoo parlors, and pawnshops."

"You're just jealous he was flirting with me yesterday after church and not you."

Theresa's shrewd brown gaze pinned Ginger. "What has he offered you?"

"None of your beeswax." Ginger stamped her purple-flip-flop-shod foot on the hardwood floor. "This isn't about just me."

"Of course it is." Theresa smoothed her pale yellow shirtdress. "Let me guess . . ." She tapped a finger on her lower lip. "A construction job for that lowlife husband of yours. I heard he'd been fired—again."

"That's a lie!" Ginger's voice rose to a high, squeaky pitch that made Skye want to cover her ears. "Flip was not fired. The company went under. He was one of the last to go." She appealed to her supporters. "You all know that things are so bad around here, the bank is sending out loan applications with REJECTED already stamped across them."

A few women tittered sympathetically, and Theresa hurriedly said, "Tough times never last, but tough people do."

"That's just BS you read on a T-shirt." Ginger's voice rose in anger. "If you weren't dumb as a post, you'd realize how stupid you sound."

Skye knew she had to stop the women, but while she was trying to figure out how, the battle continued.

"Really?" Theresa's eyes glittered with malice. "You know, I wasn't going to mention this, but your son Bert did a good job in the spelling bee we had last week."

Skye tensed at the abrupt change of subject. What was Theresa up to?

"Oh?" Ginger's expression was wary. "He didn't mention that."

"Yes." Theresa's tone was saccharine. "The winning word was *straight,* and after he spelled it correctly, I asked him what it meant." She paused, letting the drama build. "And he said, 'Jim Beam without water.' "

It took a few seconds, but once they got the joke everyone laughed, and Ginger sputtered, "You just made that up."

"Maybe." Theresa smirked. "And maybe the reason Flip has so much trouble keeping a job has more to do with his whiskey consumption and less to do with the economy."

"That's not true," Ginger protested. "Flip only drinks beer."

"Beer, whiskey, whatever," Theresa said with condescending indifference. "A drunk by any other name is still a—"

Before the teacher could finish, Ginger lunged forward and slapped her. Theresa looked stunned as a bright red handprint appeared on her cheek. A nanosecond later, she grabbed a handful of Ginger's blouse and hauled the tiny woman toward her.

The sound of tearing fabric galvanized Skye into action, and she stepped toward the two brawlers, raising her voice. "Ladies!"

No one seemed to hear her.

"Ladies!" Skye shouted, then put two fingers between her lips and whistled.

All heads turned in her direction.

Skye thought fast. "Theresa. What if one of the children saw you fighting like this? What kind of example are you setting?"

Theresa let go of Ginger and ducked her head. "You're right."

"And, Ginger"—Skye turned to her cousin— "if your mother heard about your behavior, she'd be mortified. Aunt Minnie raised you better than this."

"You're not going to tell, are you?" Ginger's voice wavered. She was nearly as afraid of *her* mother as Skye was of May. "You wouldn't."

"Not"—Skye kept her voice firm—"if you agree to discuss this in a civilized manner."

"How about her?"

"Theresa?" Skye asked.

"I don't know what got into me." Theresa's expression was sheepish. "Except I love this town and our way of life here, and if people like her have their way"—she cocked a thumb in Ginger's direction—"it'll be lost forever."

Ginger shot Theresa a look of pure loathing and said, "And if people like her have their way, Scumble River will die a slow, boring death because there aren't any jobs."

"It's a complex issue and we won't solve it at a PTO meeting," Skye stated, knowing there was no easy answer.

Although her sympathies lay with Theresa, she could see Ginger's point of view. Not as many families were able to make a living from farming as in the past, and the only factory in the area that was still in business was Fine Foods.

Employment opportunities were scarce, and in order to live in the town they grew up in, most young people had to be willing to commute an hour or longer to Joliet or Kankakee.

"Can you two agree to disagree and deal with whatever was originally on your agenda?" Skye asked.

"Only if she apologizes to me," Ginger said, crossing her arms. "She slandered my husband and ripped my best shirt."

"I apologize for my ill-advised words." Theresa's face was red. "But you struck me, so we're even regarding the torn blouse."

Skye looked at her cousin. "Ginger, are you okay with that?"

"Yeah." The tiny blonde examined the damage. "It tore on a seam. I can sew it up."

"Great." Skye smiled warmly at both women. "Then I'll leave you to your meeting."

As Skye walked away, she realized it hadn't even been forty-eight hours since Rex Taylor's announcement, and this was the second argument over the project that she had witnessed. Which did not bode at all well for the future of Scumble River.

Chapter 7

"KILLIN' TIME"

It had been raining steadily since eleven a.m., and was still pouring when Skye left the high school at four fifteen. The irony would not be lost on the farmers—when the crops had needed water, there'd been a drought; now that they needed dry conditions for the harvest, there was a downpour.

The deluge wouldn't be good for the construction at the barn-theater site, either. The workers had probably been sent home hours ago. In which case, Rex may have decided to call it a day, too.

Heck! Maybe Suzette wouldn't be there, either. Skye smacked her forehead with the heel of her hand, cursing herself for not getting a phone number from the singer. She certainly didn't want to drive out to the theater and find a note saying Suzette and her boss were somewhere else.

Wally had told Skye that the old police records —ones pertaining to cases more than ten years earlier—hadn't been put into the computer yet. They were still stored in cardboard boxes in the PD's basement. He had promised to ask one of his officers to try to find the Neal folder as soon as possible, but he couldn't swear when that might be.

Now that Skye had decided to help Suzette, she was eager to get started, and had come up with a list of questions:

1. What was the time of death?
2. When did Mrs. Neal usually take her bath?
3. Where did the Neal family live?
4. Did anyone remember Mr. and Mrs. Neal having marriage troubles?
5. Where did Mr. Neal work?
6. Was Mrs. Neal a stay-at-home mom?
7. Did they have any relatives in town?

With the file currently unavailable, her only source of information was whatever details the singer could remember about her family.

Although a useless trip would be annoying, at least the dairy farm wasn't far. As Skye turned the Bel Air onto Maryland Street, she could only hope that Suzette wanted to find her mother's killer enough to stick around, even if everyone else had left.

The Hutton dairy farm was located midway between Scumble River and the neighboring towns of Brooklyn and Clay Center, in an area Scumble River had annexed a couple of years ago, when the mayor promised the town that a trucking depot would purchase the land. That deal had fallen through, much to Dante's chagrin.

After Skye passed Great Expectations, the hair salon her brother owned, and the medical building across from Vince's shop, the scenery became rural. There were a few houses along the way, but they were separated by acres of corn and soy-beans.

During the summer and fall, when the crops were mature, those residents had complete privacy. Their neighbors couldn't see their homes or vice versa. If Rex Taylor's plans came to fruition, these people would lose that prized seclusion.

Hmm. Didn't Theresa Dugan live out here? That would sure explain the normally serene teacher's meltdown at the PTO meeting. Nothing like a personal stake in the situation to transform some-one into a community activist.

Skye wondered how many farmers and home-owners would sell out to the music promoter. She was thankful that her family's land was on the other side of Scumble River, and would be of little interest to Mr. Taylor.

Just before she reached the I-55 exit, an old sign advertising the defunct dairy loomed up on her right. As Skye pulled onto the rutted dirt road, she noted a pair of decrepit wooden gates lying on the ground, an uncomfortable reminder that agriculture's heyday was long gone. After Skye bumped down the lane for a quarter of a mile, the buildings came into view.

The once white clapboard farmhouse was situated on the left side of the property, separated from the other structures by a neglected yard and a detached garage with a large gravel rectangle in front of the doors. A row of overgrown evergreen bushes had completely blocked the front porch. The grass was nearly thigh high, and a lawn ornament, a rusted windmill, spun madly in the wind that had kicked up.

Through the sheeting raindrops, Skye could barely make out the beginning of the makeover from farm to theater. All the work seemed to be on the exterior of the milking barn and the area around it, which was being turned into a parking lot. The other buildings—house, garage, and silos—appeared untouched.

A gleaming white Winnebago had been installed next to the driveway, which was empty of cars. *Sheesh!* It looked as if everyone had left for the day, just as she had feared.

Skye parked the Bel Air as close to the trailer as possible and reached into the backseat for her umbrella. She waited for the downpour to let up, then ran to the Winnebago's door. Sitting on the metal step was a small white dog wearing a hot pink collar studded with rhinestones. It whined when she approached.

The canine was so wet and bedraggled, Skye couldn't tell if it was a purebred or not, but she could see that it was male. She held out her hand, and the dog sniffed, then leaned against her knee. The heart-shaped silver tag on his collar was inscribed with the name Toby.

Fighting the wind, which was endeavoring to snatch the umbrella from Skye's grasp, she tried to flip the tag over to see if there was owner information on the back, but the little dog danced out of her reach. Next she attempted to pick him up, thinking he probably belonged to one of the Country Roads staff, but he dodged her hands and darted between her legs.

Skye called after him, "Here, Toby. Come on, boy. I'll take you somewhere dry."

Toby stopped, blinked his dark brown eyes, and yipped, then loped toward the barn.

Skye hesitated. Should she go after the dog? No. It would probably be better to find Toby's owner, as he or she would have an easier time persuading the canine to come in out of the rain.

Turning back, Skye tried the door. It was locked. *Hmm.* Maybe if Suzette was out here alone, she felt unsafe. Skye knocked. Nothing. She knocked again, then put her ear to the door to listen, but she couldn't hear a thing.

Raising her voice, she yelled, "Suzette, it's Skye."

There was no answer. She shouted even louder with the same results. Irritation prompted her to grab the knob and rattle the door. Still no answer.

Skye looked around. There was no sign of a note. *Son of a gun!* She'd been stood up. It was just plain rude to arrange to meet someone from whom you were asking a favor, then not honor the appointment. Maybe she wouldn't help Suzette investigate her mother's death after all.

Frustrated, Skye headed back to her car. She was about to slide into the driver's seat when the little white dog reappeared in front of the Bel Air's hood. Skye slowly stood back up and moved toward him, but he scurried toward the barn. He stopped halfway and barked, then ran on, stopping every few steps to stare at her.

Skye had seen enough reruns of *Lassie* on Nick at Nite to know that Toby wanted her to follow him. But why? She doubted Timmy was trapped in a well, and she sure hoped Toby didn't want to show off a snake or a possum he had killed. Skye'd had her fill of Bingo's mouse carcass trophies.

She trailed Toby, calling out, "*Yoo hoo,* anyone around?"

The dog kept ahead of her, never letting her get within grabbing range. He paused in front of the barn, but as Skye caught up, he shot off. Did Toby want her to go inside? It sure would be easier if dogs could talk.

The barn door was closed, but not locked. When Skye entered, she saw they hadn't started work on the interior yet. She walked through the cavernous space, but saw nothing that would make Toby behave as he had.

The flight of stairs to the hayloft was steep, and Skye was not thrilled at the prospect of climbing them. She kicked off her heels and yelled, "Is anyone up there?"

No answer. She ascended the wooden steps, wincing as they creaked. If she fell and broke her neck because of a dog, her mother would kill her. May hated all animals, especially pets.

Reaching the top, Skye couldn't see anything at first because the loft was so dark. But as her eyes adjusted it was clear that there was nothing there but a century's worth of dust and a few wisps of hay.

Skye's sense of unease grew. Whatever Toby wanted to show her wasn't here. When she exited the barn, the dog was pacing outside the door. Spotting her, he woofed and trotted away.

This time he kept Skye in sight, never getting more than a few feet in front of her. He led her around the back of the building to where the parking lot was being installed. Heavy earth-moving equipment was parked haphazardly across the vast dirt and gravel square.

Once Skye caught up with Toby, he ran to a steamroller and sat beside it, whimpering. Peeking out from under the massive roller was a pair of pink cowboy boots.

A shiver ran down Skye's spine. She hesitated a long moment, praying she wasn't seeing what she thought she was seeing, then ran over to the machine. In her head she knew that whoever was wearing those boots was dead, but she crouched down anyway and tried to reach an ankle to check for a pulse.

The flesh felt cold and hard, and when Skye withdrew her hand, it was covered with blood.

Chapter 8

"I Fall to Pieces"

Skye fought to stay calm, chanting silently, *I've discovered bodies before. There's no need to panic.* She sank to the ground while a voice inside her head whispered, *But this is so much worse than anything you've seen before.* Her stomach churned and she tasted bile.

Stop it, Skye commanded herself. *You are a psychologist and a consultant for the police. You've been trained to remain detached, to distance yourself. You can do this.* She swallowed hard.

You need to walk over to your car and get the cell phone from your purse. She closed her eyes and tried to disconnect her emotions.

Before she could force herself to her feet and do what she knew she had to do, Toby crawled over and pressed his little body to her side. She scratched behind his ears as she tried to process the situation, but her psyche refused to cooperate.

Skye lost track of time as she knelt in the mud, mindlessly petting the little dog until the rain and the wind finally penetrated the fog that had fallen over her. She got to her feet, clutching Toby to her chest. He laid his head on her shoulder and sighed.

Still in a near trance, Skye walked to the Bel Air, found her phone, and dialed Wally's private line. It rang four times, then went to voice mail. She got the same response from his cell.

Skye wrinkled her brow, then exhaled noisily and dialed 911. Her mother was the dispatcher on duty and she steeled herself for May's reaction.

"Scumble River police, fire, and emergency," May answered on the first ring. "How can I help you?"

"Send an ambulance and the officer on duty to Hutton's dairy farm." Skye didn't bother giving an address. She was sure that all the cops and EMTs knew where the farm was located. "Someone's very badly hurt in the parking lot behind the barn." She was unwilling to say for sure that the person under the steamroller was dead. The emergency squad personnel should make that call.

"Skye, is that you?" May demanded. "What are you doing out there? Who's hurt?"

Pushing the END button, Skye climbed into her car, still cuddling the little dog. The fact that she had hung up on her mother showed just how truly upset she was. Having lost her umbrella at some point, she was soaked to the skin, and even though the temperature was in the mideighties, she felt chilled to the bone. Shivering, she started the Chevy and turned on the heat full blast.

As she waited for help to arrive, she put Toby on the passenger seat, where he promptly shook his entire body, spraying both Skye and the Bel Air's interior with a fine mist. As Skye dried off the dog with a wad of napkins from the glove compartment, all she could think about was the last time she had seen pink cowboy boots—on Suzette Neal's dainty little feet.

While Skye tried to convince herself that Suzette didn't own the only pair of brightly colored boots, an ambulance with its sirens blaring and lights flashing pulled into the driveway. A police cruiser skidded to a stop directly behind the ambulance and Sergeant Roy Quirk jumped out.

Quirk was in his early thirties and was Wally's second in command. The sergeant's solidly muscled body and shaved bullet-shaped head made him look like a torpedo.

He and Skye had had a run-in last fall, but they were now on good terms. Even so, she was reluctant to leave the warmth of her Bel Air to join the sergeant on the gravel drive. Talking about what she had seen would make it real.

He tugged his plastic-covered police hat down nearly to his eyebrows, trying to shield his eyes from the driving rain, and pulled open her car door. "What's going on?" Quirk hunched over so he could look into Skye's face. "May said you sounded really bad on the phone and wouldn't give any details."

"I didn't want to have to go over it twice." Skye's voice was taut, her fingers twisted in a knot. "Where's the chief?"

"He's testifying on that gas station robbery case," Quirk answered with a sigh. "He should be back anytime now. Trials usually end by four at the latest."

"Sorry." Skye tried to remember if Wally had told her he would be out of town today. "I didn't mean to sound like I thought you couldn't handle this."

"I understand." He shook his head. "I'm used to that reaction. Everyone wants Superman, and they're disappointed when Clark Kent shows up." He straightened his shoulders. "So, fill me in."

"Okay." Skye gestured with her chin to where the EMTs had disappeared around the back of the barn. "Someone . . . Someone . . ." Feeling nauseous again, she swallowed before continuing. "Under the . . . the . . ." Saying it out loud was harder than she had imagined. "Someone's been run over by the steamroller."

All expression left Quirk's face. "Show me."

Skye wanted to refuse to return to that awful scene, but she got out of the car.

While they walked, Quirk asked, "Did you recognize the victim?"

Skye had to hurry to keep up with Quirk's fast pace. "I can't be sure."

Quirk shot her a puzzled look but kept moving. "Why is that?"

Growing breathless, Skye gasped, "All I could see were the boots."

"And you called for an ambulance?" Quirk's tone was dubious, but not harsh. "Do you really think she might be alive?"

"Probably not." Skye didn't meet his gaze. "But I sure wouldn't want to be mistaken."

At the edge of the parking lot, Quirk ordered, "Stay here."

Skye nodded; then, feeling dizzy, she sank into a nearby pile of concrete blocks. Her view was a bit obstructed, for which she was immensely thankful. She did not want to see what was under that roller.

However, it was clear from the snatches of conversation she heard and the body language of the EMTs that the woman was dead.

There was a short discussion between Quirk and the paramedics regarding how to move the hulking machine.

When no one had any suggestions, one of the EMTs climbed up into the cab, but almost immediately got back down. "The key's there, but I have no idea how to run the thing."

"Okay." Quirk grabbed the radio clipped to his shoulder and thumbed the button. "Dispatch, please locate the foreman of the construction crew working at the Hutton dairy farm and have him report to the scene."

Quirk rejoined Skye, but instead of speaking to her, he took a cell phone from his pocket, dialed, and waited for his call to be answered before saying, "Reid, we have a body for you."

Skye cringed. Simon Reid, her ex-boyfriend, was the county coroner, not to mention the owner of both the local funeral home and the bowling alley. Even though she'd been engaged to Wally since the end of June, Simon had been trying to win her back with extravagant measures that included offers of exotic trips, surprise champagne lunches, and serenading her dressed as a knight in shining armor. Running into him in any situation was awkward.

When Skye focused back on the present, Quirk was calling the county crime scene techs. Once he had filled them in, he radioed the Scumble River PD to see if the chief had checked in yet. Skye was relieved when she heard her mother say that Wally was on his way.

A quick glance at her watch told Skye that it was nearly five. It would take at least three-quarters of an hour, maybe more, for the techs to arrive from Laurel. The county seat, where they were based, was a good forty-five miles away from Scumble River, and the narrow secondary roads were full of twists and turns.

Taking a deep breath, Skye rose from her seat and said to Quirk, "Unless you need me for something, I'll wait for the chief in my car."

"Good idea," Quirk agreed. "I've called in all our off-duty and part-time officers, and they'll be keeping the perimeter intact."

"Okay." Skye started to walk away. "You're sure there's nothing I can do?"

"Positive." The sergeant's lips twitched. "I don't want to get in trouble for making the chief's fiancée catch pneumonia."

"Yeah. Like I wasn't soaked before you got here." Skye rolled her eyes.

When Skye reached the Bel Air, Toby was curled up on the backseat. He barked once as she got in, so she dug a honey and oat granola bar from her purse. After he wolfed down the treat, he went back to sleep. She had checked earlier and there was no owner information on the back of his tag, but it was pretty clear that he belonged to whoever was under the steamroller. *Shoot!* What would she do with a dog?

As she waited, she dried herself off with a couple more napkins, then rooted through her tote bag until she found her brush and a scrunchie. Taking her hair from the knot on top of her head, she blotted it with the last of her napkin stash, then smoothed it into a ponytail. A dash of lip gloss and a swipe of mascara helped her feel slightly calmer, and when she leaned her head against the seat, she was able to pray for the victim's soul.

She must have dozed, because the next thing she knew, the passenger door was being opened and Wally was sliding into the car.

He gathered her into his arms. "Darlin', are you okay?"

"I am now." She snuggled for a moment, then kissed his cheek and withdrew from his embrace. "I know you have questions. Go ahead."

He released her and pointed to the backseat. "Whose dog is that?" Before she could reply, Wally added, "Hold that thought. Instead tell me why you're here."

"Don't you remember? I told you I was meeting Suzette after school today. I was going to let her know I would look into her mother's death, then get some information from her."

"I didn't realize you were meeting her at the theater site." Wally gestured to the barn. "What happened when you arrived?"

"Well . . ." Skye gathered her thoughts. "The first thing I noticed was that there were no cars, so I thought maybe she had stood me up."

"But?"

"But when I approached the Winnebago, Toby" —she pointed to the backseat, where the dog was keeping a wary eye on Wally—"was sitting on the little metal step."

"And?"

"He ran away when I tried to pick him up." Skye turned a little toward Wally, then continued with her story, ending with, "So, Toby led me to the body." Skye winced. "I really hate calling someone that, but we still don't know for sure who she is."

"Sorry. I know this is tough." Wally patted her arm. "The construction foreman got here the same time I did. He should be moving the steamroller right now."

"Do you need me to look?" Skye didn't want to do it, but she understood that the sooner they identified the victim, the better their chances of solving the case. "I can do it if you think it'll help."

"I doubt anyone will be able to make a visual ID." Wally put an arm around her. "And I've got Anthony searching for Rex Taylor."

"Of course," Skye agreed quickly. "He should know anyone who worked here. He's definitely a better option for an identification than I am and—" She snapped her mouth shut, aware she was babbling.

"It's okay, sugar. I wish you hadn't been the one to find her. Try not to think about it anymore." Wally squeezed her shoulder.

"But . . ." Skye struggled to express her thoughts, not wanting to seem weak.

"I've got it now." He held her for a few more minutes, kissing her temple.

"You're right. There's nothing I can do here." Skye drew strength from Wally's touch. "I'd just be a distraction for you."

"Only in a good way," Wally reassured her. "You know I value your insights, and once we start interviewing suspects, I'll want you there."

"And I'll be ready."

"It'll probably be several hours before we're finished here, so I'll call you in the morning before you leave for school." Wally hesitated, his expression hard to read. "I need to talk to you about something personal, but I guess it can wait until tomorrow."

"Can't you tell me now?" Skye's stomach clenched. *Something personal* did not sound like good news. "I can hang around a few minutes longer." She willed him to say what he had to say, to get it over with before her imagination ran wild.

"This isn't a good time." Wally got out of the car. "Tomorrow is soon enough."

"Okay." Skye recognized that Wally wouldn't budge on this issue, so why the heck had he even brought it up? "When you talk to Mr. Taylor, please tell him I have Toby, and find out who he belongs to, okay?"

"Definitely. The last thing you need is a dog." Before closing the Bel Air's door, Wally said, "Take it easy. Call my cell if you want me for anything."

As Skye drove away, she noted that Simon had arrived. The hearse was parked where the ambulance had been a little while ago. There was something very "circle of life" about that, she thought, but at that moment Skye was too exhausted to figure out what.

Skye made a quick stop at the police station to prove to her mother that she was alive and well. Although she was tired, five minutes of reassurance beat an entire evening of the whole family descending on her to confirm her well-being.

Another necessary stop was the grocery store for doggy supplies. She bought the minimum—bowls, food, a leash, and a box of treats, but the bill was still well over fifty dollars.

Skye finally arrived home a little before seven. Bingo greeted her at the door, hissing in surprise when he spotted Toby in her arms. The black cat skidded backward a couple of feet, then held his ground, looking like a Halloween decoration with his fur standing on end and his spine arched.

Toby woofed and tried to leap from Skye's arms. She put him on the floor, having taken the precaution of affixing his new leash before entering the house. She kept a tight hold on the leather loop as his feet hit the hardwood and he tried to lunge at Bingo.

Bingo's yowl sounded like a kindergarten orchestra tuning up, and Toby barked excitedly.

Cat and dog stared at each other, loathing in both their eyes.

Skye had hoped that the animals would get along, but clearly that wasn't about to happen, at least not tonight. Sighing, she scooped Toby back up, carried him to the second floor, filled his bowls with food and water, and locked him in the master bathroom. Once she had dealt with Bingo's needs, Toby would be getting up close and personal with a tub of soapy water.

The sound of the top of a can of Fancy Feast being popped drew the angry feline from wherever he had been hiding. Skye petted him and started to explain Toby's situation. Bingo moved to the other side of his dish, so that his back was toward her, and pretended she didn't exist.

Skye sighed. She kept forgetting that, thousands of years ago, cats were worshipped as gods, and they still expected such treatment.

Just as Skye finished telling Bingo the dog's sad story, her phone rang. Hoping it was Wally with the name of Toby's owner, she grabbed the phone without looking at the caller ID.

A genderless voice said, "Tell your boyfriend to call me at 555-324-4321. And tell him that what he wants doesn't come cheap."

Before Skye could respond, the line disconnected.

Chapter 9

"HE'LL HAVE TO GO"

Skye was startled awake. Something wasn't right, but she couldn't settle on what.

Woof! Woof! Woof!

Oh. Yeah. Her canine houseguest. Whatever would she do about him? She hoped his owner would come forward and claim him, but she had a bad feeling that wish wouldn't be granted unless a genie popped out of her milk carton later that morning during breakfast. Considering how likely that scenario was, she'd better come up with an alternative. *Hmm.* Nope. No brilliant ideas.

She'd think about that later. According to the clock, she had more than an hour before the alarm would ring. Closing her eyes, she tried to go back to sleep, but too much occupied her mind.

Last night, having decided not to bother Wally about the weird message she'd received, she'd given Toby a bath, using that time to consider her interspecies problem. The only solution she could come up with was to lock Bingo in the bedroom with her for the night and keep the little dog in the sunroom. The drawback was that none of the downstairs rooms had doors, and constructing a barricade to keep Toby contained had been a challenge. In the end she had settled for a folded card table, which she had duct taped flat across the sunroom's entrance.

As if he knew that his human was thinking about a D-O-G, Bingo meowed from the pillow next to Skye. She turned her head and discovered the cat watching her, but when she extended her hand to pet him, he moved a few inches out of her reach and meowed again.

"Good morning to you, too."

Bingo glared.

"Hey. You usually sleep with me anyway, and I lugged your litter box, not to mention your food and water bowls, up here, so what's your problem?"

Bingo rose, hopped off the bed, and sat facing the closed bedroom door, his tail twitching.

"Fine." She swung her legs over the side of the mattress. "But you're staying in here until I work out what to do with Toby."

Which reminded her—she'd better check on the dog. Thank goodness he appeared to be house-trained, but it had been seven hours since his last walk.

Skye padded barefoot down the staircase and groaned when she stepped into the foyer. Some-time during the night, Toby must have escaped the barrier she had constructed. Up and down the hall, shredded magazines and books made it look like a huge confetti balloon had burst.

In the parlor, throw pillows had been chewed and tossed around, and the air swirled with their feathery remains. But by far the worst mess was in the kitchen. Whatever had been on the counter or table was now on the floor. Canisters of flour and sugar had been knocked to the tiles and broken open. Torn tea bags were strewn everywhere, and ribbons of cloth chewed from her pale yellow place mats added a decorative touch. How in the world had a dog less than two feet tall jumped so high and done so much damage?

Following the trail of telltale paw prints, Skye found Toby asleep in the sunroom—right where she had left him the night before. Bits of what might have been her favorite candy-apple-red lace bra adorned his fur. It was obvious that Toby could not be trusted alone while she went to work.

As Skye leaned against the wall, her head spinning from the extent of the demolition, Toby opened one bright brown eye and gave her his best canine smile. Her shoulders slumped. It wasn't his fault. Yesterday had been traumatic for him, and last night she'd left him alone too long. A bored doggie was a destructive doggie.

When she scooped him up, he yipped excitedly. "Do you need to go outside?" she asked.

He yelped again, and she carried him to the back door. Shoving her feet into a pair of neon orange Crocs, she clipped on his leash and trudged down the back steps. It crossed her mind that if she were to keep Toby, she'd have to have her backyard fenced.

Once his immediate needs were taken care of, the little dog ate his breakfast and settled down for a nap. Hoping he stayed asleep, Skye cleaned up the mess he had made, then hurried upstairs to get ready for work.

After a quick shower, Skye walked into her bedroom just as the radio alarm she'd forgotten to shut off clicked on. As she stood looking into her closet, trying to decide if she could stand to wear yet another pair of black slacks to school, she hummed along with Glen Campbell singing "Galveston."

The announcer's voice distracted her from her fashion dilemma. "It's six o'clock on a beautiful fall Tuesday morning. Today's temperature will be in the high sixties, with light breezes and sunshine. And all of you will be pleased to hear the high humidity is finally gone."

Yes! Yes! Yes! Skye grinned. At last it was sweater weather.

As she reached for her zebra-print twinset, the DJ said, "Now for some breaking news. Early yesterday evening, the body of a woman was discovered at the old Hutton dairy farm. This property was recently purchased by Rex Taylor, a music promoter from Nashville, for a country music theater. Mr. Taylor hopes to turn our area into the Branson of Illinois."

Skye was tempted to cover her ears and sing *La la la,* but she forced herself to listen to the rest of the report so she'd know exactly what information had been released to the public.

"The police have verified that the victim was found under a large piece of construction machinery, but they refused to provide any further details." The announcer's voice deepened. "Murder has not been ruled out."

When the DJ switched to sports, Skye turned off the radio. Sound bites of athletes mangling the English language drove her crazy.

As she finished dressing, the phone rang. "Morning, darlin'," Wally greeted her. "Are you feeling better?"

"Yes. Much. Thank you for persuading me to leave last night." Skye wedged the handset between her shoulder and neck and sat down at her dressing table to apply her makeup. "What time did you get home?"

"Close to midnight."

"You must be exhausted." Skye examined the circles under her own eyes and reached for a tube of concealer. "What kept you so long?"

"First it took the techs forever because it was an outdoor crime scene; then we had a hard time locating Rex Taylor, and when we did find him, his wife demanded that she accompany him to the barn. After watching the guy flirt with the female EMT, I can see why Mrs. Taylor insisted on coming with him."

"Yikes." Skye stroked taupe eye shadow on her lid. "That couldn't have gone well."

"Nope." Wally's tone was not amused. "When she saw the body, the idiot woman fainted and her husband made us get the paramedics to take care of her."

"Was Rex able to ID the body?" Skye asked, almost not wanting to know.

"Yes and no," Wally answered slowly. "He was able to say for certain that the clothes the victim had on were what Suzette had worn to work that day. And Mrs. Taylor identified a necklace on the body as Suzette's. But to be absolutely certain we'll have to wait for DNA tests. When the techs went through her room at the motor court, they picked up her toothbrush and razor for comparison DNA samples."

"But for investigation purposes, you're going with Suzette, right?"

"Yes," Wally confirmed. "No one else is missing from the staff."

"Did you get a chance to ask about Toby?" Skye crossed her fingers. *Please, please, please,* she begged silently. She really wanted to be able to hand the dog over to his rightful owner on her way to work.

"Yep. He was Suzette's all right." Wally paused,

then said, "Did she mention any relatives when she talked to you the other night?"

"None that are living."

"Son of a b—!" Wally cut himself off. "Mr. and Mrs. Taylor have no idea who her next of kin might be, and no emergency contact is listed on her employment records."

"What will you do next?" Skye checked her watch. She really needed to get off the phone with Wally so she could start looking for someone to take care of Toby.

"We'll talk to her colleagues, do a background check—you know, the usual. What time will you be finished today?"

"I should be able to leave by three thirty. Why?" Skye asked.

"Because I need to get your formal statement. Come straight to the station, okay?"

"Sure." Skye bit her lip. "Uh, do you think maybe Mr. or Mrs. Taylor would want Suzette's dog?" She thought fast. "I mean, if she brought Toby to work, they might be attached to him."

"Not a chance." Wally snorted. "Mrs. Taylor called him a disgusting mutt."

"Shoot."

"What are you going to do with him?"

"I don't know." Skye had counted on someone connected with Suzette claiming him. "I guess, for now, I'll keep him. At least until the case is closed or we find a member of Suzette's family."

"*If* we find her next of kin, they may not want him." Wally's voice was gentle. "Not everyone is as willing to take in strays as you are."

"I'll deal with that when the time comes." Skye checked her watch again. "Hey—sorry to cut you off, but I've got to get going. I'll see you this afternoon."

"Bye, sugar."

As soon as she hung up, she remembered the message from the night before. Should she call Wally back? No. If it was that important, last night's caller could have phoned Wally directly. Besides, she had to find a dog sitter ASAP.

Geez! Skye couldn't believe she wasn't able to think of anyone to take care of Toby. Her first choices—Trixie, Loretta, and Vince—all worked, as did all of her friends. She briefly considered Frannie Ryan, Justin Boward, and Xenia Craughwell, recent high school grads with whom she had remained close, but they were attending college or film school classes.

A fellow animal lover, her father would have been ideal. Too bad Jed was at an estate sale hoping to buy an old grain truck for cheap. Her godfather, Charlie Patukas, owner and manager of the Up A Lazy River Motor Court, was also gone for the day—in Joliet, buying new mattresses for the cottages.

Skye's mother, who should have been the next

logical choice, would have a hissy fit when she learned Skye had taken the dog. May would tell her to give him to Animal Control. It didn't feel right asking her aunts or cousins for a favor. Skye just didn't have that kind of relationship with any of them—especially considering the very real possibility that Toby might destroy their houses as he had hers.

Which left Owen. Trixie's husband would make a perfect canine nanny. He worked at home, liked dogs, and wouldn't be overly upset if Toby chewed up his possessions. There was only one —all right, two—problems. First, Skye felt a little awkward talking to him after the incident at the concert last Saturday, and second, Trixie must have already left for work, because no one was answering the phone at the Frayne residence.

Okay, that doesn't mean he isn't there. Trixie had said he rarely stepped into the house during the day. Owen was probably in the barn. Yep. That was where he was all right—there or in one of the other outbuildings. He wouldn't be in the fields today. The corn was already in, and depending on the weather, it would be five to ten days before the soybeans could be harvested.

Blocking any alternative scenario from her thoughts, Skye gathered up Toby and his equipment and put him in the car, admonishing him, "Be a good boy and Uncle Owen will take you for a nice run."

Returning to the house, Skye sprinted upstairs and opened the bedroom door to release Bingo from his imprisonment. He was curled up on the mattress and only deigned to open one eye and yawn before going back to sleep.

"Fine," Skye muttered as she grabbed her tote bag and headed out. "Be like that."

Skye pulled into the Fraynes' driveway at a quarter after seven. She had fifteen minutes to convince Owen to watch Toby and to make it to the high school on time. *Drat!* Another day of running as fast as she could just to keep up.

The white two-story house was to her left. Its door was closed, the shades down, and there was no sign of Owen. In front of Skye was a garage and an equipment shed; to her right was the barn.

To Toby, Skye said, "I'll be back in a second. Good doggies do not chew on genuine leather seats or expensive wooden steering wheels."

Tossing a mental coin, Skye chose to try the barn first. It felt a little like déjà vu, but unlike yesterday's barn, this one was clearly a working enterprise. Bales of hay were stacked along one end of the interior and stalls lined either side. The animals had already been released into their paddocks for the day, but their odor lingered.

Skye called out, "*Yoo hoo!* Owen, it's Skye. Are you around?"

There was no answer, but as she strode through

the building, she noticed evidence of Owen's recent presence. The stalls had been mucked out; the rake, shovel, and pitchfork were back in their assigned places; and all the metal troughs were full of water.

She tried again, raising her voice. "Owen, I need to ask you a favor."

Silence. Okay, he was probably in the equipment shed. If he was anything like her father, when all the other chores were done, he tinkered with his machinery.

The shed's only entrance was a towering metal door that had to be rolled to the side. Skye managed to shove it far enough open to squeeze through, but the gap didn't allow much light. The interior was one cavernous room with a packed-dirt floor. Arranged in rough rows were tractors, combines, threshers, and a variety of implements she didn't recognize.

She picked her way carefully down the center walkway, peering into the shadows and calling out Owen's name. *Darn!* He wasn't here, either.

Crossing her fingers, Skye headed to the garage, murmuring under her breath, "Be there, be there, *please* be there."

Both overhead doors were down, which was not a good sign, but Skye forced herself to remain optimistic as she walked over to the pedestrian entrance and opened it. Inside, one space was empty, clearly where Trixie parked her Honda

Civic, but the other half was occupied by a dusty black pickup.

If Owen's truck was here, where was he? As Skye pondered that question, something nibbled at the back of her mind.

Good gravy! Owen's pickup looked just like the one that had dropped off Suzette at the trailer Saturday night. *No.* Skye shook her head and scolded herself. *Don't go there. A lot of men drive dusty black trucks.* Surely Suzette's date hadn't been Owen.

Chapter 10

"ACT NATURALLY"

Even if Skye had been willing to risk cat-canine combat and doggy destruction, it was too late to take Toby back home. The clock was ticking, and she had run out of options. Toby would have to go to school with her.

Yeah. Like that would work out well.

Sheesh! If she had known this would turn into Bring Your Pet to Work Day, she'd have left the dog at home and brought Bingo. He slept twenty-three out of twenty-four hours, used a litter box rather than the great outdoors, and rarely made a sound.

As she drove, Skye tried to look on the bright side. At least the junior high's weekly Pupil Personnel Services meeting had been postponed until Wednesday, and she could spend the entire day in one building. So, taking into account a midday potty break, she'd have to smuggle Toby in and out only twice.

Another plus was that the high school had several classrooms with doors that opened directly to the lawn. Now all Skye needed was to find a teacher with one of those rooms who would be willing to look the other way when Toby needed to be walked.

Skye was still mentally scrolling through the staff roster when she pulled into the parking lot. She chose an isolated space partially blocked from view by a storage shed, and tried to figure out a way to sneak Toby into her office.

Taking an inventory of what she had to work with, she remembered the large computer paper carton that she'd stowed in the Chevy earlier that morning. It currently contained dog food, two bowls, and a chew toy, but there was plenty of room for the little dog. If Toby would keep quiet, that would be his magic carpet into the high school.

She used a pen to poke a few air holes in the side of the box, then scanned the nearby area for witnesses. There was no one around. Quickly scooping up Toby, she tucked him inside the carton and moved the rawhide bone into his sight. He immediately curled up and started gnawing.

Before putting on the lid, Skye instructed, "Okay, boy. No barking."

Clutching her key ring, she slid her tote bag onto her shoulder and hefted the box into her arms. As she strode toward the school's entrance, she concentrated on keeping her expression nonchalant. It was fairly common for her to carry around cartons and test kits, which meant that if Toby kept his little white muzzle shut, no one would look twice.

Skye was in luck. It was a few minutes before the kids would be allowed inside, so the halls were relatively empty. At one point she saw the principal marching toward her and her stomach clenched, but he was engrossed in haranguing the custodian about dented trash cans and didn't acknowledge Skye's presence.

Almost there. Skye put the box on the floor in front of her office and inserted her key. Just as she opened the door, a group of teachers walked by, talking loudly, and Toby shoved the lid from the carton, poked his head over the side, and looked around. His eyes were bright with interest and his pink tongue lolled out of his mouth.

Skye quickly thrust the box inside the room, slammed the door, and waited. Had they seen Toby? After a few moments, when no one came around asking about the little dog, she collapsed on her chair.

Phew! That had been too close. It was only seven thirty-five and already her heart was racing and her pulse was pounding. How would she pull this off for another eight hours?

While Toby acquainted himself with every nook, cranny, and object in the room, Skye's mind galloped. Since she now had the morning free, she could stay in her office writing reports, but she had counseling sessions scheduled for the afternoon. Where could she stash the little dog while she saw students?

There weren't many staff members Skye could count as real friends. For the most part, it was easier to maintain impartiality and confidentiality if she kept somewhat distant from most of the faculty.

Past circumstance had thrown her and Alana Lowe together, and they had formed a bond, but the art teacher was too emotionally fragile to handle this sort of favor. That left Trixie.

Hmm. As the school librarian, Trixie had greater freedom than almost anyone else. She also had a workroom that she could lock. And since the three afternoon periods totaled only two hours, surely Toby wouldn't need to relieve himself during that time.

The little dog had found an old sweater Skye kept around for days when the furnace went out and had managed to wrestle it from the coatrack onto the floor. He was currently nestled in its folds, chomping on his bone. This was an ideal time to go talk to Trixie.

School had started a quarter of an hour earlier, and the students were finishing homeroom—twenty minutes in which attendance was taken, announcements were made, and a good-citizen lesson was taught. Apparently today's session was about organization, because Trixie had an image of the official assignment notebook on the overhead screen and was demonstrating how to keep track of homework due dates.

From where Skye lingered in the back of the multimedia center, she noticed that few of the kids seemed impressed with the multicolor pencil method. Most sat with their books in their arms on the edge of their seats, and when the bell rang, they bolted for the exit.

Trixie was gathering up debris when she spotted Skye weaving her way through the departing teens, and called out, "Hey, girlfriend. I was going to go look for you as soon as I had a break."

"You want to hear about the body," Skye guessed, knowing that rumors must be flying fast and furious around town.

"What else?" Trixie drew Skye into her tiny office and shut the door. "Spill."

While Skye described yesterday's experience, Trixie unwrapped a package of miniature donuts. She offered Skye one of the quartet, then bit into her own, moaning, "Oh, my goodness. These are *sooo* good."

While Skye had been off the diet roller coaster for the past five years, she still tried to eat healthfully and to exercise. So despite having missed breakfast, she resisted the donuts and stifled the urge to smack her friend. It wasn't Trixie's fault that she could consume her own weight in sugar and never add an inch to her size 4 figure, while Skye could gain five pounds watching the Food Channel.

Once both Trixie's appetite for sweets and her curiosity about the murder were sated, Skye said, "I need a favor."

"Sure." Trixie popped the last bite into her mouth. "What?"

Skye explained about Toby, then said, "So, can you keep him in the storage room this afternoon?"

"No problem." Trixie pressed the powdered sugar from inside the cardboard tray into a tiny ball and licked it from her fingers. "I can take him from after lunch until the end of the day." She crumbled the cellophane. "Normally, I'd go home on my break and drop the dog off with Owen, but he's going to some estate sale with your dad today."

"Too bad." Skye had deliberately omitted her search for Owen, since she'd been afraid Owen was AWOL again. "That would have been a great solution."

"Yeah."

As the two women got up, Skye asked, "Did Owen ever say where he was Saturday when you were looking for him?" She hadn't had a chance to talk to Trixie either Sunday or Monday, and now the coincidence of the black truck along with Owen being MIA the same afternoon that Suzette was missing troubled Skye.

"Sort of." Trixie's smile dimmed. "He said he ran into an old friend after his business meeting and they went into Joliet for a drink." She led the way into the library. "I told him I didn't care if he went out with friends. All I wanted was for him to call and tell me."

"That's a reasonable request."

"He promised to let me know next time."

"Good." Skye waved good-bye, walking away before Trixie could see the worry on her face. Could Owen's old friend have been Suzette?

During the last of the two lunch periods, Skye checked the teachers' lounge to see who was there, and thus whose classroom would be unoccupied. When she spotted Alana, Skye hurried back to her office, put Toby into the computer paper box, and snuck him over to the art room and out its exterior door.

While the little dog was doing his business, Skye's thoughts went back to Owen's truck. Had it been the one she saw? Concentrating, she tried to recall some detail that would distinguish his dusty black pickup from the one Suzette had arrived in. She knew she had seen something, but couldn't remember what. Deep in thought, she failed to notice that the marching band had assembled across the lawn from her—at least she didn't notice them until the loud bleat of a tuba startled her from her contemplation.

At the sound of the first note, Toby stiffened. His head whipped toward the assembled musicians, and with his ears twitching, he barked furiously and lunged in their direction. The leash jerked in Skye's hand and she felt something pop in her shoulder.

Despite the pain, Skye hung on tight. She reeled in the eighteen-pound dog like a trout on the end of a fishing pole, scooped him up, and dashed inside. Panting, she plastered herself against the side of the wall and hoped no one had seen Toby. Or if they did, that they wouldn't bother to find out why there was a dog taking a whiz on the school's memorial crab apple tree.

As she closed the door, Skye heard the band director shout, "Britney, quit trying to be the center of attention. Everyone can see there's no animal over there. Just be quiet and play your flute."

After the near miss, Skye was relieved to deposit Toby with Trixie and to see her first counseling client—even if it was Ian Gooding, a precocious twelve-year-old freshman whom

Skye had argued against double promoting last year due to the socialization issues she knew would arise.

Her suggestion—that Ian remain with his age group but that his curriculum be adjusted to meet his unique needs—had been rejected by the superintendent on the grounds that it would cost too much money. Since he had an IQ of over 165, his parents understandably wanted their son to be academically challenged, and they'd demanded that he skip seventh and eighth grades and go directly to high school.

Within a week Skye had been asked to see him for counseling. He had no friends and alienated nearly everyone with whom he interacted. This was their third session, and she wondered what test she would have to pass this time before he would talk to her.

In their first meeting, Skye had had to beat him at chess—thank goodness Simon had taught her well. The second time, he brought a Sudoku for her to complete. Today she was hoping for a crossword puzzle, but he surprised her by actually wanting to discuss an incident he'd been involved in on the school bus.

Skye suspected his progress had more to do with a new girl who had moved in last week than with her skill as a therapist, but she would take improvement however it occurred.

After a lengthy explanation, Ian finally got to

his real question. "What I want to know, Ms. Denison, is how I should act so that Christy will like me."

"Just be yourself." Skye smiled reassuringly at the preteen. "But maybe just a little less judgmental of other people's limitations."

"Even the really stupid ones?"

"Especially those who are less fortunate than you." Skye made sure she had eye contact. "Everyone has a place in this world. You just need to find yours."

"But I'm a geek." He ducked his head and mumbled, "Christy will never like the real me."

"She might." Skye knew that the young lady he was referring to was also gifted—not that she could share that information with Ian. Instead she said, "The people who matter won't mind if you're yourself, and the people who do mind don't matter."

Ian's expression was skeptical, but as he left Skye's office he promised to think about what she'd said.

In comparison to Ian, the next two students were easy; both were cooperative and working hard on their counseling goals. Skye sent the last one back to his classroom a few minutes before the bell rang, then headed toward the library to retrieve Toby.

Congratulating herself on having concealed the little dog's presence for an entire day, she didn't notice Homer Knapik until his hairy hand descended on her shoulder. The principal's lumbering movements, protruding belly, and the graying hair that grew on nearly every visible part of his body made him look like Hollywood's concept of the abominable snowman.

Instead of greeting her, Homer grumbled, "Why didn't you answer your phone? I've been calling you for the past hour."

"I put it on voice mail when I'm with students," Skye reminded him, perhaps for the fiftieth time. "Did you leave a message?"

"Message, smessage," Homer groused. "Come on or we'll never get this meeting over with."

"What meeting?" If she had to explain with one word why the human race would never achieve its full potential, *meeting* would be that word.

"The one you're making us late for." Homer thrust his head at her.

Skye stepped out of bad-breath range. "What's it about?"

"Mrs. Gooding wants to talk about that little brainiac of hers."

"Now?" Skye's heart sank. She couldn't stay late today. She had to rescue Toby and get to the police station. "If it's not an emergency, she should make an appointment like everyone else."

"Everyone else isn't on the school board." Homer grabbed Skye's elbow and shoved her forward. "After five years in public education, you don't still believe that everyone gets treated equally, do you?"

Skye ignored his cynicism. "Where are we going?" she asked, cringing because she already knew the answer. There was only one place in this direction where they sometimes held conferences.

"The library."

Of course. Where else? Skye tried to hang back, but Homer kept pulling.

When they arrived, Skye was relieved to see that Trixie had seated Mrs. Gooding as far as possible from the storage room where Toby was currently ensconced. As Skye and Homer were sitting down, the final bell rang, and a few minutes later Ian's teachers began to assemble.

Once everyone was present, Homer said, "Mrs. Gooding, what is it you'd like to discuss?"

"First—" A series of sneezes interrupted her. Once she found a tissue, blew her nose, and accepted a round of *God bless you*s, she continued. "I'd like to thank you all for your hard work with Ian. He hasn't complained about being bored once yet." She paused, sneezing twice more, then said, "But he has expressed an interest in dropping physical education and taking a real class in its place."

"Well." Homer stroked a tuft of hair that poked between the buttons of his shirt. "The problem with that is he needs PE credits to graduate."

"But—" Mrs. Gooding broke off, overcome by

a bout of sneezing. Once she had wiped her nose, she said, "Sorry. I can't think what's making me sneeze. The only thing I'm allergic to is dogs."

Skye stole a quick glance at the storage room. A white paw was sticking out from under the door. "It's probably mold," she suggested. "This is an old building after all." She had to get this meeting over with ASAP. "Maybe we should move somewhere else."

Homer glared at Skye. "I'm sure we're almost done. Right, Mrs. Gooding?"

"Yes." Mrs. Gooding dabbed at her watering eyes with a Kleenex. "I just wanted to speak to the math teacher about the note you sent me yesterday."

"The one about Ian's assignments?" the math teacher asked.

"Uh-huh." Mrs. Gooding nodded. "I checked with him, and he said that his homework is not missing; it's just having an out-of-notebook experience."

Skye looked to see if Mrs. Gooding was joking, but her expression was completely serious.

"Fine." The math teacher didn't blink. "Please tell Ian that his homework better rematerialize by tomorrow or he's getting a zero."

"Anything else?" Homer interjected before Mrs. Gooding could respond.

"Yes." Mrs. Gooding turned to Skye. "How is Ian's counseling going?"

"Slow but sure." Skye's tone was encouraging. "He's starting to talk more."

"About?"

"I can't discuss specifics." Skye shifted in her chair. "Remember, I told you about confidentiality when you signed the permission slip?"

"Good." Homer shoved back his chair. "Then if there's nothing else . . . ?"

"One more thing."

While Mrs. Gooding paused for another sneeze, Skye watched in horror as one of Trixie's student helpers walked up to the storage room, inserted her key, and opened the door. Toby erupted from the confined space like Silly String from a can.

Skye took off after him, but he eluded her every attempt to corral him. She and the dog did a few laps around the library. Books flew off the shelves as Skye tried to right herself while she skidded around corners. Toby took the same hairpin turns with ease. He looked back every once in a while to see if Skye was keeping up with him, but the moment she got near enough to grab him, he danced away, yipping excitedly.

Finally he grew bored with the game, abruptly changed direction, and zipped over to where everyone in the meeting was sitting. Before Skye could reach him, he ran up to Homer, raised his leg, and peed on the principal's shiny black shoes.

• • •

Toby's antics put a quick halt to the conference. Homer barely waited until everyone had fled before he laid into Skye. His tirade eventually wound down, ending with, "And I want a new pair of these exact same shoes on my desk by tomorrow morning or you're fired."

"Where—?"

"Franklin's in Clay Center. Size ten double-E. They close at six."

"Yes, sir. I'm so sorry." Skye stared at the floor as she explained her predicament. Lifting her head, she said, "It won't happen again. I . . ." She trailed off; Homer was no longer there. The only trace of him was his soaked, smelly shoes left in the middle of the table.

Having already deposited Toby in her car, Skye was walking back to her office to get her purse when the school's music teacher, carrying a large box that obstructed her view, bumped into Skye in the hall. The impact caused the contents to spill all over the floor.

"Oops." Noreen Iverson was in her late forties, with a smooth complexion and comfortable figure. "You must think I'm really clumsy."

"Not at all." Skye squatted to help the woman gather her belongings. "I drop stuff all the time."

"I guess I'm a little distracted today." Noreen's cheeks turned red. "I heard some disturbing news

116

this morning and I can't get it out of my mind."

"Oh?"

"About the poor girl who was found dead at the old Hutton dairy." Noreen picked up pages of music and stuffed them into the carton.

"Yes." Skye was thankful no one seemed to know that she was the one who had found the body.

"My niece is an EMT and she was called out there to take care of some woman who fainted," Noreen explained. "She heard one of the officers say the dead girl was Suzette Neal."

"Really?" *Great!* The news was out before the identification was official. She'd have to let Wally know. "The singer from Saturday night's concert?"

"Yes." Noreen straightened. "But I knew her when she was just a baby."

"I saw from the flyer that she was from around here," Skye said, hoping to encourage the woman to continue.

"Her father was my supervisor when I student taught here twenty-seven years ago." Noreen's hazel eyes softened. "He was such a sweet, handsome guy."

"Did he work here long?" Skye nabbed another stray sheet of music and handed it over.

"Just that one year. His wife died very suddenly —a terrible accident—and he was a changed man after that." Noreen hoisted the refilled

117

carton into her arms, adding as she walked away, "In fact, when he left, they offered me his job and I've been here ever since."

Well, that solved one mystery. Mr. Neal had been a teacher. When Skye got to her office, she pulled out the list of questions she'd made regarding Mrs. Neal's death and made a quick note. Another thing to share with Wally when she talked to him this afternoon.

Chapter 11

"MAMA HE'S CRAZY"

A few minutes later, when Skye slid into her car, Toby greeted her with a tail wag and a happy woof. For a second, she relaxed and stroked his soft white fur, but then the memory of Wally saying he wanted to talk to her about something personal intruded.

She had deliberately refused to think about what he'd said, and had even managed to stop herself from asking him about it when he'd called that morning. Now that she was on her way to meet him, there was no avoiding the panicky feeling in the pit of her stomach. If the news had been good, he would have told her right away, which meant it must be bad. Just how bad was the question.

When Skye arrived at the police station, the municipal parking lot it shared with the city hall and library was full again. Unless Dante and the music promoter were having another meeting, this late in the afternoon there should have been only four automobiles present: one belonging to the dispatcher, one to the officer on duty, one to the librarian, and one to the city clerk. So why was the tiny lot suddenly packed?

As she circled the small patch of asphalt looking for an empty spot, Skye noticed a white van with a huge antenna sticking up from the roof taking up two spaces. A few vehicles down, a similar van also hogged multiple slots, and another, a little way from that one, had parked over the painted lines as well. In front of the last van, the drummer and keyboard player from Flint James's backup band were being interviewed by a reporter.

Hmm. Now Skye knew why, when she'd tried to call Wally a few minutes ago to let him know she was on her way, all the police lines had been busy, even his private number. The media had invaded Scumble River.

Evidently, as Father Burns had said in one of his sermons, even though there are no new sins, the old ones are getting a lot more publicity than in the past. They'd been fairly lucky that previous deaths involving somewhat well-known individuals hadn't attracted as much notice. In those cases, either the celebrities had been too minor for reporters to bother, or word of the murder hadn't spread until after the case was solved. Up until now, the over-the-hill supermodel's murder had been the worst, with reporters stealing trash from the crime scene, but this all-out blitz went way beyond that coverage.

While Suzette was far from a household name, it was clear that the manner of her death or the fame of the others involved—or both—had chummed the water, and a feeding frenzy was in progress.

A door on one of the vans was flung open, catching Skye's attention. She turned in time to see a tall, skinny young man with a massive camera perched on his shoulder bolt out of the vehicle, followed by an overly made-up young woman clutching a microphone.

Holy crap! They were coming straight at her. Skye revved the Bel Air's engine and slammed the gas pedal to the floor. Bitter experience had taught her that any contact with reporters was to be avoided at all costs.

Her tires squealing, she sped out of the lot, then tore down Maryland, hanging a right on Kinsman. Once she was out of view, Skye slowed and turned into the driveway of Holy Redeemer, a recently defunct nondenominational house of worship. After parking as far from the church as possible, she exited the Chevy.

With Toby on his leash, she started across the

grassy strip separating the PD and the church's parking lot. This time she not only had to smuggle a dog into a building; she had to sneak herself in as well.

As she walked, she dug through her tote looking for the key to the police garage's back entrance. Thank goodness Wally had given her one after a recent mix-up. Of course, the little piece of metal was at the very bottom of her bag, hidden by a gum wrapper, an expired cat food coupon, and a crumpled tissue.

When Skye neared the steel door, Toby stiffened and started barking. At first she thought he had caught the scent of a squirrel or a rabbit, but as she scanned the area, she noticed a journalist lurking near the corner of the building. *Duh!* Of course, someone would cover the rear of the station.

She tightened her hold on Toby's lead and asked him loudly, "What's there, boy?"

The little dog growled.

"Is it a nasty reporter?" Skye stuck the key in the lock and turned it.

The growling increased.

"If anyone tries to push his way inside with us," Skye said, scooping up Toby, "bite him."

She darted over the threshold and slammed the heavy door behind her. Looking around, she noted that both squad cars and the chief's cruiser—Scumble River PD's entire transportation fleet—were parked in the garage. No one was out patrolling.

Skye threaded her way among the vehicles and into the station's rear entrance, which led to a short passageway. To her right she could hear loud voices coming from the reception area. She wasn't sure who she felt sorrier for—her mother, who was the dispatcher on duty, or the journalists trying to get past May.

The cubicles that lined the hallway, usually empty, were filled today with officers on the phone or the computer, or both. From the snatches of conversation she overheard, half of the officers were looking for background information on Suzette, while the others were handling calls from the media.

As soon as those in the latter group hung up, the telephone would ring. They'd pick up the receiver, listen for a moment, and repeat, "We have no more information at this time."

Shuddering, Skye was glad she hadn't been assigned to that duty. She and Toby hurried to the back of the building and trotted up the steps. They paused at the top as she glanced uneasily through the archway. She was half afraid the mayor would pop out at her like a malevolent jack-in-the-box, so when she saw that Dante's office door was closed, she took a relieved breath. She felt even better when she saw that there wasn't any light coming from underneath his door.

Her uncle must have left for the day or was downstairs talking to the media. Either way, Skye was glad she wouldn't have to deal with him. Since she'd been the one to discover the body, she was sure the mayor would find a way to blame her for any bad publicity Scumble River received.

Skye's heart turned over when she saw Wally behind his desk. He exuded a masculine magnetism that reached out to something inside her. As she got closer and saw the lines of exhaustion etched around his eyes and mouth, her chest tightened. While she had been home resting last night, he'd had to stay at the grisly crime scene, dealing with everyone involved and all that went into an investigation of this magnitude.

At the first sight of Skye, Wally rose to his feet. In one swift movement he met her halfway across the office and gathered her to his chest in a fierce embrace.

She kicked the door closed, locked it, and dropped Toby's leash, then buried her face against the strong, warm column of his throat. It was a rare moment of pure pleasure, and she enjoyed it fully.

With his lips against her hair, Wally whispered, "I've been thinking about holding you like this all day." His large hands framed her face and held it gently while his dark eyes caressed her.

"Me, too." She wound her arms around his waist and stroked his back.

"In that case, maybe I should make your dreams come true right now."

"Here?" Skye was distracted by his thumb stroking her jaw.

"Well, your ghost makes it risky to try to make love at your place." His words were teasing. "Half the time she even blocks my phone calls."

Skye knew Wally didn't really believe it was the spirit of Alma Griggs that caused things to blow up, catch on fire, or flood every time they went beyond a chaste kiss on the cheek at her house, but Skye wasn't so sure. Just to be on the safe side, they'd gotten into the habit of hanging out at Wally's.

"Guess I need to sprinkle some holy water around," Skye murmured. "Or maybe get Father Burns to perform an exorcism." The jolt of electricity where Wally's thigh brushed her hip made it hard to breathe, let alone concentrate on forming a coherent sentence.

"Or," he purred as he tugged off her cardigan, leaving only the thin camisole she wore underneath, "you could move in with me." He nipped at the sensitive cord running from her ear down her neck.

"I don't think we should . . ." Skye tried to bring both of them to their senses. "I mean, what if someone . . . ?" She lost her train of thought when he arched her body into his and locked his hands against her spine. "It wouldn't be good if someone . . ." There was a reason they shouldn't be doing this, but darned if she could think of it.

"True." His lips hovered above hers as he spoke. "But right now I don't care."

Skye stopped trying to resist and pressed her open mouth to his. He needed no further invitation and his kiss devoured her.

A few minutes or hours or days later, a bright flash of light exploded in front of her. Wally's head whipped around and he swore violently. Careful to keep Skye behind him, he turned toward the intruder.

At the same time, a white blur rocketed past the couple, launched itself at the guy standing in the open door wielding the camera, and knocked him down.

"Get this freaking animal off of me!" Kicking and screaming, Camera Guy tried to dislodge the little dog from his leg. "It's trying to kill me!"

Before Skye could respond, footsteps thundered up the stairs and her mother rushed over to the fallen cameraman. May attempted to haul him to his feet, but her five feet, two inches and 120-pound frame was at a disadvantage against the much bigger man.

"Citizen's arrest!" May yelled at him as she struggled, making it clear that her intent was not to rescue him, but to take him into custody. "Citizen's arrest."

Close on May's heels were the officers who had been working the phones.

Anthony, a part-timer, reached them first. His face was beet red and he was stammering. "Uh, Chief, I, uh, we're, uh . . . This weasel slipped through the gate when I went to help Mrs. Denison with those dang reporters. He must've hid somewhere real fast, 'cause he disappeared. We looked everywhere, and were checking in the garage when we heard the ruckus up here."

Skye stepped around Wally and grabbed Toby. Searching for a place to contain him, she finally gave up and tied his leash to the desk. After admonishing the little dog to stay, she turned and saw Wally pulling May off the downed cameraman.

Once he had separated May from the guy, Wally took the man by the arm and announced to his employees, "Okay, everyone. I'll handle this. You all can get back to work."

But Skye's mother stood firm, with her arms crossed over her chest and a stubborn expression on her face.

"May"—Wally's voice was cool and unyielding —"I meant you, too."

At one time Wally and Skye's mother had been close, but May's objection to his engagement to her daughter had introduced considerable tension into that relationship. May believed Wally wasn't young enough to father a sufficient number of grandchildren for her; plus he was divorced, an additional mark against him. He was trying to get an annulment, but there was little he could do about his age.

"I want to press charges against this jerk." May narrowed eyes that were the same emerald green as her daughter's. "He broke into the station, pushed me out of the way, and when I fell against a file cabinet, I tore my best uniform pants."

"Are you all right?" Wally and Skye asked in unison.

"I guess." May's words were grudging. "But there's going to be a bruise."

"Okay, then. That's assault, breaking and entering, and trespassing." Wally thrust the young man into a chair and handcuffed him to the arm. "In these parts we don't go around shoving older ladies or forcibly entering clearly marked restricted areas."

"Who're you calling an old lady?" May's lower lip pooched out.

May had turned sixty in August and was a tad sensitive about that milestone.

"Mom." Skye stepped between her mother and her fiancé. "He said older, not old."

Wally ignored May and Skye's exchange, concentrating on the man sitting stiffly on the visitor's chair, clutching his camera to his chest with his free hand. "What do you have to say for yourself?"

"You're violating my first amendment rights." The guy's expression was defiant.

"How's that?" Wally's tone was mild, but his mouth was a hard line.

"By not giving me access to the officers. By everyone hiding behind locked doors. And by refusing to tell what happened."

He sounded like the kids on the school paper that Skye and Trixie cosponsored. For the first time since he'd appeared, she took a good look at him and realized he was much younger than she'd first thought.

She put her sweater on, then shot a glance at Wally, seeking permission to participate in the interrogation.

When he nodded, she moved in front of the prisoner and asked, "Who do you work for?"

He stiffened but remained silent. When she repeated her question, he dropped his gaze to the floor, scuffed the toe of his beat-up sneaker on the carpet, and mumbled something she didn't catch.

"What?" She stepped closer. "Lift your head and speak clearly."

"I'm freelancing."

Skye and Wally exchanged a relieved look. A picture of them in the *Chicago Tribune*, locked in a passionate embrace the day after a gruesome murder, would be bad for both their careers.

"Son"—Wally leaned a hip against his desk—"I'll make you a deal."

"What kind of deal?" Suspicion oozed from the young man's voice.

"We aren't going to arrest you for trespassing or breaking and entering or assault, and you're going to apologize to my dispatcher, buy her a new pair of pants, and hand over the memory card from your camera."

"Can you believe that little peckerhead had the nerve to admit he picked the lock on my office door?" Wally ground out between clenched teeth. "Who does he think he is, Woodward and Bernstein?"

The cameraman had been escorted out of the police station and onto the front sidewalk half an hour ago, but Wally was still enraged. Even though Skye had tried to calm him down, he continued to pace back and forth in front of her, Toby trotting at his heels.

"He's lucky I didn't let May take him out to the woodshed and beat the crap out of him."

Skye opened her mouth to respond, but Wally was on a roll. "Did he really think no one would notice him running around a police station taking pictures?"

"His problem was he didn't think." Skye finally managed to get a word in edgewise.

"That's for damn sure."

"At least you destroyed the memory card. Everything's fine." She lost patience when she saw Wally continue to scowl. The problem was solved and it was time he got over it. Maybe humor would do the trick. "And I'm sure Mom will eventually forgive you for calling her a little old lady."

"Yeah." Wally's lips turned up at the corner in a tiny grin. "Right after she forgives me for not being Catholic."

"She'll come around once the annulment goes through." Skye's tone was uncertain.

"Actually"—Wally pulled up a chair in front of Skye and took her hands—"that's what I need to talk to you about. You see—"

He was interrupted by the ringing of his private line. The one to which only Skye and the mayor had the number.

Chapter 12

"WHERE WERE YOU?"

Skye sat frozen, her face expressionless, trying not to give any indication she was upset. But Toby seemed to sense her distress and leaned against her leg, whimpering. She absently petted him while she listened to Wally on the phone.

"No, Dante. There's still nothing definitive from the medical examiner." Wally sat on the edge of his desk. "Yes, I'm sure there's no way it could have been an accident. Steamrollers do not move without someone in the driver's seat and people do not lie down in their path and allow themselves to be flattened like a pancake."

He listened as the mayor's voice blasted from the receiver, then said, "Hell, no. I wasn't trying to make a joke. I don't even know what a crêpe suzette is."

Skye could hear her uncle screaming something about bad publicity, but she caught only every other word of his diatribe.

"Believe me, no one around here wants to talk to the media," Wally interjected when Dante took a breath. "We're directing all questions to you."

Skye couldn't stand it any longer. This waiting was killing her. She got up. "I'm going to get a soda. Do you want one?" Wally shook his head. "Okay. I'll be right back."

When Skye returned juggling a can of Diet Coke, a bag of Cheetos, and a Kit Kat bar, Wally was just hanging up the receiver, saying, "Yeah. I'll call you right away if I hear anything."

"That sounded fun," Skye commented, laying her loot on the desktop.

Wally ran his fingers through his hair. "Your uncle's gone crazy."

"I'll bet it was a short trip." Skye resumed her seat, grabbed the soda, and popped the top. "He's had the map to that location for years."

Wally chuckled mirthlessly. "Rex Taylor has

him convinced we need to spin this as an accidental death."

"Right." Skye swallowed a sip of Diet Coke. "Has he suggested blaming the whole thing on gremlins or a poltergeist?"

"I'm sure that's next." Wally picked up the Cheetos and pulled open the bag. "It sure would help if the ME got his report in."

"When do you expect it?" Skye unwrapped the Kit Kat bar.

"The preliminary one should be here anytime, but it'll be three to seven days before we get the DNA tests." Wally crunched a bright orange puff of cheese. "Too bad it's not like those shows you like. I bet *NCIS* would have had the results before the first commercial."

"Probably," Skye deadpanned. "They have Abby on their team and she's a lot smarter than our lab guys." She knew Wally thought the forensics on TV dramas were bogus, but she still enjoyed the programs. "So what were you going to tell me before the phone rang?"

"Maybe we should wait until later, when we're home, to talk about that." Wally's expression was apprehensive. "You know, stick to business while we're here. We have a lot to discuss about the case."

"Actually . . ." Skye faltered. She had just remembered Homer's ultimatum. "I have to get over to Franklin's in Clay Center and they close in half an hour."

"You want to go shopping now?" Wally's brows disappeared into his hairline.

"Not want, need." Skye enlightened Wally about her afternoon and Toby's indiscretion, finishing with, "So, you see, it's those shoes or my job."

"A dog is a big responsibility." He glanced down at the culprit in question, who was staring at the Cheeto Wally was holding. "Maybe you need to find someone else to take care of him."

"I told you this morning, I'm only keeping him until you find Suzette's next of kin."

"I just want you to think of the consequences of your decision."

"Fine." Skye narrowed her eyes.

"Fine." Wally pressed the intercom button. "May, have Anthony come up to my office."

"What are you doing?"

"I'm going to send him to get Homer's shoes." Wally crossed his arms. "I need you here and I can spare him, so it makes sense."

"You can't have him run my errands." Skye wondered at Wally's uncharacteristic behavior. He was usually obsessively careful not to exploit his position as chief of police. "Not on the city's dime."

"I wasn't going to." He shot her a quizzical look as he reached into his back pocket and took out his wallet. "His shift is almost over, so I'll take him off the clock and pay him myself."

"It's my problem." Even though they were

engaged, Skye felt uncomfortable letting Wally spend his money on her this way. "I'll pay him."

"Fair enough."

While Wally worked out the details with Anthony, Skye phoned the store to see how much the shoes cost. "You're kidding me."

The clerk's voice was amused. "No, ma'am. That particular brand is two hundred and twenty-nine dollars."

"Holy mackerel!" Skye's shriek drew Toby's, Wally's, and Anthony's attention. She covered the receiver and repeated the price. The little dog yipped in sympathy, but the men seemed unimpressed.

"Lady, I've got customers waiting. Do you want them or not? I only have one pair in that size."

Yeah. Skye rolled her eyes. Like there were hundreds of people clamoring to buy butt-ugly size 10 double-E clodhoppers that cost more than a new set of tires.

"Yes, I want them." Skye gritted her teeth. What choice did she have? "Can I give you my credit card number to pay for them now?"

"Knock yourself out."

Skye stopped herself from suggesting that the man take his own advice, and instead she said, as civilly as she could manage, "A friend of mine will be there in twenty minutes to get them. His name is Anthony."

"Is he cute?" Before disconnecting, the clerk

added, "Never mind. Even if he's Brad Pitt, we close at six on the dot and I'm not sticking around if he isn't here."

After Anthony left for Clay Center, Skye and Wally were silent for a few minutes.

Finally Wally seated himself behind his desk. He opened a folder, picked up pen, and said, "Shall we get down to business?"

"Well . . ." Skye ate a section of the Kit Kat bar while she considered insisting Wally tell her about whatever he was avoiding. Deciding it would be better to handle their personal issues somewhere else, she said, "Okay. Where should we start?"

"Why don't you write out your statement, so May can type it up for you to sign while we talk?" Wally pushed a legal pad and ballpoint over to her.

"Already done." Skye whipped several sheets of paper out of her tote bag and slid them across the desktop toward him. "I wrote it last night after I got home so it would be fresh in my mind."

"Good thinking." He picked up the pages and flipped through them. "Is there anything here that you remembered after we spoke? Anything you didn't tell me?"

"Nothing about finding the body." Skye made a couple of notes on the legal pad. "But I did discover some information today."

"Great." Wally leaned forward. "We sure haven't made much progress on this end." He absently fingered a letter opener. "We did brief interviews with the Country Roads employees and we told them all to stick around town until we give the go-ahead to leave. Though if anyone consults a lawyer, they'll find out we can't really hold them here."

"From what I overheard Uncle Dante telling you on the phone earlier, it doesn't sound as if Rex has any intention of altering his plans to open a music theater," Skye reassured Wally. "Which means I doubt he'd let any of his employees leave town."

"True." Wally flipped to a fresh page on his legal pad. "So tell me what you've got."

"First"—Skye held up a finger—"the bad news. The EMT who attended to Kallista Taylor's fainting spell heard someone mention that the victim was Suzette, so that cat's out of the bag."

"Oh, well." Wally shrugged. "We knew we'd never keep it quiet." He grimaced. "But I can't make an official announcement until the ME confirms the DNA samples, which will drive the reporters crazy."

Skye nodded sympathetically. "Number two, I discovered that Suzette's father worked at the high school for a year as a music teacher."

"How did you find that out?"

"The current music teacher told me." Skye explained how Noreen had come to confide in her, finishing up with, "I'll talk to her more about Mr. Neal tomorrow, and also find out from her if there's anyone else still around town who would have known him back then."

"That's great information to have, especially because Martinez couldn't find the case file on Mrs. Neal's accident." Wally tapped his pen on the desktop.

Zelda Martinez was the newest, youngest, and only female officer on the Scumble River police force. She'd started less than five months ago, straight from the academy, and was still considered a rookie, which meant she was given all the boring assignments.

"Do you think they didn't write up the case?" Skye could believe it. The chief before Wally had been hired because he was the previous mayor's cousin, not because he was the best candidate for the job.

"No. I'm sure the file exists. The problem is the chaos in the storage room." Wally ran his fingers through his hair. "I told Dante a couple of years ago we needed to get those records in the computer, but he refused to give me a budget to hire someone to do it, and with only one officer and one dispatcher on duty per shift, there's no time."

"Sounds like the school system." Skye walked around the desk and rubbed his shoulders. "Something is never important enough to spend money on until it's an all-out emergency."

"Right." Wally blew out a puff of exasperation.

"Dante only pays attention to whatever is hot now. Then it's asses and elbows, but once the crisis is over he goes back to his same old neglectful ways."

"Remind me again why we chose to be civil servants." Skye smiled wryly.

"Because we're too idealistic for our own good."

"That brings me to the third piece of info." Skye gave his muscles a final squeeze and sat back down. "The one I'm not sure I should share with you."

"Why's that?"

"Because it's only a hunch." Skye pursed her lips. "Actually, not even a hunch—just a possibility. An extremely unlikely possibility."

"That's never stopped you before." Wally grinned. "In fact, that's your specialty."

"You are so not funny." Skye shot a rubber band at him, then sobered. "The difference this time is that I could hurt a friend."

"I promise to move cautiously"—Wally put his hand over his heart—"and try to keep whatever I can out of the written reports."

"Okay." Skye inhaled sharply. After keeping a secret from Wally in their last case, she had vowed never to do it again. She had to tell him, no matter how bad she felt doing so. "Owen Frayne disappeared last Saturday afternoon and didn't reappear until early that evening."

"So?"

"He told Trixie he went to Joliet for a drink with a friend."

"But?"

"But I think he may be lying and he really might have been with Suzette." Putting her suspicions into words tied Skye's stomach into knots. "She was missing during the same period of time Owen was gone. And when she did finally show up at the concert, I saw her being dropped off by someone in a dusty black pickup." Skye blew out a breath. "Just like the one Owen drives."

"There are a lot of dirty black trucks in the area," Wally pointed out. "What was the make and model?"

"I have no idea," Skye admitted. "And I'm hoping it wasn't Owen's, but the fact that he and Suzette didn't show up where they were supposed to be on the same afternoon . . ."

"Yeah. And even though their dual absences could be a coincidence, we need to check out Owen, as well as the other owners of black trucks in the area." Wally made a note on his pad. "Here's what I'll do. I will personally have a talk with him, telling him that we're meeting with everyone in the area who drives a black pickup."

Skye chewed on a thumbnail. "You're not going to tell him it has anything to do with Suzette, are you?"

"No," Wally assured her. "I'll tell him we're investigating a hit-and-run during that time that involved a black truck. If he gives me the name of his friend and that person confirms his alibi, we can clear him without causing any collateral damage."

She tilted her head, thinking, then nodded. "Yeah, that should work."

"Anything else about the case?" Wally asked.

"Yes." Skye crossed her legs. "I was thinking about yesterday when the EMT climbed up on the steamroller to see if he could move it."

"And?"

"And he came right back down and told Quirk that even though the key was there, he couldn't figure out how it ran."

"Right." Wally leaned back in his chair. "The construction foreman had to be called."

"Exactly." Skye nodded. "So, driving a steamroller is a skill requiring special training. And whoever killed Suzette had to have had that training."

"Shoot. I should have asked about that last night at the scene." Wally picked up the phone and punched a couple of numbers. "Martinez, I want you to contact the construction foreman and get a list of his workers who know how to operate heavy equipment, in particular a steamroller. When you finish that, run a background check to see if any of the Country Roads people ever worked in an occupation where they might have learned to drive a steamroller."

Wally hung up and Skye asked, "Have you established a timeline yet?"

"According to the foreman, he dismissed most of his workers around twelve thirty because it didn't look like the rain would let up anytime soon. They were all gone when he left the site at three o'clock."

"Any evidence Suzette was still alive at that time?"

"Yes. The foreman stopped at the office trailer and spoke to Taylor. He said he saw Suzette."

"Does Taylor confirm that?" Skye asked.

"Not only him, but Suzette was on the phone with the mayor, so Dante verifies it, too." Wally read from the file in front of him.

"Suzette didn't have her own transportation," Skye remembered. "Did Taylor say why he left her alone out there without a ride to town?"

"He claims that when he left at three thirty, she told him someone was picking her up."

Skye swallowed hard. "She must have meant me."

"That was my guess."

Skye was silent. Would Suzette still be alive if she hadn't stayed around to meet Skye?

"So that puts the time of death between three and four thirty." Wally looked up from his notes.

"So, who doesn't have an alibi for those ninety minutes?"

"Most of the construction workers claim they

were at the Brown Bag Bar all afternoon, but with the amount of alcohol they consumed, I really don't trust their memories."

"How about the music people? The guys in the band, the sound techs, the roadies?"

"Only three of them were alone during that time."

"That narrows it down."

"To a certain extent. But most of the ones with alibis were part of a big group at a bar, so they might have slipped away. Or the killer could be someone we're not aware of. We've learned little about Suzette's background. And so far, we haven't found anyone who can think of why someone would want to kill her."

Skye opened her mouth to mention Kallista and Flint's animosity toward Suzette, but she was interrupted by the telephone.

While Wally answered the call, Skye took Toby out back for a walk. She definitely didn't want a repeat of the incident that afternoon, although Wally's shoes couldn't possibly cost as much as Homer's.

Wally was off the phone when she got back. "That was the ME."

"Oh?"

"He finished his preliminary examination. The victim was probably immobilized by a blow to the head before she was run over by the steamroller."

"So she might have been dead or at least

unconscious before being crushed?" Skye thought about it. "That makes sense. No one would just lie there and let that happen."

"The ME's sent all the samples he obtained to the lab."

Skye couldn't read Wally's expression. "That's what you wanted. Right?"

"Right." Wally nodded. "And although the DNA evidence on the exterior of the body was compromised by the conditions, the ME's exam did give us a lead to follow."

"Which is?" Why was Wally hesitating? This couldn't be good news.

"He found semen inside the body."

"Yikes!"

"Exactly." Wally rubbed his chin. "Now the question is, did she have consensual sex or was she raped?"

"The ME couldn't tell?"

"The body sustained too much damage."

"Of course." Skye shivered. "How stupid of me." She kept trying to put the image of Suzette under the steamroller out of her mind, but there was always some reminder of it.

"You realize that this changes everything." Wally's voice held a trace of reluctance as he added, "Whoever Suzette was with Saturday is now a prime suspect."

"Why?" Skye wrinkled her forehead. "If the ME found semen, she would have had to have sex just prior to her death, not forty-eight hours previously."

"True," Wally agreed. "However, since no one has mentioned that she played around, a reasonable assumption is that Suzette was probably only involved with one man. And if that guy was Mr. Black Pickup Truck, he very well may have visited her at the construction site after Rex Taylor left."

"Oh." Skye had a sinking feeling she knew what Wally was getting at. "You mean Owen might be . . ."

"Yes."

Chapter 13

"If You've Got the Money, I've Got the Time"

While Skye tried not to think about the consequences of Owen being a suspect in Suzette's death, Wally phoned the Frayne residence to see if he was around. Trixie answered and said her husband wasn't available, but promised to have him call Wally's cell as soon as he returned. Not wanting to alarm Trixie, or alert Owen to his status as a person of interest in a murder investigation, Wally agreed to that plan.

A few minutes later, after Anthony delivered the shoes and was paid for his time, Skye and Wally left the police station via the garage's back exit. To avoid any chance of the reporters following them, Wally decided to ride with Skye rather than follow her home in his police cruiser, as was his usual practice. The minor inconvenience of being without his squad car, should there be an emer-gency, was outweighed by the major annoyance of the press recording their every move.

They considered stopping at the Feed Bag, Scumble River's only non-fast-food restaurant, for supper, but when Skye pointed out that would mean Toby would have to wait in the car, they decided against it. The air had cooled off and there was no sun to heat up the vehicle's interior, but neither one of them was comfortable leaving the dog by himself. The poor thing had been through enough.

Instead, following a quick stop at the super-market to purchase ingredients for their meal, they headed straight to Skye's house. She and Wally were both silent during the five-minute drive, and even Toby, who was draped across the backseat, seemed subdued.

When Skye turned into her driveway, Wally said, "Tell me again why we didn't go to my place?" He glanced at the two-story house to his left, then frowned when a curtain on a second-floor window appeared to move slightly. "Did you see that?"

"What?" Skye looked where he was pointing, then shook her head. "I don't see anything." Skye parked next to the front walk. "And to answer your first question, because it's not fair to Bingo to leave him alone for so long. Toby's been with me all day."

"But Bingo sleeps most of the time." Wally got out of the Chevy, carrying the grocery bag.

"True." Skye joined him, then whistled for the little dog, who jumped into the driver's seat, then into her arms. "But he'll be awake now."

"I'm worried that you're getting too attached to Toby." Wally frowned as Skye cuddled the little dog. "You do realize that keeping him isn't a good idea, right?" Wally patted the canine's head with his free hand. "I'll grant you he's cute, but dogs are a lot more work than cats."

"I know." Skye climbed the steps. "If we find a next of kin for Suzette, and that person won't take him, I'll try to find him a good home." She paused, and tilted her head. "Hey, maybe you could adopt him."

"No."

"Why not?" What was up with Wally's attitude toward Toby? He loved Bingo. "I thought you liked animals."

"I do, but it's not fair to a dog to leave him alone for hours and hours at a time. They're pack animals, and they need companionship."

"Then I need to find him someone who is either at home a lot or has a job that allows them to bring pets to work." Skye dug her keys from her pocket.

"What are you going to do with him in the meantime? Clearly he can't go to school with you again." Wally took the key ring from Skye's hand. "You said he and Bingo don't get along, and that Toby destroys his surroundings if he gets bored."

"Those are problems," Skye admitted, scratching behind the little dog's silky ears.

"Then I suppose you'd better study up on how to introduce a dog into a cat household." Wally fitted the key in the lock. "Have you thought of spread-ing tuna on Toby's back or sprinkling him with catnip?"

"Actually, I had Trixie do some research online for me about that." Skye patted her tote bag. "It's what to do with him during the day while I'm gone that's my real concern." She frowned. "If only Mom liked animals or Dad wasn't so busy right now."

"Well, a short-term solution might be that new Doggy Daycare place out on Robin Road across the street from the spa." Wally swung open the front door for Skye. "The problem is that I heard it's really expensive since it's mostly aimed at the spa's clientele. And I'm guessing you won't let me pick up the tab for you."

"You're guessing right. I can pay my own bills." Skye smiled to take some of the sting from her words, then made sure she had a tight grip on Toby's leash. "When did the place open and why didn't you tell me about it this morning?"

"A couple of weeks ago." Wally moved back. "And when you didn't bring it up during our conversation, I figured you had already arranged for someone to watch him."

"Oh, yeah." Skye thought back. She hadn't mentioned her canine babysitting problem to Wally. "Sorry." She crossed the threshold and braced herself for an explosion.

Bingo sat immobile in precisely the middle of the foyer's hardwood floor. He looked at Skye, then flicked an ear and stared at the dog. Toby barked excitedly, but the black cat only sneered. Swishing his tail back and forth, Bingo deliberately turned his back on the canine.

Skye and Wally exchanged glances.

"What do you think?" Skye asked.

"Let's see what happens if you let Toby approach Bingo," Wally suggested, putting the grocery sack on the hallway bench.

Skye kept a firm hold on the leash. "Okay." She stepped closer to the cat.

Wally followed, angling to get behind Bingo in case of trouble.

"They're nearly the same size," Skye commented as she watched.

148

Toby uttered a couple of sharp woofs, then sniffed at the cat.

Appearing to ignore the dog, Bingo lifted his rear leg and began licking it.

"Interesting." Wally cocked his thumb at the two animals. "They seem okay."

Toby's nose twitched and his stubby tail started to wag.

"Should I let him off the leash?" Skye asked doubtfully. "I don't want him to hurt Bingo."

"I doubt Bingo is in any danger." Wally appraised the pair. "I'd be more worried about the dog."

"You're probably right," Skye agreed. "Grandma had Bingo's front paws declawed, but he's far from defenseless. And I'd like to see if they'll tolerate each other."

"Go ahead." Wally crouched down next to the cat, ready to intervene. "If there's trouble, I'll grab Bingo; you go for Toby's leash."

"All right." Skye let go of the lead, ready to snatch it back up at the first sign of hostilities.

Toby circled the cat while Bingo continued his bath. After two or three orbits, the dog lay down next to the feline and sighed. Bingo stopped his ablutions, gave Toby's ears a couple of licks, then rose and stretched. Once he was sure everyone was watching, he sauntered down the hall, pausing halfway to see if the humans were following.

"Well, I'll be darned." Wally's expression was bemused.

"The old wives' tale must be true," Skye said half to herself as she rushed to the feline's food bowl, popped open a tin of Fancy Feast, and gave him the entire can for being such a good kitty. "Every now and again, cats decide to humor us because they feel guilty that their ancestors ate ours." She giggled at her own silliness.

A moment later, when Toby trailed Wally into the kitchen, she rewarded the little dog with his mushy food, too.

With the animals fed and behaving themselves, Skye fetched the groceries from the foyer and said to Wally, "How about making a tossed salad while I cook the salmon?"

"Sure." Wally took off his gun belt, unknotted his tie and slid it out from under his collar, then draped both over the back of a chair. "There. That's better."

Skye noticed he appeared years younger as he shed the accoutrements of his job. Smiling, she promised herself that later she'd get him out of the rest of his uniform.

Once the meal was ready, Skye asked Wally, "Can you open a bottle of wine for me, please?"

"You're drinking?" Wally's tone was quizzical. Skye rarely drank on a school night.

"Yep. It's been that kind of day." Skye gathered

the plates, cutlery, napkins, and stemware. "Let's eat in the sunroom."

"Okay." Wally followed her, carrying the salad and merlot. After they were settled on the wicker settee, Wally poured them each a glass of wine.

They were both hungry, and ate in silence for the first ten minutes. Finally, they spoke at once.

"I forgot—" Skye said.

And Wally said, "So, what I—"

"You first." Skye waved her hand in his direction, put down her fork, and leaned back. "You've been trying to tell me something for the past twenty-four hours and I can't stand the suspense any longer."

Wally chugged the rest of his merlot, then cleared his throat. "So you know that last month after Father Burns told us the address I gave him for Darleen wasn't any good, I traced her to another town in Alaska and sent a registered letter there?"

"Yes." Of course she knew. How could she not know? The fact that they couldn't find Wally's ex-wife to get her statement was holding up the annulment process.

"A week or so later that letter also came back marked 'Moved, no forwarding address.' And I hadn't been able to unearth even a new phone number for her."

Silently, Skye was screaming, *Get to the part I don't already know,* but aloud she said in an encouraging tone, "Yes?"

"So, yesterday—" Wally broke off at the sound of an insistent buzzing from the hall.

Whoever was at the front door was jabbing the bell repeatedly, causing Toby, who had been lying at Skye's side, to leap to his feet and run out of the sunroom, barking wildly. Bingo, who had been asleep on the settee cushion next to Wally, opened one eye and turned over.

Geez! Skye ignored the ringing. "Go ahead," she ordered. "Tell me what happened yesterday."

"It might be one of my officers about the case." Wally rose from his seat and strode toward the foyer. "You know my cell doesn't always work in this house."

Skye followed, easing past him to brush aside the curtain covering the front window. She peered out, sighed in frustration, then swung the door open.

Trixie burst into the entrance hall. "Owen's disappeared again," she cried. "I can't find him anywhere. Something terrible has happened—I just know it!" She flung herself at Skye, sobbing hysterically.

It took half an hour and most of the rest of the bottle of wine, but Skye and Wally finally managed to calm Trixie down enough for rational conversation. They had seated her on the settee in the sunroom next to Skye, while Wally took the matching wicker armchair.

Skye put her arm around her friend and asked

gently, "Are you ready to tell us what happened?"

Taking one last gulp of merlot, Trixie wiped her mouth with the back of her hand and said to Wally, "After you called at six thirty wanting to speak to Owen, I got worried about what you wanted with him." She glared at Wally. "You wouldn't tell me why you needed to talk to him."

"Sorry." He crossed his arms. "As I said before, it's confidential."

"Right." Trixie hiccupped. "Anyway, about a half hour ago, I decided to go get Owen, so he could call back and find out what was going on. I looked in the barn and the tractor shed, and even though it was too dark to be doing anything in the fields, I even checked there. Finally, I noticed that his truck wasn't in the garage."

Skye and Wally exchanged uneasy glances. Had Owen somehow gotten wind of the autopsy results and realized he might be a suspect in Suzette Neal's murder?

"And that's unusual?" Skye asked, not sure what was normal for the couple.

"Yes." Trixie nodded emphatically. "Generally, we eat at five; then Owen takes care of the animals and works around the barn or shed for another two or three hours. Although lately he's been staying out there until bedtime."

"Which means, typically, if I hadn't called, you wouldn't have been concerned if he didn't come inside until ten or so?" Wally asked.

"Right," Trixie agreed, a troubled expression stealing over her face.

"You're sure he hasn't phoned you?" Skye asked. "Is your cell on?"

"Yes. I checked just before I left home," Trixie affirmed. "And there are no messages from him."

"Could you have forgotten a meeting he said he was attending?" Wally inquired.

"There's nothing on the calendar." Trixie shook her head. "And the only regular meeting he attends is the Farm Bureau on the second Wednesday of the month."

They were silent as Skye searched for a rational explanation for Owen's disappearance. Finally, she noticed that Trixie had her eyes closed and her lips were moving.

She poked Trixie with her finger. "Are you awake?"

"Yes. I'm praying for the wisdom to understand my husband," Trixie enlightened Skye, then added, "Also for love to forgive him and patience to deal with his inconsiderate actions."

"You're not praying for strength?" Skye asked, thinking Trixie might need it.

"No," Trixie said tartly. "If the Lord gave me strength, I might end up beating the crap out of my husband."

Oops! Skye hurriedly thought of an explanation for Owen's absence. "Maybe he went to get a tractor part." She glanced at her watch. It was eight twenty-nine. "Farm and Fleet doesn't close for another half hour."

"Well." Trixie's shoulders relaxed. "I suppose he might have gone over to Kankakee. But he should have told me. Heck, maybe I would have wanted to take a ride with him." She scowled. "This does it. He's getting a cell phone whether he wants one or not. And he darn well better use it or there'll be hell to pay."

As Skye walked Trixie out to her car, Trixie hugged her and said, "Thanks for always being there for me."

"That's what friends are for." Skye hugged Trixie back. "We're sort of like Spanx; we never let you droop and are all about support."

Once Trixie left, Skye started to clear the mess from dinner. While she filled the sink with hot water, she asked Wally, "Where do you think Owen really is?"

"Well . . ." He put the leftover salad in a Tupperware bowl before placing it in the refrigerator. "The only thing we know for sure is he's not with Suzette."

"Unless . . ." Skye squirted soap under the running water and watched the bubbles foam. "The body isn't Suzette's and they ran away together."

"I suppose anything's possible." Wally selected a dish towel from the drawer. "But then, who was under the steamroller?" He dried a plate and placed it in the cupboard. "No one else is missing."

"True." Skye washed a handful of silverware. "Besides, I can't really see Owen doing something that wild. Heck—I can't picture him having an affair."

"Sometimes the quiet ones fool you." Wally finished putting away the dishes.

"Yes, they do. They do, indeed." Skye turned to stare at Wally. "So, what were you trying to tell me when Trixie arrived?"

"Let's sit down." Wally led her to the kitchen table and pulled out two chairs. He cleared his throat before saying, "Darleen contacted me yesterday just before I left for Laurel to testify in court."

"That would be good news." Skye smiled hopefully. "Wouldn't it?"

"That depends." Wally wrinkled his brow. "She said I owe her for all the money I should have paid her when we got divorced."

"Oh?" Skye remembered Wally saying his ex-wife hadn't received a penny from the divorce due to the airtight prenuptial agreement she had signed.

"She claimed that now that she has some powerful friends she's going to get what she deserves from me."

"And?"

"And if I want her cooperation in writing a truthful letter to support my request for an annulment, I need to bring her two hundred and fifty thousand dollars."

"To Alaska?"

"No." Wally shook his head. "To Chicago. She's back in Illinois."

Chapter 14

"PLEASE REMEMBER ME"

"Did you agree to give her the cash?" Skye asked Wally, studying him carefully.

"No. I was in a hurry and I told her I had to think about it." Wally took Skye's hands and kissed both palms. "Do you want me to?"

"I'm not sure what I want." Her first instinct was that Wally shouldn't give in to Darleen's blackmail. While Skye was considering how she felt about the matter, she remembered last night's call. "Oh, my God!"

"What?"

"Someone phoned me last night and left a message for you. He said, 'Tell your boyfriend what he wants is expensive.'" Skye leaped up, ran to the counter, and grabbed the notepad where she'd jotted down the information. "Here's the number he left."

"You said 'he'—so it wasn't Darleen?" Wally tore off the page and examined it, then tucked it into his breast pocket.

"I'm not sure." Skye pursed her lips. "It almost sounded like a robot."

"You can get a gadget from Radio Shack that will disguise your voice." Wally narrowed his eyes. "Maybe Darleen's trying to up the ante by involving you."

"Do you think she's telling the truth about her 'powerful' friends?" Skye asked, part of her not believing Darleen, whom she was convinced was mentally unstable, but another part of her worried that getting mixed up with the wrong kind of people was exactly what Wally's ex would do.

"Hard to tell." Wally patted his pocket. "I'll see if I can have this number traced tomorrow, but odds are it belongs to a disposable cell."

"I guess we really have no choice but to wait and take it from there."

"Even if Darleen is telling the truth—which is a big if—and she does have some tough guy backing her up, he's most likely just egging her on," Wally reassured Skye.

"True." Skye bit her lip. "Maybe he thinks getting money from the rich ex will be easy. I wonder if Darleen mentioned you were the chief of police."

"That is the sort of detail she'd leave out." Wally squeezed Skye's hand. "That, and the fact that although my father is rich, I'm not."

"So where does Darleen think you'll get the cash?"

"The amount she's asking for just happens to be the exact sum my mother left me." Wally's smile was rueful. "Darleen was always ticked that only my name was on that account, and she couldn't get her hands on any of it without my permission."

"Which, of course, you didn't give her."

"No." Wally shook his head. "We were already not getting along and I didn't think letting her blow my inheritance would strengthen our marriage."

"True," Skye agreed. "Well, we can't do anything about Darleen until you try to trace that phone number."

"Right."

"So, what's our next step in investigating Suzette's murder?"

"I'll talk to Owen first thing in the morning." Wally pulled the pad of paper closer and made a note. "And since we have no other leads, I'll have my officers tear apart the storage area in the basement and find the file on Suzette's mother's death."

"Shall I talk to the music teacher about Suzette's father?" Skye asked.

"Definitely."

"Anything else you can think of that I should do?" Skye asked.

Wally rose from his chair, pulling Skye along with him and into his arms. "I can think of one or two things." He leaned down and pressed his lips to her ear. "Let's see if your ghost will let us try them."

Mrs. Griggs's spirit must have been out on an otherworldly errand, because for the first time ever Wally and Skye were able to enjoy a pleasurable night in her antique four-poster bed without any household disaster occurring.

By six a.m. Skye had already dropped off Wally at his place so he could change clothes before going to talk to Owen, and had driven to Doggy Daycare. The pale purple building with black paw prints stenciled across the entrance was easy to spot. In the center of the lawn, a six-foot-tall pink fire hydrant topped off by an equally large sparkly tiara acted as a beacon to passersby. And lest someone fail to get the message, there was also a baby blue water bowl the size of a kiddie pool and a bone big enough to have come from a T. rex's thigh.

Skye clicked Toby's leash to his collar and led him up the front steps. When she pushed open the glass door, chimes played "How Much Is That Doggy in the Window?"

A thirtyish brunette wearing a lavender T-shirt with the Doggy Daycare logo embroidered across her chest greeted them from behind a rose marble counter. "Welcome to your darling's home away from home. My name is Puppy Pointer."

"Poppy?" Skye was sure she couldn't have heard correctly.

"No, Puppy. P-U-P-P-Y." The woman enunciated each letter carefully.

"What a cute nickname." As a school psychologist, Skye had heard a lot of unusual, astonishing, and sometimes downright bizarre monikers, but, surely, Puppy was not on this woman's birth certificate.

"It's my legal name." Puppy raised a bushy eyebrow, daring Skye to comment further. "Now, which of our wonderful services can I offer you today?"

"Uh." Skye was stunned by the opulence and variety of merchandise on display, not to mention the set of white pointy ears that seemed to emerge directly from the top of Puppy's head.

"I bet your precious pet is here for a spa day." Puppy's tone was perky.

"No. Sorry." Skye gave an apologetic little cough, wondering what a spa day for a canine consisted of, let alone cost. "I just need to board him until four thirty."

Puppy studied Toby. "At least let us give him a cut and style."

"No, thanks." Skye dug her wallet from her tote bag. "How much for the day?"

"I'm afraid we need to fill out some paperwork

161

before we know what the charge will be." Puppy held out a rhinestone-encrusted clipboard.

"Fine." Skye glanced at the questionnaire. Beyond the first few lines, which requested her name, address, and phone number, there was little she could fill in. "Um, I've only had Toby for a couple of days, so I don't know his mother's name or any of the rest of this stuff."

"Unfortunately, we can't take him without that information."

"Couldn't you make an exception?" Skye pleaded. "Just for today?"

"Well . . ." Puppy eyed Skye thoughtfully. "Perhaps."

"I'd really appreciate it." Skye held her breath. What would she do if Toby didn't qualify for Doggy Daycare? "How can we make it happen?"

"Because we don't have proof of his immunizations, we'll have to keep him separated from our other guests, so we'll have to charge you an additional fifty dollars beyond our normal daily fee."

"Fifty *more?*" Skye squeaked. "That seems like an awful lot to feed him and take him out a few times. How much is your regular price?"

"Forty-eight dollars." Sharp little canines showed as Puppy smiled.

"So ninety-eight total?" *Hell's bells!* At the rate she was hemorrhaging money, Skye wasn't sure she could pay her bills this month.

"And there's a nonoptional eighteen percent gratuity." If Puppy had a tail, it would have been wagging. "The total bill is payable in advance."

"That's highway robbery!" Skye's face turned red and she badly wanted to slap those cute little ears right off Puppy's head.

"It's not my fault you don't know your own dog's history." Puppy shrugged. "Without the completed forms, Toby's care will be a lot more work for me." She curled her lip. "Take it or leave it."

Skye wished she could walk out, but what would she do with Toby? Her only option would be to call in sick, and she couldn't do that. Too many meetings would have to be canceled and rescheduled.

Vowing that she would find another solution by tomorrow, Skye asked weakly, "Do you take credit cards?"

"Of course." Puppy straightened her faux ears. "But the extra fee is cash only."

Skye's shoulders slumped and she reluctantly placed her credit card, a twenty, two tens, a five, and four singles into Puppy's outstretched paw.

"You owe me another dollar."

Skye sighed and dug through the change at the bottom of her purse, coming up with two quarters, four dimes, a nickel, and five pennies.

Puppy handed her a receipt and said, "I hope you don't mind me saying so, but you look really frazzled. You should do what I do when I'm feeling tense."

"What?" Skye asked before she could stop herself.

"I handle stressful situations like our canine friends do." Puppy's expression was serious. "If you can't eat it or hump it, pee on it and walk away."

After politely agreeing that Puppy's stress relief idea had merit, Skye said good-bye to Toby and hurried out of the building. It was now seven o'clock, and since all she had left in her wallet was a coupon good for twenty-five cents off a bottle of salad dressing, she had to hit the ATM before going to school.

There were only two ATMs in Scumble River, and one was, thank goodness, on Skye's way to work. She parked in front of the Scumble River Savings and Loan and hurried into the foyer. The bank's interior was dark, but the area containing the ATM was brightly lit.

Skye rushed up to the machine, her debit card at the ready. She punched in her PIN number, then hesitated. How much cash should she take out?

At the pace she was spending money, she should probably get the limit—five hundred dollars—but she decided to be cautious and take only half of the maximum allowed. Her purse would probably be secure in her desk drawer, but better safe than sorry.

She waited impatiently for the bills to come out of the slot, then tucked the cash inside her tote bag and grabbed the receipt. Whirling around, she bit back a scream.

"I guess you didn't hear me come in." Simon Reid stood a few feet away from her, a charming smile on his handsome face. "Maybe they should install chimes over the door."

Skye nodded in agreement, waiting for her heart to return to its normal rhythm before trying out her voice. Simon had always been able to sneak up on her. If she didn't know better, she'd swear he floated above the ground instead of walking like a normal person.

"Sorry I scared you." Every strand of Simon's short auburn hair was in place, his cheeks were freshly shaved, and his black wingtip shoes were so perfectly polished he could use them to check that his tie was straight.

Instantly, Skye became conscious of her own rumpled appearance. She tugged at the empire waist of her plum-colored knit dress and brushed white dog hair from its elbow-length bell sleeves.

"Are you on your way to school?" Simon's finely sculpted features hinted at an elegance and sophistication that were rare in Scumble River.

"Yes." Skye glanced down at her black tights. The buckle on Toby's collar had caught in them, so there was a huge run that started from the top of her ballet flats and disappeared under the hem of her skirt. She'd planned to change into the emergency panty hose she kept in her desk drawer as soon as she got to school.

"I'm glad I ran into you." Simon's warm tenor washed over her. "I wanted to talk to you."

"In your role as coroner?" Skye stopped fussing with her clothes and met his gaze. "Is there some evidence about the murder you want to share?"

"No." Simon's hazel eyes were hooded. "I'm sure Boyd has filled you in on those facts." He paused. "Although I do have a question about Suzette."

"What?"

"When you first met her, did she look familiar to you?" Simon wrinkled his brow. "When I saw her perform last Saturday night, she reminded me of someone, but I just couldn't put my finger on who."

"Not really." Skye tried to remember if she had thought Suzette looked like anyone. "Her parents only lived here a year, and that was back in 1978."

"Then there's no way I could have known her mother or father. I would only have been eight years old at the time, and I didn't move to town until 1998, when I inherited the funeral home from my uncle." Simon massaged one temple. "Does she have any relatives in Scumble River?"

"No. As far as I know, the police haven't been able to locate any family."

"I see." Simon shrugged. "I guess she just had that kind of face."

"That could be it."

"Back to the reason I was glad to run into you," Simon said. "I hear you have a houseguest who needs alternative accommodations."

"Who told you that?"

"Trixie mentioned it to Frannie yesterday afternoon at the drugstore. Then Frannie told Mom when she got to work last night." Frannie was a waitress at the bowling alley that Simon owned and his mother, Bunny, managed.

"I should have known. There are no secrets around here." Skye twisted a strand of the gold chain that hung past her scoop neckline. "I suppose Bunny told you the whole story."

"About Homer and the shoe baptism? Yes, she did." Simon chuckled. "That must have been quite a sight."

"Yes." Skye giggled. "I've never seen Homer so upset, and that's saying a lot."

"Anyway, if you still need someone to take care of the dog, I'd be glad to do it."

"Why?" Skye asked, wondering if this was another of Simon's schemes to win back her affections.

"I've been thinking of getting a pet." He examined the crease in the pants of his olive green wool suit. "And this would be a good way to see if a dog is right for me. A bit like being a foster parent."

"Well . . ." Skye was suddenly reluctant to give up Toby. "I'm not sure—"

"How about I take him during the day while you're at work," Simon suggested. "You can pick him up on your way home after school, and if you need me to take care of him longer, just give me a call."

"You'd have to keep him with you," Skye warned. "Believe me, you do not want him bored and alone in your house, or anywhere else."

"So I heard." Simon grinned. "Actually, that works out perfectly for me, since most wakes are held in the late afternoon or evening."

"How about interments or when you have to consult with the bereaved?" Skye was still not sure this was a good plan. She didn't want to owe Simon a favor.

"I'll set up one of the empty rooms for him at the funeral home with a bed and some toys." He stuck his hands in his pockets. "Xavier can help."

"I'm so glad you talked Xavier into coming back to work for you after he quit last month."

"Me, too." Simon shuffled his feet. "So, what do you say? Will you trust me with the little guy?"

"Yes." Skye realized she really couldn't afford to turn down his offer. "He's already set for today, but I'll bring him over to your place between seven and seven fifteen tomorrow."

"Thank you." Simon stepped close to Skye and softly kissed her cheek. "I'm looking forward to the companionship."

"Toby can definitely provide that." Skye tried to lighten the mood.

"That's good." Simon's expression was pensive. "Now that we're not together, it seems I no longer like my own company as much as I used to."

"I'm sorry to hear that." Skye kept the sympathy out of her voice, not wanting to mislead him about her feelings.

"Thank you." Simon grimaced. "It's just that I never thought of myself as a person who'd ever be lonely."

Chapter 15

"A Boy Named Sue"

Half an hour later, Skye sat on an uncomfortable molded-plastic chair in an overheated office, still wearing her ruined tights. She had intended to drop off Homer's new shoes with the school secretary and escape without having to deal with the principal, but Homer had pounced on her as soon as she entered the building.

While the principal propelled her through the lobby, past the front counter, and into his inner sanctum, he grumbled about a new student who was moving into their district. Woodrow Buckingham was being enrolled that morning and his parents were arriving in ten minutes to brief them on their child's needs.

After a quick scan of the six-inch-thick file Homer thrust into her arms, Skye said, "We really need to have the physical therapist, occupational therapist, speech pathologist, and nurse at this meeting."

"Right." Homer sneered. "Since the OT, PT, and speech path are only assigned to this building half a day a week and we get the nurse three afternoons—if we're lucky—I suppose you want me to ask Harry Potter to borrow his magic wand. Or do you have a better suggestion about how I should get them all here at the last minute?"

Fortunately for both Homer and Skye, Mr. and Mrs. Buckingham arrived before Skye could tell the principal what he could do with Harry's wand. For the next two hours Mrs. Buckingham talked about her son's special needs. Skye took notes, trying to make sense of all the medical jargon, but in the end her yellow legal pad looked as if she'd been writing in Swahili.

After the meeting was over and the door finally closed behind the couple, Homer said, "That woman's train of thought needs a caboose."

Skye sat stunned, contemplating what she'd been told. It was difficult to comprehend all it would take to educate Woodrow in regular classes. She could only imagine what this poor kid had to cope with every day of his life.

From what Skye could piece together from Mr. and Mrs. Buckingham's lengthy description, Woodrow was in a motorized wheelchair and had the use of only two fingers on his left hand. His speech was difficult, sometimes impossible to understand, and he had a moderate hearing loss in his right ear. He also had other significant health issues.

Woodrow would definitely be the most challenging student Skye and Homer had ever attempted to mainstream. Although he had an above-average IQ, it was extremely difficult for him to perform even the smallest physical task. The personnel and materials he would require to be integrated into regular classes were astronomical.

Homer caressed a tuft of hair growing from his ear and said, "What are we going to do with him? Where do we even start?"

"I wish I knew." Skye felt numb. "I'll study his file and start making a list of the equipment and services we'll need."

"We have to have a plan before he can start classes." Homer grimaced. "Didn't the mom say they expect him to start next week?"

"Yes, both parents were adamant about that. At least Monday is Teacher Institute, so no students." Skye made a note on her legal pad. "But come Tuesday, he'll need a specially outfitted bus."

"Shit." Homer closed his eyes and started to move his lips in and out.

"Listen." Skye could tell that the principal was going to his happy place, and if she didn't pull him back right now, he would stay there until she had solved his problem. "You need to contact the special education cooperative and get the coordinator assigned to us out here for a consultation."

Homer didn't open his eyes. "You call."

"No." Fighting the temptation to toss her legal pad at Homer's head, Skye stuffed her notes into her tote bag. "He won't listen to me, and the only way we can get access to all the apparatus and staff we'll need is through him."

Homer grunted and reached for the phone, which Skye took as both agreement and dismissal.

She quickly stood, moved to the door, and said, "I'll be around until one thirty; then I'm heading to the junior high."

Homer waved her off. As she exited, she heard him say, "Opal, get me the sped coordinator right now. Tell him it's an emergency."

Although Skye didn't like the special education coordinator—he lacked a sincere interest in the students and harangued Skye for becoming too involved with them—he was the only person who had the authority to help them. That is, of course, if the jerk could be motivated to actually do his job.

As Skye headed down the hall, she tried to come up with ideas to help Woodrow fit in and make friends. Which classmate would be a good buddy for him? Who was popular enough and had sufficient self-confidence and compassion to get the other students to accept the boy?

Skye's deliberations had brought her to a junction in the corridor. If she went left, she'd arrive at her own office; if she went right, she'd pass the music room. It was ten twenty-three; third period ended in two minutes and fourth period was Noreen Iverson's plan time, which made it the perfect moment to talk to her about Suzette's father.

As Skye headed right, she rationalized that she needed to speak to Noreen about Woodrow. His mother had mentioned that he loved music, and it should be assigned as his scheduled elective. If Noreen brought up Mr. Neal and Skye got a lead in the investigation of Suzette's murder, she figured that would simply be a twofer.

Noreen's room was in the oldest part of the school, in the fine and practical arts wing. Although the heating was iffy and there was no air-conditioning, it did have the coveted advantage of windows, real walls versus curtain separators, and spaciousness.

Skye expected to hear the familiar notes of flutes, violins, and drums, but instead she heard shouting. She couldn't make out the words, but accelerated her steps as the voices grew louder.

Afraid that fists would be swinging soon, Skye dashed into the room and stopped abruptly when she saw several students lined up on a dais in front of the class. Noreen stood facing them, using a conductor's baton to point to each in turn. As she did so, each teen spoke a word; then the next person uttered the same word, only louder.

At that moment the bell rang, and Noreen said, "Excellent work, everyone. We'll pick up here next time. Class dismissed."

Skye hesitated, not sure what she had seen. What in the world was Noreen teaching?

Once all the students had left, Noreen approached Skye. "Is everything okay?"

"Yes." Skye's cheeks reddened. "I'm so sorry for bursting in here without knocking." She knew she'd breached the unwritten rule that each teacher was king or queen of his or her classroom.

"No problem." Noreen's lips twitched. "I bet you thought the kids were about to start throwing punches."

Skye nodded.

"We're so isolated in this wing, I didn't even think of what the lesson on voice as an instrument would sound like to someone in the hall." Noreen patted Skye's arm. "Sorry for frightening you."

Skye blew out a breath. "I need to stop letting my imagination get the better of me, and seeing crises around every corner."

"Don't we all," Noreen agreed. "So, were you coming to see me about something?"

"Yes." Skye tipped her head toward a small table. "Do you have a minute?"

"Sure." Noreen led the way and took a seat. "But I need to grade papers for my next class while we talk."

"I won't keep you long." Skye sat down. "We're getting a new student who wants music on his schedule as his elective course."

"Oh?" Noreen raised a brow. "So where does the school psychologist fit into that picture?"

Skye explained about Woodrow's special circumstances, ending with, "Which means we don't know yet exactly what he'll require, but at a minimum he'll have a teacher assistant with him at all times."

"Then everything should be fine." Noreen reached for a stack of papers. "I'm sure his aide will know what to do, and I'll be happy to make any accommodations or modifications suggested."

"That's great." Skye relaxed. "Thanks." Some teachers were more comfortable than others with students who had special needs.

"I learned to be flexible during my student teaching." Noreen smiled fondly. "One of the first lessons Quentin Neal taught me was that music teachers eventually have every kid in the school in their class, and we'd better be able to handle all types."

"It sounds as if he was a terrific trainer." Skye couldn't believe her luck; Quentin was exactly who she really wanted to talk about.

Noreen nodded, then asked, "Have you heard anything more about his daughter's death?"

"Not much so far, but the police and I are working on it," Skye said, taking out her notepad. "Maybe you can help us out a little. Would you mind answering some questions about the Neals?"

"Sure." Noreen picked up a red pen. "But I don't remember much."

"Anything you can tell me would be helpful," Skye assured her. "Do you remember where the Neals lived?"

"Hmm." Noreen closed her eyes. "They rented a house on that street behind where the McDonald's is now. Singer Lane. I remember thinking how appropriate the name was."

Skye made a note. "Did Mrs. Neal work outside the home?"

"I don't think so."

"How, uh, was . . ." Skye wasn't sure how to ask the next question. "Did you ever hear anything about Mr. and Mrs. Neal's marriage?"

"Well . . ." Noreen hesitated, clearly deciding whether to tell Skye what she knew. "Quentin put in a lot of hours directing the Catholic Church choir, and Paulette was a little unhappy with that, but no, nothing else."

"Can you think of any friends or relatives of the Neals who might have more information?"

"No. He didn't talk much about his personal life." Noreen uncapped her pen. "And they hadn't been here very long. You know it takes a while for native Scumble Riverites to warm up to newcomers."

"True." Skye searched for something more to ask. "Was anyone who's currently on staff here around the year Quentin was teaching?"

"Hmm." Noreen chewed the top of her pen. "Homer and Pru are the only ones I can think of who have been here that long."

"Great." The two people Skye most didn't want to have to question.

"I wish I knew more."

"The biggest obstacle so far is that we can't locate a next of kin."

"That's terrible." Noreen made a sad clucking sound with her tongue. "I remember Quentin mentioning that both he and his wife didn't have any siblings."

"Darn! That means Suzette didn't have any aunts or uncles or even first cousins."

"Yeah." Noreen pulled a quiz from the stack, read a line, then put a red check by number one. "That was why Quentin and Paulette were so happy they'd had twins. They didn't want to risk raising an only child."

"Suzette had a sister?" Skye's voice rose and she nearly smacked the music teacher. Why hadn't Noreen mentioned that fact in the first place?

"A brother," Noreen corrected. "They were fraternal twins."

"What was his name?" Skye demanded.

"I don't remember." Noreen squeezed her eyes shut, then shook her head. "Nope. Sorry. Quentin always just called him the boy."

"I wonder why there's no record of him in her life," Skye mused out loud, then thought to herself, *And why didn't Suzette mention him when she asked me for help?*

"I have no idea." Noreen frowned. "After Paulette died and Quentin moved away, I never heard from him again. I don't think he wanted any reminders of Scumble River."

Chapter 16

"WHEN YOU SAY NOTHING AT ALL"

Skye hurried out of the junior high school as soon as the final bell rang. She had several items on her to-do list, but two tasks were competing for the number one spot—picking up Toby before Puppy charged her overtime and tracking down Wally. She'd been calling and leaving messages for him every chance she had, which wasn't all that often since she'd been stuck in a PPS meeting most of the afternoon.

Using cell phones wasn't allowed in the school building, but as Skye's foot hit the parking lot pavement, she dug hers out and powered it up. Before she could hit speed dial, she saw she had a missed call. Punching in her super-secret code—456—she put the tiny silver rectangle to her ear and tapped her fingers against the metal case as she waited for the chance to press the correct number, after which she might actually get to hear what her caller had to say.

Skye couldn't understand why people thought voice mail was superior to an old-fashioned answering machine. Instead of facing forty-two options—most of which she would never use—a push of a button, and your messages played.

Finally, Wally's voice said, "Sorry we keep missing each other today, darlin'. My cell bit the dust early this morning and I wasn't able to get a new one until three o'clock."

Ah. Skye yanked open the car door. That explained why he'd never called her back.

"One of the reasons it took me so long to replace my phone is that someone leaked the news that semen was found in the body and reporters are camped out at the PD again."

Terrific! She slid into the driver's seat. Just what they needed: more media attention.

"So instead of coming to the station, meet me in back at the church parking lot at four thirty. We have a road trip to make. Love you. Bye."

Heck! Wally hadn't mentioned anything about his interview with Owen. Having checked with Trixie, Skye knew Owen had returned before bedtime last night, saying he'd gone for a ride to look at the neighbors' fields. But Skye didn't buy that explanation any more than Trixie had.

Skye glanced at her watch. Ten after four. Oh, well; at least she'd see Wally in twenty minutes or so. She could probably contain her curiosity for that long—but just barely. She turned the key, threw the Bel Air in gear, and stomped on the gas.

Doggy Daycare was mobbed with parents retrieving their canine children. The wait was so long, Skye was considering calling Wally to say she'd be late when she finally reached the front of the line.

Puppy smiled widely at Skye and said, "I've got a surprise for you."

"Oh?" Skye answered cautiously. Considering Puppy and Doggy Daycare, Skye was afraid they had bronzed Toby's poop as a memento.

"I'll be right back." Puppy disappeared behind a half wall and returned seconds later with Toby in her arms.

At least, Skye thought it was Toby. She

examined the little white dog carefully. His fur had been clipped so close he looked like a sheared lamb—except for the giant round cotton ball–like puff at the end of his tail.

Tentatively, Skye fingered the bright blue bows adorning his head. Those would have to go. But how in the heck were they attached? She had a feeling their removal would require scissors, or maybe even a scalpel.

"Wow." It had taken Skye a moment to realize that Puppy was staring at her, anxiously awaiting her reaction. "He really looks different."

"Do you like it?" Puppy asked. "I had some extra time, and I felt a little bad about how much you had to pay for him to stay here, so I fixed him up." When Skye didn't respond, Puppy added, "It's on the house."

"It's amazing." Skye figured that was the only honest answer that wouldn't hurt the woman's feelings. "Thank you."

After thanking Puppy again, Skye headed toward her rendezvous with Wally. When she rocketed into the church's parking lot a few minutes later, Wally was leaning against the front fender of his Thunderbird. Not quite the undercover vehicle Skye would have chosen to avoid reporters, but a step up from a police cruiser.

Wally pushed upright as she squealed to a stop a few feet away. While Skye fumbled for her tote bag and Toby's leash, Wally opened her door. She handed him the dog, got out, and gave him a quick kiss.

"What the hell happened to this poor little guy?" Wally held Toby up and away from him as if the dog had on a dirty diaper.

"It's a long story," Skye answered with a sigh. "Suffice it to say the owner of Doggy Daycare wears a headband with fake dog ears attached, wags her backside like a tail, and calls herself Puppy Pointer."

"You're kidding." Wally did a double take. "What's her real name?"

"That's it." Skye shrugged. "Apparently she had it legally changed." Skye paused to reflect on the absurdity of a grown woman called Puppy, then asked, "So what did Owen have to say?"

Wally cocked his thumb at the T-bird. "I'll tell you all about it on the way."

"Okay." As she climbed in, Skye asked, "Where are we going?"

"That self-storage place halfway between here and Laurel." Wally settled Toby on Skye's lap— the sports car didn't have a backseat—and slid behind the wheel. "Turns out all the files aren't in the PD's basement after all. Warehousing of the older records was outsourced when I was still a rookie."

"Who's the owner of that place related to?" Skye asked with a sidelong glance. "Nepotism is the only explanation for the city using a business located outside the city limits."

Wally smirked. "You."

Skye wasn't at all surprised to hear it was one of her family members. She was kissing cousins to half the county, and that was just on her mother's side. "Which of my many relatives is the proprietor?"

"Our esteemed mayor." Wally turned onto the road that would take them toward Laurel.

"Oh!" If Skye didn't know how small-town government worked, she might have wondered how the chief of police could be unaware of where all the files were stored. But in a good-ol'-boy regime, unless you knew the right question to ask, no one would volunteer the information. "How did you find out there were more records than just the ones in the basement?"

"Dante told me when he called to ream me out for not wrapping up this case fast enough."

"He is truly a pain in the butt," Skye commiserated. "If it's any consolation, he acts the same way with the family."

"You know, he's one of only a very few people I'd be willing to name a building after." Wally grinned. "Of course, he'd have to be dead first."

Skye laughed, then asked, "So how did the storage issue come up?"

"I lost my temper." Wally's expression was sheepish. "I made it plain that if the police board had allowed me to have all the records digitized, as I had requested several years ago, maybe I could access the information I needed to solve Suzette's murder."

"I'm sure my uncle took that well. He so loves criticism." Skye hid a smile. "Is that when Dante revealed the hush-hush location?"

"Yes. It seems that when the rent came due for the previous facility, Dante had the city hall custodians move everything to the place he owned. That must have been when the ones in the basement got all messed up, since he instructed them to reshuffle the boxes and leave the most recent ten years' worth at the PD." Wally scowled. "Of course, no one thought to mention any of this to me."

"What a shock." Skye snickered, then demanded, "Now, what about Owen?"

"He told me the same thing about his absence on Saturday afternoon and evening that he told Trixie." Wally stopped for a grain truck turning into a field. "He ran into an old friend after his business meeting and they went into Joliet for a drink."

"What was the name of the friend?" Skye asked. "Did that person confirm Owen's story?"

"Owen wouldn't identify his companion. He hemmed and hawed, and said he'd rather not involve anyone else." Wally's expression was rueful. "He did, however, give me permission to look at his truck so I could see that there was no damage from any accident."

"Rats!" Skye stopped petting Toby. "Did you promise him that whatever he told you would stay between the two of you?"

"Yes, but I could tell he didn't trust me." Wally glowered. "And when I pressed him, he wouldn't budge. That guy is more stubborn than ants at a picnic."

"Double crap!"

"Furthermore, since everything that points to him as a suspect is circumstantial, I have no way to compel him to tell me." Wally tapped his fingers on the steering wheel. "Plus, my hands are tied because I really don't want to alert him to the fact that he might be a suspect."

"Well, that stinks." Skye scratched behind Toby's ears, causing the little dog's tail to thump like a metronome and his hind end to wiggle in ecstasy. "On another note, did you get my message about Suzette's twin?"

"Yes." Wally concentrated on navigating the T-bird around a curve. "Good work."

"Thanks." Skye basked in Wally's praise. "Have you found out his name?"

"Not so far. Like everything else to do with this case, the light at the end of the tunnel always turns out to be glowing eyes with claws and teeth." Wally blew out an irritated breath.

"Discovering the brother's identity is turning out to be harder than it should be."

"Can't you just get ahold of his birth certificate?" Skye asked.

"I put Quirk on that as soon as I got your message. But since we don't know where Suzette and her twin were born, he hasn't had any luck."

"So, what is Quirk doing now?"

"He's checking state by state"—Wally's lips formed a thin line—"starting with Illinois and moving outward. So far, he hasn't found any male with the last name of Neal who shares Suzette's birthday."

"Is there any other way to find Suzette's twin?" Skye asked.

"The county crime scene techs have her laptop and are looking through her e-mail and files. And the Nashville police are talking to her friends and neighbors, so maybe they'll come across someone who can help us identify her brother." Wally shook his head. "They already searched her apartment and didn't find anything helpful —no birth certificate or passport or personal correspondence."

"So if there's nothing on her computer and none of the people in Nashville know anything, what next?"

"If the name of her son isn't in Paulette Neal's file, I'll try the federal databank."

"What's that?"

"It's a database of birth records of all fifty states." Wally frowned. "Unfortunately, budget cuts, red tape, and not having the full name of the person for whom the information is being requested means there'd be a long wait for requests to be processed. It could be more than a month before they get back to us."

"Oh." Skye felt frustrated by yet another roadblock; then she had a thought. "Hey, I ran into Simon at the ATM this morning and he mentioned he thought Suzette looked familiar."

"So?"

"So, if we ask him to think about it some more, maybe he'll remember something."

"I won't hold my breath, but it's worth a try," Wally agreed. "I'll have Martinez run a picture of Suzette over to Reid tomorrow."

"Good." Skye opened her mouth to tell Wally that Simon would be dog sitting for her, but decided later might be a better time to reveal that piece of information. Sometime when Wally was more relaxed.

"We need to get Owen's DNA," Wally said after a few minutes of silence. "But I don't want to come right out and ask for it."

"Because, as you said earlier, you don't want him to know he's a suspect?"

"Right." Wally twitched his shoulders as if his neck were stiff.

"I really would like to be able to look him in the eye again, without having that nagging doubt in my mind."

Wally passed a slow-moving combine, waving to the driver. "Too bad there's no legal way to get his blood without his knowledge."

"Yeah." Skye stroked Toby, letting her thoughts wander; then, as Wally guided the T-bird into the self-storage lot, she blurted, "The Red Cross."

"What?"

"The Farm Bureau had a blood drive this past Monday, and Owen always gives." Skye twisted to look at Wally. "That means, if you can get his blood from them, you don't need a warrant for it. Once he donates it, he gives up all expectations of privacy."

"How do you know that?"

"I saw it on some TV program," Skye admitted. "But surely the show's writers would have to get something like that correct."

"Maybe." Wally sounded unconvinced. "I'll check with the city attorney."

While Wally made that call, Skye examined the storage facility. It looked a little like a fifties-style motel, albeit a windowless one surrounded by a six-foot-high chain-link fence with razor wire strung across the top.

There appeared to be two types of spaces available: one the size of a single-car garage, and the other twice that large. The siding was a dirty tan, and paint was peeling off the steel doors.

Skye and Wally were parked in front of one of the larger units. She couldn't see any other vehicles, and the facility was silent except for the sound of Wally's voice as he talked into his cell phone.

Several minutes later, he clicked the sleek black device shut, exited the T-bird, and opened Skye's door. "Ready to investigate?"

"Yep." Skye wiggled out of the low-slung sports car, conscious of her skirt riding up, and asked, "Is it okay to bring Toby inside?"

"Sure. There's nothing in there he can hurt."

Once Wally took the key from his pocket and opened the lock, Skye preceded him into the dark interior. It had an eerie, deserted vibe, and she was glad when Wally reached past her and pulled a chain attached to a bare bulb, flooding the room with light.

Now she could see the labyrinth of cardboard boxes surrounding her. The entire unit was stacked with bins, crates, and cartons as far as Skye could see. A narrow path wound through the maze, but Skye could make out only a few feet in front of her.

"Where do we start?" Skye tried to keep her voice even, and not reveal how overwhelmed she felt by the sheer volume of records.

"Let's do a walk-through." Wally's tone was grim. "Maybe there's some organizational method that isn't obvious at first glance."

"Okay." As Skye navigated the warren, she read the words hand lettered in black on the sides of the boxes. "It looks like they're arranged by year."

"That's something." Arriving at the back of the space, Wally pulled the chain on another bare bulb, then motioned to a long table against the rear wall. "We can sort through the cartons on this."

"Sure." Skye gripped Toby's leash; he'd begun trying to tug her forward. "I wonder if anyone's been here since they dropped off the records."

"I doubt—" Wally broke off and pointed to the floor, then said softly, "I guess they have, and I'd say fairly recently, too."

A fresh trail of footprints disturbed the thick layer of dust that covered the floor. The prints led away from where Skye and Wally now stood and into an aisle they hadn't been down yet.

Skye started to reply, but Wally put a finger to his lips and motioned her behind him. He unsnapped his holster and rested his hand on the butt of his gun, then moved forward.

Skye picked up Toby and followed. The cartons near the door bore dates beginning in the 1990s, and as she moved down the second aisle, she saw boxes marked 1980, then 1979.

Wally stopped abruptly. He stood motionless, but everything about his stance screamed that he was on high alert. Suddenly, he tilted his head, and at the sound of a door easing closed, he took off running.

Toby whined and tried to leap from Skye's arms to follow him, but she tightened her grasp and clamped a hand over the canine's muzzle. Should she go after Wally? No, better to stay here and not distract him from his pursuit. It wasn't as if she could run fast enough to catch anyone, not while wearing high heels, a dress, and carrying a dog.

Skye crept forward a few steps and saw papers scattered across the floor. Taking out a bag she'd tucked into her pocket to dispose of any future doggy deposits, she slipped it over her right hand. Using one plastic-covered finger, she fanned out the sheets and glanced through them. They were records concerning a twenty-seven-year-old bicycle theft from the park's bike rack.

Next, she righted a carton that was lying on its side and saw black Magic Marker numbers scrawled across the edge. She squinted until they came into focus—1978. Underneath the year, MAY—JUNE was written in smaller print.

Glancing around, she noticed an empty file folder crumpled in a corner. She gingerly moved it toward her with the toe of her shoe. A white label across the top read PAULETTE NEAL.

Chapter 17

"HEY GOOD LOOKIN' "

The windows along Scumble River's main drag were dark when Skye and Wally drove back to town. Wally hadn't been able to catch the intruder, who had presumably stolen the contents of the Neal folder, so he'd had to call in a county crime technician to dust the empty box and the other files for fingerprints. By the time the tech arrived, did her job, and departed, it was close to eight thirty, which meant Skye and Wally didn't get home until after nine.

Skye's stomach growled as Wally turned the T-bird into the church parking lot. Both she and Toby were starving, and she'd bet Bingo would be yowling for food as well.

"You sure you don't want to get a bite at McDonald's?" Wally asked, opening her door.

"No." Skye slid behind the wheel of her Bel Air and deposited Toby in the backseat. "I have a hungry cat waiting for me."

"Okay." Wally kissed her cheek. "Then I'll stay here and work on the case awhile." He jutted his chin toward the police station behind him. "Although I'm not sure where to start."

"Yeah." Skye sighed in sympathy. "I imagine it's hard to figure out who had a motive to kill Suzette when you have so little information about the real person behind the public persona."

"Exactly." Wally shoved a hand through his hair. "We're not aware of any Scumble Riverites with whom she had more than casual contact, although we're still looking. And so far, all of the owners of black pickups we've located have alibis. We've interviewed the Country Roads employees and the laborers who were on the theater construction site, but everyone says she kept to herself."

"Even Kallista Taylor and Flint James?" Skye asked, then said, "Dang it! I never did tell you the negative things they said about her Saturday night, did I?" Skye described the scene in the trailer, ending with, "So both Flint and Kallista were jealous of Suzette. For Flint it was professional; for Kallista it was personal."

"No one mentioned a word about that yesterday or today in any of the interviews we conducted with the Country Roads people."

"Of course not." Skye crossed her arms. "Who would volunteer that kind of information about the star or the boss's wife?"

"Nobody who wanted to keep his or her job." Wally's eyes were cold. "But tomorrow will begin round two of the interrogations, and this time I have something specific to ask them.

193

Especially since neither of them has an alibi."

"I am so sorry I forgot to tell you about that conversation. I didn't realize they were two of the three Country Roads people who couldn't account for their time." Skye felt she had let Wally down. "What kind of psych consultant am I if I don't remember the important details?"

"You overheard Flint and Kallista before the murder, when what they said wasn't that important. Then you had a nasty shock when you found Suzette in that horrific condition." Wally leaned into the Chevy and embraced Skye. "No one could expect you to be at the top of your game after seeing that." He rested his cheek against hers. "Besides, it's only been two days."

"Thanks for understanding and not being mad." She hugged him back. "But I promise I'm over it now. Simon is going to dog sit for me, and I'll concentrate on helping you find the killer."

Skye held her breath, wondering how Wally would take the news of Simon's involvement.

"Why would you ask your ex-boyfriend for help?" Wally's voice was soft, but it had an edge that made Skye flinch.

"Actually, Simon volunteered." Skye hastily explained the conversation they'd had at the ATM. "I have a feeling he might end up adopting Toby if they get along and no one else claims him."

"Yeah." Wally nodded thoughtfully. "I can see

that." After a few seconds his face relaxed. "Reid will need the companionship." Wally kissed her, then straightened. "Because he's not getting you back."

"That was my thinking. Do you want me to help with the reinterviews tomorrow after I get out of school?"

"Definitely." Wally's smile was predatory. "I'm going to save the two major players for you. And instead of bringing Kallista and Flint into the PD, we'll approach them in their home territory, where they're apt to be less careful of what they say."

"I can't wait." Skye started to close the Chevy's door, but stopped. "Hey—how about Darleen? Were you able to trace that number I gave you?"

"Just like I figured, it came back to a disposable cell." Wally crossed his arms. "And no one answered when I dialed it, not even voice mail."

"Guess whoever called isn't in much of a hurry for the money." Skye studied Wally's tired expression before asking, "Have you decided if you're going to pay her or not?"

"I don't think it's a good idea." Wally leaned a hip against the car. "But if you want me to, I will, because getting to marry you is worth more than a measly quarter million dollars."

"That's such a sweet thing to say." Skye beamed at him. "But I'd never encourage you to give in to blackmail."

"I'll try calling that number again tomorrow." Wally's shoulders hunched forward. "Maybe we can work something out."

"Well, whatever you decide, I'm behind you a hundred percent." Skye started the Bel Air's engine. "If we don't get a letter from Darleen supporting your request for an annulment, it may take a bit longer, but it will still come through and we'll still get married."

Skye had been praying it wouldn't come to this. She'd been sure they'd find the name of Suzette's brother last night in the police file. But now that the file was officially stolen, that hope had vanished.

Noreen had said only two people currently at Scumble River High were at the school when Quentin Neal worked there—Homer Knapik and Pru Cormorant, the English teacher. Voluntarily spending time in Homer's company was bad enough, but questioning Pru ventured into the realm of appalling.

Pru hadn't liked Skye when she had her as a student, and she disliked her even more as a colleague. The animosity was mutual, especially since last month when the English teacher had tried to shut down the newly opened bookstore in town, claiming the romances it sold were pornography and the horror novels were satanic.

Skye had been putting off the discussions with

Homer and Pru all day. But by the afternoon, when the elementary school student she had scheduled for testing was absent, Skye had run out of excuses and reluctantly headed over to the high school. Pru wouldn't be available until eighth hour, which was her second planning period, but Homer was almost always free.

The session with Homer went remarkably well. Having successfully turned over the administrative problems pertaining to Woodrow Buckingham's integration to the special education coordinator, the principal was in a mellow mood.

Homer answered Skye's questions with only a few snide remarks, but he could add nothing to what Noreen had already reported. Homer's sole recollection of Quentin Neal was that he had done his job and kept out of trouble.

When the seventh-hour bell rang, Skye waited for the kids to leave before approaching Pru's room.

"Hi, Pru," Skye called from the open doorway. "Got a minute?"

The English teacher was facing a six-foot-high double-door metal cabinet. At Skye's greeting, she swung around and scowled. "Did Mrs. Cook complain about that note I sent home yesterday?"

"What note?" Skye asked cautiously. Homer usually sent her to deal with Pru when the teacher ticked off a parent, but he hadn't mentioned a problem.

"The one I wrote that said, 'Your son sets low standards and then consistently fails to achieve them.'"

"Holy smokes!" Skye blurted out. "What possessed you to send a parent something like that?"

"I know you think I'm crazy," Pru snapped, "but I've just been in a very bad mood for the past twenty-odd years."

"Of course I don't think you're crazy," Skye soothed, thinking, *Mean as a polecat, but not crazy.*

"Fine." Pru crossed her arms. "Which of your little darlings needs special treatment this time?"

"No one at the moment." Skye forced a smile. Pru thought everyone should be treated equally —that is, everyone but the two or three students she selected as her pets every year. "However, I always appreciate your cooperation when I do have a request."

The English teacher narrowed her wintry blue eyes and twitched her pointy nose. "Then to what do I owe the pleasure of your company?"

Skye held on to her smile. "I understand you knew Quentin Neal. He was a music teacher who worked here quite a while ago."

"He was here only for a year, so I wouldn't exactly say I knew him," Pru quibbled. "Especially since he taught a fluff subject."

"I understand. But is there anything at all you

can recall about him?" Skye was fairly sure that Pru, who acted as gossip central for the school, kept track of all the new teachers, even the ones she dismissed for teaching superfluities like music and art. "Maybe who his friends were?"

"I do remember he was a handsome man." Pru gave a small shrug, her expression contemptuous. "All the young females on the staff, and several of the older ones who should have known better, were atwitter."

"Did he chirp back?" Skye asked, wondering if Pru had been one of the cheeping flock. "I imagine that kind of adulation would be tempting to him."

"No." Pru smoothed her stringy dun-colored hair back into its chignon. "He was pleasant, but he kept his distance."

"Did you ever meet his family?" Skye asked. "I understand he had twins."

"Yes to both your questions. And since the girl was just murdered here in town a couple of days ago"—Pru's smile was superior—"I imagine she is why you're so interested in Quentin."

"That's true," Skye admitted, not allowing herself to be baited. "Do you remember his son's name?"

"Let me think." Pru tapped a bony finger on her receding chin and pursed her thin lips. "It wasn't an *S* name like Stephen or Scott, as you'd expect with twins."

"Did it rhyme with Suzette?" Skye asked, realizing the absurdity of the suggestion before the last word slipped from her lips.

"What boy's name ends with *ette?*" The English teacher glared in contempt at Skye's stupidity.

"Oh." Skye ground her teeth, angry she had given Pru an opening to ridicule her. The woman had done enough of that when Skye had been in her class twenty years ago. "Right."

"Let's see." Pru *tsk*ed. "I almost had it when you interrupted me."

"Sorry." *Uh-oh.* Being interrupted was one of Pru's major pet peeves.

"I remember thinking the name was appropriate." Pru's pause was indisputably for effect. "The little boy was such a hellion."

Skye held her breath, waiting for the big revelation to which Pru was building up.

After several seconds, Pru shook her head. "No." She rubbed her temples. "I'm afraid it's flown out of my head."

Sheesh! What a letdown. "Well, thanks for trying." Skye barely refrained from shaking Pru until the teacher came up with the name. "If you think of it, let me know or call Chief Boyd. The police would be grateful for your cooperation in this matter."

"Of course." Pru looked meaningfully at the wall clock, then glowered at Skye. "Now, if you don't mind, I'd like to use the few minutes left of my planning period for my own work, instead of yours."

As Skye walked back to her office, she processed what Pru had told her. What boy's name could be associated with the word *hellion?*

"Adolph?" Wally guessed. It was four thirty and they were in his Thunderbird on the way to the Up A Lazy River Motor Court to talk to Flint James. "Damian?"

"That's a good one." Skye had been thinking of names since she'd left Pru. "Attila?"

"Fidel?" Wally parked the Ford in an empty slot next to a red Maserati.

"I've got it." Wally exited the T-bird, walked around the hood, and held out his hand to Skye. "Cain. Wasn't he the ultimate hellion?"

"Yes. I'd have to say killing your brother qualifies you for that title." Skye marched up the sidewalk to cabin number two and knocked, paused, then knocked again when there was no response. "That's odd. He should be here. When I called Uncle Charlie just before we drove over here, he said that Flint James was in his room. He'd pulled in a few minutes before I phoned."

Wally moved Skye out of the way, stepped closer, and pounded on the door.

This time they heard a muffled voice yell, "Be right there!"

While they waited, Skye spotted the bass player

from Flint's backup band peering out his cottage's window. She waved and he let the curtain drop. Turing to Wally, she said, "Speaking of Cain, do you think Suzette's brother might have killed her? After all, the media has been all over this murder and he hasn't come forward. Maybe that's why."

Before he could respond, the door was flung open and Flint James in all his nearly naked glory stood on the other side of the threshold.

Skye swallowed hard, her mouth suddenly dry. The small bath towel that Flint wore wrapped low on his hips didn't leave much to the imagination. She caught herself hoping for a strong gust of wind.

"Sorry." The singer grinned and hitched the terry cloth rectangle a little higher. "I wasn't expecting company. Rex had me on the dog and pony show circuit all day and I needed to wash off the sleaze."

"No problem, partner." Wally got his Texas on and he slung his arm around Skye. "We were on our way to dinner, but I saw your car and thought this might be a good time to clear up a few things."

Skye hid a smile. So that's why Wally was dressed in jeans and cowboy boots and they were using his private car. He had said they would try to keep this laid-back to throw the suspects off, but she hadn't realized they were going in disguise.

"If you don't mind, could we come in and talk for a minute?" Wally asked.

"Sure." Flint stepped back. "Make yourself to home." He headed toward the bathroom. "Let me throw on some clothes."

While the star was dressing, Skye whispered to Wally, "I take it my role in this little performance is as the dumb girlfriend."

"Not necessarily dumb." Wally leaned his backside against the desk. "Just not as smart as you really are, at least at first."

"Gotcha." Skye sat on the only available chair and studied the room. It contained a double bed, a dresser with a TV on top, and two nightstands. She noted that Flint's belongings were all neatly arranged.

A few seconds later Flint returned, toweling his hair. "What can I do you for?"

Wally asked routine questions about the singer's activities on Monday afternoon, where he'd been at the time of the murder, and what his relation-ship with Suzette had been like.

Flint's answers were exactly the same as in his first interview. He'd been alone in his room from two until five, and he and Suzette were friendly colleagues.

Finally Flint said, "Man, I answered all these questions before. If you don't have anything new, I need to get ready for an evening gig and I'd like to rest for a couple of hours before then."

"Right. Of course." Wally straightened but subtly put pressure on Skye's shoulder, indicating she should stay seated and that it was her turn to take over the interrogation. "We surely don't want to keep you from that. Thanks for your patience."

"I'm happy to cooperate with the police." Flint held out his hand.

"Mr. James," Skye spoke from behind Wally. She could see the singer, but he could only glimpse her. "Before we go, I just wanted to tell you how much I enjoyed your concert last Saturday night."

"Why thank you, little lady." Flint's baritone was as smooth as twelve-year-old scotch. "I truly love singing to a live audience."

"You know"—Skye let her voice drop as if imparting a secret—"for a while there I was afraid the concert wasn't going to happen."

"Oh?" Flint's expression was neutral. "Why is that?"

"Folks here in Scumble River are pretty impatient and I thought they'd leave when it didn't start on time." Skye giggled. "Good thing there was all that free booze available." She put her hand over her mouth, pretending to be embarrassed. "No offense."

"None taken."

"But the concert was nearly half an hour late." Skye shook her head. "Some people thought that was downright rude of you all."

"I agree." Flint's ears were red. "I hate speaking ill of the dead, but the delay was entirely Suzette's fault. I was there early."

"I know." Skye stood and moved around Wally until she was facing the singer. "I overheard you talking to Mr. Taylor before she arrived."

"How did you—?" The beautiful bronze skin of Flint's face became a jaundiced yellow. "Where were you? I mean—what did you hear?"

"I heard you say that you didn't trust Suzette. That she was a schemer and had sweet-talked Mr. Taylor into giving her one of your best songs." Skye moved closer to the singer. "Is that what you call being friendly colleagues?"

Chapter 18

"YOUR CHEATIN' HEART"

Flint stuttered for a moment or two, then took a breath, smoothed his hair, and pulled his celebrity persona around him like Superman's cape. His trademark sexy grin appeared, and in a sensuous drawl he said, "You must have misunderstood me, darlin'."

"I don't think so." Skye stared coolly into his

molten toffee eyes and crossed her arms. "I was only a few feet from an open window."

"Have you been around many performers?" Flint intensified his smile.

"That depends on what you mean by *performer*." Skye allowed her lips to curve slightly. "I'm a school psychologist and deal daily with teen- agers, parents, teachers, and administrators— many of whom are putting on an act for my benefit."

Flint's chuckle was forced. "Real artists usually blow off steam before a live gig." His expression was now little-boy earnest. "Everyone knows it's just nerves and we don't mean anything by it."

"Really?" Skye persisted, not swayed by Flint's attempt to charm her. "Does that include Mrs. Taylor? She seemed to share your opinion of Suzette."

"Kallista is a singer, too. As soon as her throat is better, she'll be back onstage."

"Maybe sooner rather than later, now that Suzette's gone," Skye suggested, testing to see if Flint would offer up Kallista as an alternative suspect.

He seemed to think about it for a couple of seconds, but straightened his shoulders and said, "You're not even close." His charisma slipping, he sneered, "Suzette was far from the sweet young thing she pretended to be. As my grandpa used to say, she had honey on the lips, but vinegar in the heart."

"Yet only you and Kallista have spoken badly of her," Wally said, the Texas twang now gone from his voice.

"No one who wants to make it in show business is as nice as she pretended to be." Flint gave a hard, bitter laugh. "And I'm sure I wasn't the only one who had a problem with her."

"Fair enough." Wally moved into Flint's personal space. "But when I asked you that the first time we spoke, you said Suzette kept to herself. Were you lying then or are you lying now?"

"Neither. She kept to herself, but she was ambitious, so she had to have made enemies."

"Right." Wally flicked the singer a scornful glance. "You need to wipe the corner of your mouth. Some BS is stuck there."

"I'm telling you the truth."

"Name someone."

"Figure it out for yourself." Abruptly Flint's manner changed from cajoling to confrontational and he thrust his face close to Wally's. "I'm looking out for number one, and that doesn't include doing your job for you."

"My job requires the public's assistance." Wally held his ground. "We're asking all the men connected with the Country Roads tour and the construction crew to give us DNA samples. Can we count on your cooperation?"

"Will it get you out of here?"

"You bet."

"Then, sure." Flint shrugged. "Whatever."

"I'm shocked Flint is willing to give us his DNA," Skye whispered as they left the cabin. "Have the others agreed so easily?"

"He's the first one I asked. And I'm contacting the county tech to come get it now before he changes his mind." Wally grinned. "Tomorrow I'll see if I can parlay James's cooperation into making the other men look bad if they aren't prepared to follow his lead."

"I'm a little surprised you didn't try to get everyone's specimens after the semen was discovered," Skye commented as they reached the car.

"I wish I could just check them all, but there's a huge backlog at the lab. I have to pick and choose whose DNA I request expedited, and I've been saving one spot for Owen's." Wally's expression was frustrated. "On the other hand, now that I have a good pretext for requesting the samples, I'd rather get them while the getting is good, even if they never get tested."

After Wally finished phoning the techs, Skye asked, "What do you think he meant when he said that Suzette wasn't the innocent she seemed to be and that other people had problems with her?"

"It's hard to say."

"Was that his way of pointing the finger at

Kallista without getting in trouble with her husband?" Skye slid into the T-bird. Earlier, she'd asked Simon to keep Toby overnight, and now she was glad she had. It was a mighty tight fit when both she and the dog had to share the passenger seat of the tiny sports car.

"Maybe." Wally started the Ford's engine and put it into reverse. "I've got Anthony keeping an eye on Kallista's RV. As soon as she gets home, he'll call me. Then we can go talk to her and find out."

"What will we do until then?" Skye asked. Wally hadn't mentioned interviewing another suspect.

"Until then, we'll have some supper." Wally trailed a caressing finger from her shoulder down her side and onto her thigh. "I feel like a jerk for starving you yesterday, so tonight I'm prepared."

A couple of minutes later, Wally stopped the car next to the riverbank. He popped the trunk and lifted out a gingham-covered basket. Walking with one arm around Skye, he guided her toward a picnic table. From there they could see the cerulean blue water and the tiny waves lapping the rocky shore.

Wally spread the cloth on the table, arranged the food, and waved his hand toward the meal. "Your feast awaits, my love."

"Thank you." Skye took a bite of her sandwich —both the bread and the roast beef were obviously homemade—and mumbled, "Dorothy?"

Dorothy Snyder was Wally's part-time house-keeper and a fantastic cook.

"Of course." Wally scooped a mound of creamy yellow potato salad onto his paper plate. "I asked her to drop the chow off at the PD."

"Yum." Skye gestured at the surrounding trees whose leaves were beginning to change to the gold and red colors that were the very essence of autumn. "This is perfect."

"Yep." Wally took her hand. "When I heard the temperature was going to be in the sixties today, I realized this might be our last chance for a picnic."

"You are so thoughtful." Skye squeezed his fingers. "Even in the middle of an investigation you think of us."

"You're always on my mind," Wally said.

"But if Anthony calls, we can pack up and leave immediately." Skye's gaze was shrewd. She knew Wally was too good a cop to let even her interfere with a case.

"Yes, but in the meantime"—Wally opened a can of caffeine-free Diet Coke for Skye and a Dr Pepper for himself—"we can have a nice dinner in a romantic setting. Maybe we can even pretend we're on a regular date rather than hunting down a stone-cold killer."

"That sounds wonderful. I'll try my best." Skye managed to forget the murder and every-thing else for the next half hour as they ate and talked, but when Anthony's call came in alerting them to Kallista's presence at the trailer, Skye knew the fun was over—at least for a while.

While they were repacking the basket, throwing away their trash, and loading the T-bird, Skye asked, "Did you get any info today from the Nashville police or on Owen's Red Cross blood or about the victim's DNA or the fingerprints from the self-storage?"

"No, no, no, and no." Wally started the sports car and headed toward Kallista's RV, which was still at the park. "The ME promised me the victim's DNA results tomorrow. The city attorney is still looking into the legality of your suggestion about Owen's donated blood. There have been no hits on the fingerprints. And the Nashville police haven't found anybody who knows anything about Suzette's past."

"Darn."

"That's putting it mildly," Wally agreed. "Except for reinterviewing the Country Roads and construction employees, which yielded zilch, the only thing I accomplished today was talking to Owen and rechecking where he was during the murder."

"Is he aware yet that he's a suspect?" Skye asked.

"I don't think so. I told him that a black pickup had been involved in another accident during that time period, but this time someone got a partial plate and it fit his license number."

"Did Owen believe you? Did he come up with an alibi?"

"Maybe and no. Since he was alone working at the farm that Monday afternoon, he couldn't think of anyone who'd seen him." Wally turned onto the gravel road leading to the Country Roads Tour Airstream. "Too bad the animals can't talk."

"That's for sure. Toby could solve the case for us." Skye chuckled. "I take it Owen continues to refuse to say who he was with last Saturday."

"Yep. He's maintaining that we have no right to ask him for that information."

Skye was silent for a few seconds, then offered tentatively, "I have an idea about finding Suzette's twin. But I don't know how good it is."

"I'm all ears," Wally encouraged. "Since this case isn't a priority—no imminent danger suspected—the federal database has informed me that they won't have any information for at least two weeks."

"How about those genealogy sites online? Couldn't you use those to track down Suzette's brother?"

"That's not a bad idea." Wally thought for a moment. "I'll have Martinez check out a couple sites tomorrow."

Skye hated to bring up the subject of Wally's ex-wife, but she had to know the status of that situation. "Anything new with Darleen?"

"Around noon today I tried that number you

gave me again. This time, a guy answered on the first ring." Wally pulled the car next to the silver trailer but made no move to get out. Instead, he turned to Skye and took her hands. "He said basically the same thing he said to you."

"Basically?"

Wally sighed. "I told him that if Darleen wouldn't provide a truthful account of our married life without being paid, I'd just wait for the annulment process to continue without her input. He said in that case Darleen would write a letter disputing my claims about the marriage and I'd never get an annulment."

"Is that possible?"

"I'm guessing that if such a document surfaced, it would be my word against hers." Wally wrinkled his brow. "The guy said to call him tomorrow night at seven and have the money ready to hand over to him."

"I'll call Father Burns in the morning and make an appointment for after school. We need to check what he has to say about the situation." When Wally was silent, Skye asked, "Right?"

"Yeah." Wally frowned. "I guess that's the logical next step. We'll decide what to do after we talk to him."

"Okay." Skye kissed Wally's cheek; then as she was getting out of the T-bird, she said over her shoulder, "One thing at a time."

It was nearly six o'clock when Skye and Wally

climbed the trailer's steps. Skye lifted her fist to knock, still thinking about what Wally had just told her, when Wally's hand closed over hers and gently pushed it down to her side.

She turned and saw that he had his finger to his lips and his head inclined toward the door. Once she moved closer and concentrated, she could hear an argument coming from inside the RV.

The sound was muffled by the trailer's walls, but Skye heard a man shout, "All I'm saying is that we need to cool it for a while."

"Fine. If you're going to be a jerk about it, maybe we should cool it for good."

Skye figured the second voice had to be Kallista's. She mouthed the name to Wally, who nodded.

"Baby, you know I don't want that," Mr. Jerk wheedled. "I love you."

"You sure aren't showing it," Kallista screeched. "You've got your eye on that sound-and-lights chick, don't you?"

"Of course not, sweetie pie." Mr. Jerk's baritone dropped into bass range. "You're my one and only. You know I want to marry you as soon as all the papers with the music theater deal are signed and we can both get shed of Rex. You can get a divorce and I can get free of my contract."

"Then why don't you want to see me any-more?" Kallista sobbed.

"Baby doll, I'm just trying to protect you,"

Mr. Jerk sweet-talked. "Rex is acting suspicious and I don't want you to get into trouble. We both know he's got a temper."

"Yeah." Kallista's voice faltered. "But he's mostly just a lot of hot air, and he doesn't care if I have my little flings, as long as the guy isn't any threat to his ego." Her tone brightened. "Which is why I let him think I was messing around with one of the boys in the band. And since he doesn't know which one, nobody gets hurt."

There was a lengthy silence, and just as Wally raised his hand to knock, Kallista said, "It would have been so much better if Rex was the one under that steamroller instead of that bitch. If he was dead, I'd inherit it all and we wouldn't have to wait anymore."

Another lengthy silence, then Kallista said, "You'd better go. Rex might come back any minute."

Before Skye could react, the door swung open and Flint James nearly plowed her down in his haste to exit the Airstream.

He stopped abruptly, stared at Skye and Wally, then blurted, "Excuse me. I was . . . uh . . . just checking to see if Rex wanted to ride with me to tonight's meeting." He pushed past them and disappeared in the direction of the footbridge that led from the park to the motor court.

Kallista moved out of the shadows, took in

the situation, and fluttered her lashes at Wally. "Why, Sheriff, I almost didn't recognize you out of uniform. I mean, in regular clothes." She giggled. "Although I bet you'd look mighty fine out of them, too."

"It's 'Chief,' ma'am." Wally tipped an imaginary hat. "But thank you."

"What can I do for you, Chief?" Kallista moistened her glossy pink lips.

"Well, I was hoping you'd have a few minutes to talk with me."

"I surely do, Chief." Kallista wiggled past Skye, entwined her arm with Wally's, and drew him inside. "Can I get you a beer?"

"No, but don't let me stop you." Wally beckoned for Skye to join them.

Skye obliged, noting that the door opened directly into the living room. She chose a straight chair that was nearly hidden behind a red-lacquered three-panel screen stenciled with black dragons.

Kallista tugged Wally to a black leather sofa and playfully pushed him onto the cushions, joining him after fetching a Corona for herself. She continued to act as if Skye were invisible, petting Wally's biceps with one hand and slugging back the beer with the other.

Skye gritted her teeth, but remained quiet. While Kallista manhandled Wally, Skye glanced around the Airstream's interior. It was much roomier than she had expected, and all the furniture looked expensive.

Kallista gave a high-pitched laugh, and Skye focused back on the woman pawing her fiancé. The blonde was running her tongue along the neck of the beer bottle while caressing the bottom half.

While Kallista flirted, Wally went over the same questions with her that he had with Flint. What were her activities on Monday afternoon and where had she been at the time of the murder?

And like Flint's, Kallista's answers matched her previous ones. She had spent Monday afternoon in Joliet and was at the movies at the time of the murder.

"Did you ever find that ticket stub we talked about?" Wally asked.

"No." Kallista shook her head. "I probably threw it away."

"If we show your picture, would the theater employees remember you?" Wally persisted. "Maybe the ones at the candy counter."

"Do I look like I eat candy?" Kallista ran her hands down her flat stomach. "I save my calories for this." She held up the Corona.

"Good choice." Wally smiled, then said, "Pardon me for asking, but when we got here it sounded as if you were having some marriage trouble. Isn't Mr. Taylor a good husband?"

217

"He could be." Kallista finished off her beer. "But he stinks at doing impressions."

"I see." Wally laughed politely. "What was your relationship with Suzette like?"

"She was my husband's gofer. We didn't have a relationship." The blonde hiccupped. "*She* did what she was told and that was that."

"I understand she kept to herself, but was there anyone she was close to?"

Kallista narrowed her unbelievably violet eyes. "You mean besides my husband?"

"She and Mr. Taylor were friendly?" Wally encouraged the woman to continue. "In what way?"

"She wanted him to make her a star and he wanted into her pants."

"Do you believe what Kallista said about Rex wanting to sleep with Suzette?" Skye asked the minute she and Wally were back in the car. "Or that Suzette might have had sex with him to get ahead?"

"No one but Kallista has suggested anything like that regarding Suzette." Wally put the T-bird in gear. "But I think Taylor's the kind of guy who tries with every woman he meets."

"Really tries or just sort of tries?" Skye fastened her seat belt. "I mean, from what little I know about Rex, he does appear to be the type, and I did see him attempt to hug Suzette at the meeting in the mayor's office last Sunday."

"He's like the guys you see in a casino. They put a quarter in nearly every slot machine they walk past. If it hits, great, and if it doesn't, they go on to the next one."

"You might be right, because he didn't appear upset when Suzette shrugged off his arm."

"Exactly." Wally made a U-turn and headed out of the park. "Each time I've seen Taylor, he's coming on to one woman or another, but it seems more of a habit than a serious effort."

"How about Kallista and Flint? Their affair certainly complicates matters." Skye paused, thinking. "What if Suzette found out about Flint and Kallista's plans to run away together, and they killed her to stop her from telling Rex?"

"Except for the lovers' quarrel or rape scenario, that's the best motive I've heard so far." Wally tapped his fingers on the steering wheel. "On the other hand, why would Flint have sex with her first?"

"He's a jerk?" Skye closed her eyes. "Or Flint was having an affair with both women." Her lids popped open. "And Kallista discovered them in the act. In a rage, she killed Suzette—whom she considered her competition for both men in her life."

"I suppose that's possible, but did she act alone or did James help her?"

"My money's on Kallista." Skye wrinkled her nose. "Obviously she didn't like Suzette."

"Judging from the way she treated you, I don't think Kallista likes any other women." Wally squeezed Skye's hand. "And by the way, thank you for going along with that whole production."

"No problem."

"Because Kallista is just a screen saver, not the real deal like you."

"Screen saver?" Skye's expression showed her confusion.

"Yeah." Wally winked. "She looks good, but she's useless."

Skye smiled. "Anyway, I trust you and I appreciate you trusting me when I told you about having Simon take care of Toby."

"Speaking of Toby, since he's not an issue, and you stopped and fed Bingo before we went to see Flint, how about spending the night at my place?"

"Well . . . I think that's a fine idea." Skye stroked Wally's thigh. "Especially since there was one thing missing from our picnic."

"What's that?"

"Dessert."

Chapter 19

"I Can't Stop Loving You"

Friday afternoon Skye felt as if her good luck might be back. So far, there had been no emergency parent conferences and no inconvenient student absences. If the next hour went well, she would be able to leave work at quitting time and make her four thirty appointment with Father Burns with time to spare. And since the priest had said he didn't mind if she brought a dog along to the meeting, she didn't need to ask Simon to keep Toby for another night.

Glancing at the clock, Skye saw she had fifteen minutes to grab a cup of coffee before she needed to fetch the boys for her group. She locked the file she'd been working on in the cabinet, gathered up the material she needed for the session, and headed for the staff room.

The lounge was located in the back half of the basement, and Skye wound her way through a warren of construction paper rolls hung on huge cylinders, a massive cage containing balls of various sizes, and several racks of cleaning supplies. The scent of dust, sweat, and ammonia mingled in her sinuses, and she sneezed three times in rapid succession.

From somewhere in the labyrinth a male voice yelled, "God bless you!"

"Thank you, Cameron," Skye shouted back. The young custodian was often heard but not seen.

When Skye pushed open the door to the teachers' lounge, she saw Yvonne Smith facing a bulletin board at the rear of the empty room. The plump middle-aged woman with a halo of brown and gray curls, half-glasses, and baby blue eyes was the epitome of everyone's favorite teacher. The fact that she taught special education was a true bonus for children with special needs.

"Hi, Yvonne," Skye said cheerfully. "How are you this afternoon?"

"Oh, my!" The teacher spun around, clutching her chest. "You startled me."

"Sorry." Skye wrinkled her brow. What was up with Yvonne? She was usually one of the most unflappable teachers Skye dealt with. "Is anything wrong?"

"No." The older woman's voice was sheepish. "I've just received a strange call."

"Really?" Skye walked over to the coffee machine, put down the equipment she was carrying, and poured the dark brew into a cup. "What happened?"

"A parent was upset because her eight-year-old

came home and told her he'd learned how to make babies in my class yesterday."

"Okay—I know you aren't teaching sex ed, especially to third graders." Skye opened two packs of Sweet'N Low and shook them along with some powdered creamer into her coffee. "So why would her son say that?"

Yvonne shook her head. "Yesterday I taught a lesson on plurals, and told them that to make the word *babies* from *baby* you change the *y* to an *i* and add *es*. My question is, why didn't the mom ask her son what he meant?"

"Because that would have been too easy." Skye stirred her coffee.

"True," Yvonne agreed, then added, "I'd better get going." She strode toward the exit, pausing to say, "I'll send my aide down with the boys for your group as soon as we finish our after-recess quiet time minutes."

"I'd appreciate that." Skye snapped a lid on the cup and gathered up her supplies. "I'll be waiting for them in the usual spot."

"You're more than welcome." Yvonne smiled. "I'm grateful that you're seeing them. Those three are a handful. It will be nice to have a little uninterrupted time to devote to the others." She waved and hurried away.

Skye followed at a slightly slower pace. Not having to fetch the kids from the far end of the building gave her a few extra minutes.

Emerging from the basement stairway, Skye balanced three game boxes, a bag of rewards, and her cup, then hiked down the main hall. Near the office she noticed a handmade poster that read:

**The fifth graders will be presenting
Shakespeare's *Macbeth* in the gym
Friday at 7:30 p.m.
The staff is encouraged to attend this tragedy.**

Wondering if whoever made the sign had actually read it before putting it up, Skye giggled to herself as she headed into the elementary school's oldest section. The smell of mildew hit her full force as she turned into the corridor, making her eyes water.

Previously this wing had been rented out to a church group, but they had found a better facility and moved. Three years later, the school board was still trying to figure out whether to bring it up to code for classroom use or to tear it down and start over.

It was not the best location for a group session —stifling in the spring and fall and freezing in the winter. What's more, it was isolated and dreary. However, the principal had assured Skye that this was the only space available, and since there was no way she could squeeze three lively eight-year-old boys into her tiny office, she had to make-do. Conditions were rarely ideal when one worked in public education.

Here, at least, she was able to use a room that was the correct size. She had learned the hard way that when dealing with active children, a space that was too big was just as bad as one that was too small. When she had started the group, she had cleared out the pastor's old office and brought in a low table and four chairs. The walls were bare and there were no windows. Another lesson she had quickly learned was that it was best to have an area without many visual stimulants.

Skye set up the first game—one designed to encourage cooperation—then took a sip of her coffee as she waited for her group to arrive. After a couple of swallows, she became aware of an unsettling silence. Usually schools were full of noise, but she was totally on her own here.

The isolation made her think of Suzette's mother—supposedly alone in the house, with a three-year-old as the sole witness to her accident. What had really happened to Mrs. Neal all those years ago? And what had happened to her daughter a few days ago? Skye hastily scribbled down thoughts as they occurred to her.

1. Did Mrs. Neal's death have anything to do with Suzette's murder?
2. Did Suzette's brother have anything to do with either death?
3. Why use a steamroller to kill Suzette?

Before she could come up with more questions, her clients burst into the room. The teacher's aide hurried after them, a harried expression on her face. She nodded at Skye, then turned on her heels and fled.

The boys were definitely unusual. Clifford, the brightest of the three, handed Skye a white square of paper.

She thanked him, unfolded it, and read: *The opinions expressed by this child are not necessarily those of his parents.* Fighting to keep a straight face, Skye stuffed the paper into her pocket.

Glaring at Skye, Clifford sat down and slammed a thick hardcover *Harry Potter* into the middle of the game board. Playing pieces scattered everywhere.

Skye silently looked at him until he dropped his gaze; then she checked on the other boys. Alvin, who was tall for his age and built like a mini-linebacker, immediately got down on all fours. He crawled after the tokens, making excited yipping noises.

For an unprofessional moment, Skye wondered why Alvin insisted he was a dog named Spot instead of a singing chipmunk. At least the cartoon Alvin talked; her Alvin communicated only by barking.

The third boy had his back pressed to the door and was waving a can of Lysol in the others' direction, as if warding off mosquitoes. Duncan —or, as the kids called him, Mr. Clean—liked everything to be perfectly orderly and hygienic. So much so that he had insisted on having his head shaved so no hair would ever be out of place. Skye still couldn't believe his mother had gone along with that.

Clifford, aka Book Boy, glanced around and smiled contentedly. He retrieved his novel, flipped it open to the bookmarked page, and started to read.

Needless to say, none of the three kids had been able to make any friends, which concerned both their parents and the school staff. At their Individual Education Plan conference last fall, Skye had volunteered to provide a socialization group. This was their second meeting. Clearly she had her work cut out for her.

Reaching over, Skye plucked the book from Clifford's hands, swiftly put it on her chair, and sat on it. Then, in a mild tone, she said, "Would you all please help collect the pieces so we can begin our game?"

Alvin picked up one of the larger tokens in his mouth, trotted over, and dropped it into Skye's hands. Duncan gingerly approached a few pieces, sprayed them with Lysol, and brought them to the table. Clifford stared at Skye without moving.

Ignoring the recalcitrant boy, Skye showed the other two boys the rewards they could earn for taking turns, following directions, and speaking in their indoor voices. Once she had their interest, she got them started on the game.

Less than ten minutes had passed when Clifford grabbed a token and put it on the board. Alvin growled and Duncan aimed his Lysol can at the intruder.

"Should we let our friend Clifford join our game?" Skye selected a small rubber ball from her reward bag. "Alvin, do you think Clifford should get a turn?"

The large boy cocked his head, nodded, and said, "Woof."

Skye gave him the ball. "Good job on taking turns, Alvin."

"Duncan, do you agree we should let our friend Clifford join us in our game?" Skye held up a miniature container of hand sanitizer.

"Yes, Ms. D." Duncan reached for the bottle. "I want to take turns, too."

"Excellent decision." Skye checked her watch. The group was scheduled to last a half hour, and they still had ten minutes left. She handed the dice to Clifford and said, "Your friends agree it's your turn."

The rest of the time went well, and the boys were putting the game pieces away in the box when the same teacher's aide who had brought the boys to the session eased the door open. "Sorry to disturb you, Ms. Denison, but Mrs. Smith needs you. Two of the older children are having a disagreement about the proposed music theater and she's afraid it's about to turn physical."

"Oh, my." Skye swiftly stood and hurried out of the room, leaving the aide to supervise the boys.

Once she had helped the special education teacher with a conflict resolution exercise, Skye picked up her counseling equipment, then headed back to her office. As she walked down the hall, she thought about the similarities between the students' disagreement and the argument between Ginger and Theresa. It was sad that the kids had behaved better than the PTO board. The boys hadn't hit each other, shredded any clothing, or called each other names.

Skye's lucky streak continued, and she was able to leave school on time, which meant she had a luxurious half hour in which to pick up Toby and get over to the rectory. Skye thought she might even have a chance to talk to Simon about Suzette. If he hadn't been able to figure out why the singer looked familiar, maybe Skye could nudge his memory.

Simon swung open the front door of his house as soon as Skye knocked, almost as if he had been waiting for her in the foyer. She cringed. Had Toby destroyed a valuable antique or misbehaved so badly that Simon couldn't wait to get rid of him? No, that couldn't be it. The little dog sat obediently at Simon's feet, neither barking nor jumping.

"Hi." Simon smiled warmly. "Do you have time to come in, or are you in a hurry?"

"Well . . ." A small voice inside her warned that being alone with Simon in his home might be misconstrued by both her ex and Wally. But it had been a month since Simon's last over-the-top stunt in his quest to win her back, and she was hoping he'd finally realized his continued pursuit was futile. "I have a few minutes before I have to be at the church."

"Great." Simon stepped back so she could enter. "I want to show you a trick I taught Toby." He led her down the hall, through the kitchen, and into a screened-in porch, gesturing for her to take a seat.

She chose a bronze wrought-iron chair with black-and-tan-plaid cushions. Simon perched on the end of a matching chaise longue.

"Look." Simon made a motion with the flat of his hand and Toby trotted over. Another gesture and the little dog sat in front of Simon.

"How did you do that?" Skye asked, totally wowed by the performance.

"His mistress must have trained him, because as soon as I figured out the correct signals he was terrific." Simon grinned. "Now watch this." He pointed his finger at the dog and mimicked shooting a gun. Toby immediately fell over, all four paws pointed upward.

"Wow." Skye beamed. "That puts a whole new twist on playing dead."

"Yeah." Simon reached into the pocket of his khaki pants and gave Toby a treat. "He's extremely smart." Simon scratched behind the dog's pointy white ears and crooned, "Aren't you, boy?"

"He sure seems that way when he's with you." Skye was pleased to see Simon so happy. It had been a rough year for him because of her engagement to Wally, as well as a friend's betrayal. Maybe now that he wasn't obviously trying to sweep her off her feet, they could be pals. "I'd say you two are getting along like gangbusters."

"We are." Simon stroked the dog's silky fur. "He loves my fenced-in backyard." Simon pointed through the screens. "And I really like having him around to talk to."

Skye swallowed. She hated that she had caused Simon pain. He was a good man, and for a while she had thought she loved him. She remembered one evening together when he had brought her to his house for dinner. A trail of rose petals had greeted her at the door and led into the dining room, where the table had been set with a crisp white linen tablecloth.

Delicate china, sparkling crystal, sterling flatware, and candles in silver holders had contributed to the beautiful table setting, and a mouthwatering meal waited in the kitchen. But the gourmet food had grown ice cold before they ever got around to eating it.

Skye knew that too much had happened since

then to go back, but she exhaled a long sigh of regret before refocusing on the present and asking, "Did the police drop off a picture of Suzette a day or two ago?"

"Yes. That new officer, Martinez, brought it over yesterday." Simon rubbed his temples. "I've stared at it and stared at it, but I just can't shake loose why she looks so familiar to me."

"Could you get the photo?" Skye asked. "I want to try something."

"Sure." Simon left the room, returning almost immediately with a glossy head shot of the dead singer. "What's your idea?"

Skye took out a legal pad from her tote bag and ripped off a sheet. Eyeing the picture, she carefully tore a face-size hole in the paper, then laid it over the photo. "Now look. Does that help any?"

She had remembered a facial recognition test she used with younger children in which the removal of hair and background made a difference in their ability to identify faces as being the same.

Simon studied the altered image for several seconds, opened his mouth to speak, then pounded his forehead with the heel of his hand. "This is so frustrating. It's on the tip of my tongue."

"Do me a favor." Skye glanced at her watch. "Leave the picture covered like that; then after you've forgotten about it, look at it again." It was twenty after four. "Memory is a tricky thing. Sometimes if you stop thinking about something, it will come to you."

"Absolutely," Simon agreed. "I'll keep trying and I'll call if anything clicks."

"Thanks." Skye stood and scooped up Toby. "And thanks for taking care of this guy, too." Simon looked bereft, but she had to go.

"Anytime." Simon walked her to the door and waved. "He's a good little buddy."

Chapter 20

"DESPERADO"

Skye rushed up the steps to the rectory and came to an abrupt halt. A piece of paper taped to the pillar read:

Members of the Low Self-Esteem Group are reminded to use the back door.

Seriously? What was Father Burns thinking?

Skye shook her head and hurried inside. Wally was already waiting in the vestibule, sprawled on a wooden bench. His head rested against the beige wall and his eyes were closed. Not wanting to disturb him if he was catching a nap, she and Toby sat a few inches away from him.

Between the frustration of having no leads on the murder and the circumstances surrounding Darleen, Skye knew Wally hadn't been sleeping well. At least the media furor had settled down for the time being. Thank goodness the reporters had been distracted by another Chicago politician caught with his hand in the till and his mistress hitting the talk show circuit.

"I'm awake." Wally's lids opened. "You can scoot closer." His brown eyes looked affectionately at Skye. Once she was next to him, he said, "We now officially know the identity of our victim. The ME called this morning and confirmed she was Suzette."

"Was there ever really a question in your mind?" Skye asked.

"No." Wally shook his head. "Otherwise I would have conducted the investigation differently."

"That's what I figured."

"I was just sitting here trying to figure out if there's something I'm missing," Wally explained. "Something I've overlooked in all the confusion."

"I know what you mean." Skye made a wry face. "Was she raped? Was her murderer someone from her past? And where is this mysterious brother of hers?"

"There's nothing new from the Nashville police," Wally said, putting an arm around her, "so I guess until we get the DNA results we're stuck. And I could only request a fast turnaround for two of them, so if I chose wrong, the whole process could take a lot longer."

"So all the guys you asked today agreed to be tested?" Skye asked.

"The construction crew was fine with it, but Taylor wasn't too thrilled with the idea. Although he did it when I pointed out that matching the semen was our best chance at finding the killer and closing this case." Wally smiled thinly. "Once he heard that, he said he'd issue an order to all his employees to cooperate."

"I'm sure Rex wants the murder solved and forgotten so it doesn't taint his big Branson of Illinois plans." Skye leaned her head on Wally's shoulder. "Did you tell him that his wife and James were the only people without alibis?"

"Nope."

"Anything new from Darleen or her boyfriend?"

"No." Wally ran his thumb down her cheek. "I'm not expecting any communication from them until I call tonight."

"Right." Skye snuggled closer. "Have you thought about what you'll do if Darleen sends a statement disputing what you've said about your marriage? If she writes the wrong kind of letter—a dishonest one—you might not be able to get an annulment."

Before Wally could respond, Father Burns

swung open his office door and ushered them inside. He was in his early sixties and had been the pastor at Saint Francis for as long as Skye could remember. It was unusual for a priest to remain in a parish for so long, but his flock loved him and would be devastated if he was ever reassigned.

Once the priest was introduced to Toby, and Skye and Wally were seated on leather wing chairs facing the desk, Father Burns said, "I understand you have a question about your annulment, Wally."

"Yes. Something unusual has come up." Wally explained the situation with Darleen in a neutral voice, but his jaw tightened when he asked, "Would a letter like that slow down the annulment or prevent it altogether?"

"Since it would clearly be a document written to punish Wally for not giving her money and would, in fact, contain blatant lies, would it even be considered, Father?" Skye took Wally's hand and squeezed it.

"I'm afraid so." His ageless face was grave. "Although, with corroboration from other witnesses that the document was spurious, it would only delay the process, not halt it completely."

"In other words"—Wally narrowed his eyes— "it would be best if an untruthful letter was never written?"

"Yes, better to have no input from your ex-wife than one that differs from your view of the marriage." Father Burns sat motionlessly, his gaunt body ramrod straight. "Not that I'm advocating paying Mrs. Boyd or her companion in order to accomplish that goal."

"Of course not, Father." Skye reached down and stroked Toby. "That would be wrong."

"But," Wally said, without looking at Skye, "if things turn out badly, we may need to reconsider our decision to wait for an annulment before marrying."

Father Burns was silent for a moment, his dark, serious eyes studying them; then he said, "As I explained the last time we met, the Church's stance is that matrimony is both binding and lifelong. The annulment procedure is used to determine if an essential element, which prevented the sacramental union promised, was missing when the couple entered into the marriage."

"Understood," Wally acknowledged. "But since Darleen left me for another man, we should have that covered—with or without any comment from her."

"It will help." Father Burns fingered the Bible in front of him. "Although what you really need to prove is that you had prior knowledge that there was a missing element or something was fundamentally wrong right from the very beginning of your marriage."

"Okay." Wally didn't hesitate. "I advised you

the last time we were here that I wanted to back out of my marriage to Darleen on the eve of the wedding, but I didn't inform you that I told my best man that same thing the night before the ceremony. We aren't on good terms now, so I didn't want to have to involve him, but he'll cooperate by confirming that."

"Excellent. A witness is always good." The priest nodded solemnly. "Anything else?"

"Darleen and I fought almost from the first day of our marriage." A flicker of impatience crossed Wally's eyes, but his voice was unruffled. "It'll be awkward, but any number of people can testify to that."

"I'm sorry for your embarrassment, but those people's statements will help to disprove a letter such as the one you described." A corner of the priest's lips turned up slightly. "I do understand that for a non-Catholic such as you, this process must appear absurd, but without it your marriage to Skye will not be valid in the eyes of the Church."

"Believe me, I understand how much this means to her." Wally looked at Skye, who nodded.

"This great act of self-giving love will only make your marriage stronger." Father Burns looked heavenward and added, "God doesn't always give us only what we can handle. But He does help us handle what we are given."

Skye heard Wally grind his teeth, so she

hastily rose from her chair. "Thank you, Father. We won't keep you any longer."

As the priest ushered them to the door, it occurred to Skye that he might have known Quentin Neal. "Do you have one more minute, Father?"

"Certainly, my dear." The priest paused with his hand on the knob.

"Do you remember a man by the name of Quentin Neal?" Skye held tight to Toby's leash as the little dog lurched toward the exit. "He was active in the choir about twenty-seven years ago."

"He doesn't sound familiar." Father Burns stepped over to a wooden stand and opened a large book, flipping through the pages. "Ah, that's why I don't remember him. He was here only ten months in 1978, and that was the year I was on sabbatical in Rome."

"Rats!" They just couldn't catch a break. "Are the names of his family members listed?"

"No. Sorry." The priest ran his finger over the paper. "Only he was a member."

"How about an address?" Skye crossed her fingers that she could narrow down the location. Noreen had remembered only the name of the street.

"That is here." Father Burns leaned forward and read, "Thirteen oh eight Singer Lane."

"Terrific."

Just before Skye and Wally stepped across the

threshold, Father Burns said, "Something to think about. Everyone wants to live on top of the mountain, but a lot of happiness and self-growth happen while you're climbing it."

After thanking the priest, Skye and Wally strolled out to the parking lot together. The leaves were finally changing colors. A shower of rust, orange, and yellow rained down on them as they walked beneath a massive old oak tree. Skye giggled and Wally brushed them from her hair and shoulders. They lingered there for a few minutes, enjoying the beauty of their surroundings and each other.

Eventually Skye turned serious. She gave Wally one last lingering kiss and said, "You aren't going to pay Darleen, right?"

"No." He shook his head. "If she writes that negative letter, I'll round up the witnesses that support my view of the marriage."

"And you'll be willing to wait for the annulment?" Skye persisted as they walked toward their cars, Toby prancing by her side.

"Yes." Wally cupped her cheek and gave her a serious look. "But if that happens, I'd like you to consider us living together."

"If it's more than a year delay, I will consider it," Skye promised.

"It's a deal." Wally kissed her forehead. "Do you want to get a quick bite before I go back to work?"

"No." Skye opened the Bel Air's door. "I'm going to knock on doors near that address on Singer Lane. Maybe one of the neighbors will remember the Neals and their children."

"Okay, but be careful." Wally kissed Skye and patted Toby. "I'll come over to your house after I make the call to Darleen's boyfriend."

"Good." Skye put the dog in the Chevy's backseat and slid behind the wheel. "I'll pick up some food from the grocery store deli, and we can have a late supper."

Skye drove to McDonald's and parked her Bel Air in the back lot. After crossing Stebler Road, she and Toby hiked the length of Singer Lane—all two blocks of it. When she got to the end at Chestnut Court, she turned around and walked back, this time on the opposite side of the street.

No one was outside, which wasn't surprising since it was a few minutes before six and most folks would have just finished dinner. The average Scumble Riverite ate lunch at noon, supper at five, and then settled down in front of the TV for the rest of the evening.

The address Father Burns had provided was located in the middle of the second block, a nondescript ranch with beige vinyl siding. Near the sidewalk, a FOR RENT sign with a plastic tube attached was staked into the meager brown lawn. Skye flipped open the cap and took out one of the flyers. When she saw that it contained a floor plan, she stuck the leaflet into her tote bag, thinking it might come in handy.

After trying the neighbors on either side of 1308, Skye was discouraged. The woman on the right had lived there for only a couple of years and the one on the left had moved in that summer. Both women said that most of the houses on Singer Lane were rentals.

Skye looked down at Toby. "Shall we try a few more?"

The little dog yipped, which she took as an affirmative. Crossing the road, she knocked on the door directly across from the Neal family's former residence. This house was slightly bigger than the others on the street, and much better maintained. The trim was freshly painted, the leaves raked, and the cement walk crack free.

A man wearing sweatpants and a Bears jersey opened the door a cautious inch, and she said quickly, "Hi. My name is Skye Denison." She reached in her pocket and handed him her card. "I'm the Scumble River Police Department psychological consultant."

"I'm Hank Vanda." He let the door swing open a little wider. "Are you here about those druggies on the end of the block?"

"No. Sorry, but I will tell the chief about your concern," Skye assured the man. "I'm trying to find someone who lived in this area back in 1978."

"Let's see." He tugged on his chin and his lips moved silently. At last, he said, "We moved in when I was two, so that would be 1977."

"Oh." Skye's heart sank. Finally someone who had lived on Singer Lane during the right time period, but he'd have been too young to remember anything that happened back then. "Well, thanks anyway."

"Don't you want to talk to my mom?" Hank cocked a thumb behind him.

"Oh, yes." Skye brightened. "That would be wonderful."

"Well, then you better talk fast. Her programs start at six thirty and she doesn't let anything interfere with her television time."

"Thank you."

As she followed Hank through the living room, Skye noticed a pair of binoculars resting on the sill of a picture window facing the street. A worn recliner, its back to the rest of the room, was stationed nearby. She doubted the field glasses were used for bird watching. If Mrs. Vanda was the snoop, Skye might be in luck!

The kitchen walls were painted a bright red, with images of apples decorating the curtains, place mats, and canister set. Even the linoleum was imprinted with the fruit. Hank's mother stood at the sink washing dishes.

After her son introduced Skye, explaining who Skye was and what she wanted, the woman wiped her hands dry on a terry cloth towel hanging from a drawer handle and said, "I'm Jenny Vanda."

"Nice to meet you. What a cheerful kitchen."

"Thanks. I decorated it myself." Jenny gestured to a chair whose cushion was also festooned with apples. "Have a seat. Would you or your puppy like something to drink?"

"No, thank you." Skye sat. "I don't want to take too much of your time."

"Fair enough." Jenny glanced at the red plastic clock hanging on a soffit over the sink. "Who do you want to know about?"

"The Neals. They lived across the street from you in 1978." Skye patted Toby, who lay quietly at her feet. "I'm trying to find out the little boy's name. Do you remember it?"

"*Hmm.*" Jenny twisted the dishcloth she still held. "Let me think." She squeezed her eyes shut, then exclaimed, "Suzie! That was the girl." She tried again but shook her head. "Nope. I can't recall the boy's name." She made a wry face. "Nowadays my mind works like lightning. One brilliant flash and it's gone."

"Shoot!"

"Sorry. It was so long ago and the Neals weren't much for neighboring. The mother never let the kids play outside."

"Do you think your husband might remember?" Skye asked, crossing her fingers.

244

"He might have. Henry had a good memory." Jenny sat back. "But he died last year."

"I'm so sorry for your loss." Skye could have bitten her tongue.

"Thank you. The damn fool tried to beat a train across the tracks." Jenny's expression was hard to read. "My son moved back in to keep me company."

"I'm sure that was a blessing."

"Are you?" Jenny raised an eyebrow. "You know the old saying about setting something free?"

"Yes."

"Well, it needs to be revised. Because if that something sits on your couch, hogs your TV, eats you out of house and home, and doesn't seem to understand you set it free, then chances are you gave birth to it."

Skye chuckled sympathetically. "Is there anyone else on the street who might remember the Neal boy's name?" Skye asked, then added, "Or can you think of anyone at all who might know it?"

"We're the only ones who've been here for more than five years. The others . . . well, they come and go." Jenny paused, then leaned forward and whispered, "Quentin Neal's mistress might know."

"Who was that?" Skye fought to keep her expression neutral. No one else had mentioned a mistress. Quentin must have been good at keeping secrets.

"I only saw her twice," Jenny confided. "The

first time when she dropped him off in front of the house one afternoon when his wife and the kids weren't home."

"Maybe it was just a friend, another teacher, or someone from the choir."

"Friends don't spend twenty minutes making out in the front seat." Jenny crossed her arms. "She drove a fancy Cadillac, and they even disappeared from view a few times. It was real obvious what they were doing in that car, and it wasn't grading papers or singing solos."

"How about the second time?"

"Funny. Now that I think about it . . ." Jenny scratched her head. "It was the day of his wife's accident. In fact, not too long before the ambulance arrived."

"What did his lover look like?" Skye asked. "Was there anything special about her that you remember? Anything special about the car?"

"Well, she had ash blond hair that she wore in one of those chignon thingies. Plus her clothes looked expensive. And I'd say she was several years older than he was. She seemed real stylish, like she lived in the city, not Scumble River."

Chapter 21

"Friends in Low Places"

Jenny Vanda hadn't been able to answer any more of Skye's questions, but she promised to call her if she thought of anything. Next on Skye's agenda was a stop at the supermarket. After picking up cold cuts, macaroni salad, and more dog food, Skye got into the checkout line.

Ahead of her, paying for his purchases, was the fiddle player from Flint James's backup band. He looked at Skye, cocked his head as if he should know her, then shrugged and walked away. He appeared to be in his late teens, and Skye certainly hoped Kallista hadn't told Rex that this boy was her lover.

The pear-shaped young man sacking her purchases peered at each package as he deposited it in the bag. When he handed her the sack, he said, "You know, all this processed food isn't good for either you or your dog." He stroked his barely-there goatee. "You really should be eating organic."

"Thanks for your concern." *Geesh!* Since when had the bag boy become a nutritionist?

As Skye drove home, she tried to figure out the identity of the mysterious other woman in Quentin Neal's life. Still thinking about Jenny Vanda's information, Skye parked the Bel Air in the garage, left Toby in the car, and carried her groceries into the house.

She fussed over Bingo until he'd had enough affection, then fed him his Fancy Feast. Only then did she return to the Chevy to get Toby and bring him inside. Skye still didn't quite trust that he and Bingo would coexist peacefully, but he trotted over to his dish, which she quickly filled with Canine Cuisine, and he chowed down without giving the feline a second glance.

While the animals were occupied with their dinners, Skye changed out of her work clothes. She had already put on a pair of jeans and was pulling an emerald green sweatshirt over her head when she heard the muffled sound of the doorbell ringing.

It was going on seven thirty, around the time Wally had said to expect him. Had he forgotten his key? That wasn't like him at all.

Curious as to who could be dropping in on a Friday night, she ran down the stairs, pushed aside the curtain covering the front window, and caught her breath. What was Darleen Boyd doing on her front porch?

There was no love lost between Skye and Wally's ex-wife, so when she opened the door, she kept the chain on. "Darleen, what a surprise."

"I'll bet." Darleen was nearly six feet tall and cadaverously thin. "I need to talk to you, woman to woman. Can I come in?"

Skye hesitated. It was probably best to exercise a certain amount of caution. "I'm sort of busy right now. Maybe we could meet for coffee tomorrow morning at the Feed Bag, or the new bookstore in town has a café that serves fabulous baked goods and cappuccinos."

"Please." Darleen held out a hand, and Skye could see that her nails were bitten so short they looked raw. "It needs to be tonight."

Skye couldn't think of an excuse to turn Darleen away. Wally's ex-wife might dislike her, but she'd never been violent. "If it's important—"

"I promise I'll make this short." Darleen was shivering uncontrollably, and her baby-doll minidress revealed skeletally thin arms and legs.

"Well . . ." Why wasn't Darleen wearing a coat? Skye bit her lip. It went against her nature to turn down someone in need, especially such a waif-like creature. Darleen looked as if a stiff wind would blow her away, and October was known for its blustery weather.

"Please, just five minutes." Darleen's voice was desperate, but her expression was hard to read. "Really. I'll be in and out before you know it."

"Okay." Skye nodded, unhooked the chain, and swung open the door.

Instantly, a man who had been standing just out of Skye's line of sight propelled Darleen over the threshold, crowding in right behind her. He was huge, with bulging biceps and long blond hair tied back in a ponytail. An enormous cross hung from a thick gold chain around his neck.

Darleen stepped aside and Mr. Muscles grabbed Skye so that his forearm rested against her throat. She screamed and tried to wiggle free, kicking back at his shins and clawing at his arm, but the Incredible Hulk seemed impervious to her efforts to free herself.

He swung Skye around so that she was facing the staircase, and ordered over his shoulder, "Dar, don't just stand there like an idiot. Check out the place and make sure we don't have company."

"Uh, sure, Gary. Sorry," Darleen stuttered, then disappeared up the steps.

Realizing she would not accomplish anything by struggling, Skye decided it was time to use her skills as a psychologist. "If you tell me what you want, I'll be happy to get it for you—then you can leave. We don't need all this drama."

Gary snorted but otherwise remained silent, still holding Skye prisoner. While they waited, she tried to think of an escape plan. Just before the creep had grabbed her, Skye had noticed that neither Darleen nor her boyfriend had closed the front door. If she could get loose, she could make a run for it. But where would she go?

While Darleen was searching the second floor, Skye tried to think of a place to hide if she managed to free herself from Gary's chokehold. Too bad it wasn't as warm as the previous week; she could have headed for the river and swum away from her captors.

Darleen's whiny voice broke into Skye's thoughts. She scuttled down the staircase, complaining, "You should see the fancy bathroom this bitch has. No wonder Wally refuses to give me the money I deserve. He's spending it all on her."

"Hey." Skye couldn't let that pass. "I paid for that myself by working for my cousin. And believe me, that job was no piece of wedding cake."

"Yeah. Right." Gary made a scornful noise. "Now, ladies, if that's settled, was anyone up there? Or did you spend all your time in the bathroom, Dar?"

"Oops! Sorry, Gary." Darleen covered her mouth. "It's all clear."

"Then check the rest of the house." Gary's voice took on an impatient edge, and as Darleen ran toward the kitchen, he sneered, "What a dimwit."

"She has a college degree, so she can't be too dumb," Skye retorted. She hated it when men talked badly about their girlfriends.

"That was before the coke and the weed and the pills." Gary snickered. "That's why I don't take none of that shit. Did you see that commercial on TV with the egg? The one that says, 'This is your brain on drugs'?"

"Yes." Skye heard Toby barking. When he abruptly quieted, she flinched. What if Darleen had hurt the little dog? She knew Bingo would be okay. The cat would have fled at the first sign of an intruder. "Glad to see the public service announcement made an impression."

"I like to be in control," Gary confided. "If you're high, you're not in control."

"Very true." Since he was chatting, Skye tried once more to talk her way out of the situation. "I noticed your cross. Do you really think God would approve of what you're doing to me?"

"Probably not." Gary gave a mocking laugh. "See, I figure it like this—God may be my copilot, but the devil makes a better bombardier."

Cripes! What was it about her that attracted all the psychos? So much for her counseling skills. Maybe if she could find out what the goon wanted, she could hand it over and get him out of there. "If you're looking for cash or valuables, you picked the wrong person to rob."

"You're the valuable, sweet cheeks." Gary chuckled at his own wit. "Your man may not be willing to pay to get that letter you two want, but from what Dar says, and from what I've seen this week while I was watching you guys, he'll hand over some serious cash to get you back in one piece. That dude is so damn gaga over you

252

he'd probably even take a bullet to save you."

"That's the first smart thing you've said." Wally's voice came from behind the thug's back. "Now take your hands off my fiancée, or I'll shoot."

Skye turned her head as much as she could, and out of the corner of her eye she saw that Wally had his gun pressed to the creep's temple.

Gary howled a string of profanities, and Wally snarled, "Don't give me an excuse to pull this trigger." His .38 "accidently" slipped, clipping the creep on the side of the head. "I may not have a license to kill, but I do have a learner's permit."

"I can snap her neck in a second," Gary threatened, tightening his grip on Skye.

"Not before I put a bullet in that pea-size brain of yours." Wally's voice was menacing. "You have until the count of three. And think about this—I'd love to save the county the cost of your trial. One."

The guy didn't move.

"Two."

He wavered, his arm loosening slightly. "Come on, man. Just a little—"

"Thr—" Wally interrupted the thug's plea.

Gary swore and released Skye. As soon as she was free, she darted behind Wally.

A second later Darleen rushed into the foyer holding her arm, which was dripping blood. "Look what that little mutt did to me when I tried to put him outside." She stumbled to a stop, her eyes bulging. "What the f—?"

"Both of you lie down, face to the floor, hands behind your back," Wally commanded as he waved Darleen over to her boyfriend.

"What did you do to Toby?" Skye tried to rush past Wally, but he grabbed her shoulder.

"I opened the back door and he ran out." Darleen's tone was triumphant as she and Gary obeyed Wally's orders. "I hope he gets run over by a car or eaten by a coyote."

Skye tried to get past Wally again, but he said, "We'll deal with that later. Toby'll be fine. I'm sure he's waiting on the step. Okay?"

"Okay," Skye agreed, but she cast a worried glance toward the backyard.

"Is it just the two of them?"

"I think so."

"Here. Take my gun and keep it pointed at the guy's head." Wally handed her the pistol and snatched the handcuffs from his gun belt.

Once he had patted down the prone man for weapons and cuffed him, he turned to Darleen and patted her down as well, then used a white plastic strip to fasten her hands. Stepping away from the trussed couple, Wally took the .38 back from Skye and used his radio to call for backup.

Only then did he address Darleen. "Here's the deal. Your boyfriend is going away for a long, long time. Assaulting a police employee is a felony. You, on the other hand, can do some good for yourself."

"How?" Darleen gave Wally a calculating look. "Do I have to testify against Gary?"

The goon protested, but Wally pointed his gun at the guy's knee and said, "If you make another sound, you'll be limping the rest of your life." He turned his attention back to Darleen. "Yes. You'll need to testify, and you'll also need to write that letter I requested—the truthful version, not the lies you threatened to write."

"Not without the money you owe me." Darleen's skin was pasty and she had dark circles under her eyes. "I need it. I'm not well."

"What's wrong with you?"

"I'm sick." Darleen's face had turned an unhealthy shade of red. "Isn't that enough?"

Skye noticed Wally's expression soften, so she quickly said, "Her boyfriend mentioned she's been using cocaine, marijuana, and some form of pills."

"You bitch!" Darleen screamed, tears running down her cheeks. "You've got my husband—isn't that enough? His father's a fricking millionaire. All I want is what's rightfully mine. What I would have gotten if I hadn't been so damn naive and signed that prenup."

"Your *ex*-husband," Skye reminded her. "I'm not trying to take anything from you, but we can't give you money to buy drugs."

"On the other hand," Wally said, "if you write a letter telling what *really* happened in our marriage, not the false account you tried to use to blackmail me, I will pay for you to go to rehab and I won't charge you as an accomplice."

"Rehab is for quitters."

"Darleen." Wally's voice had a steel edge.

"You win," Darleen bleated, laying her head down on the floor. "You always win."

After Darleen and her boyfriend were picked up by Sergeant Quirk and taken to the Scumble River jail, Skye rescued Toby, who was indeed waiting on the back step. Then she and Wally took their food to the sunroom and ate their long-delayed supper. Toby was sitting at Skye's feet and Bingo at Wally's. Both animals were on red alert, watching for any scraps that might fall.

"How did you know I was in trouble?" Skye asked. "Was it the strange car in my driveway?"

"There's no vehicle out there." Wally shook his head. "They must have hiked in. My officers found a stolen SUV parked a few feet down the road." He smiled at her. "It was the open door that tipped me off. You're a creature of habit and you always keep it shut."

"Oh." Skye pursed her lips. She was happy Wally had rescued her, but she hated being so predictable. Tomorrow she would definitely come up with a plan to be spontaneous. "Is it really a felony to assault a police employee?"

"A police officer, yes, but your position is unique, so I'm not sure." Wally shrugged. "Anyway, I have no problem lying to the bad guys if it means putting them behind bars or saving you from harm."

"Thank you." Skye smiled. "I'd do the same for you, even though I'm not a great liar."

"I know. You're better at avoiding the truth." Wally took the last bite of his sandwich, swallowed, then asked, "Does drug rehab really work?"

"Sometimes."

"What do you think Darleen's chances are?" Furrows appeared in Wally's forehead.

"Not great." Skye slumped back in her seat. "But it's probably her only hope."

"Yeah. I guess I owe her that much." Wally put his arm around Skye. "Even if she was the one to leave me for another man, in reality I was never a good husband because I couldn't fully love her. My heart always belonged to you and I think she sensed that."

"You really are a special kind of guy—to not only admit you might have been at fault, but to recognize it in the first place. That's why I love you so much." Although Skye felt a warm glow at Wally's words, she felt more sympathy for Darleen than she ever had before. Knowing you were second best had to be a horrible way to live your married life. "But why me?"

"Darlin' "—Wally tilted her chin up—"that's hard to put into words."

"I know you're the silent cowboy type," Skye teased him, "but try."

"Okay." Wally grinned. "You remind me of a good wine. Full bodied with just the right amount of nuttiness."

"Very funny." Skye whacked his biceps, then sobered. "You know, until tonight, it never dawned on me that as the fiancée or wife of a potentially wealthy man, I could be a target." Shuddering, she nestled closer. "If I'm ever kidnapped, I don't want you to pay the ransom."

"I appreciate that." Wally stroked her hair. "And even though the odds aren't in favor of a kidnap victim, I would still have to try. You are my whole world and I couldn't live with myself if I didn't do everything in my power to save you."

"Aww. You are the sweetest man."

Some moments later, Skye was almost asleep when she remembered what she had found out. "I have some info about Suzette's father. He was having an affair." Skye explained what she'd learned from Jenny Vanda, finishing with, "So, do you think the mystery woman killed Paulette?"

"Anything is possible."

Skye nodded. "I just remembered. Hank Vanda mentioned a drug house in his neighborhood."

"I'll put Quirk on that in the morning." Wally grabbed the bottle of Sam Adams from the coffee table. "Too bad Mrs. Vanda didn't know the name of Neal's lover." He took a slug of beer, then mused, "I wonder how many sophisticated-looking blondes driving Cadillacs were around here back in 1978."

"At least one."

Chapter 22

"WHEN I CALL YOUR NAME"

The next day, Wally left right after breakfast. He usually had the weekends off, but this Saturday morning Darleen and her boyfriend were being transported from the Scumble River jail to the county facility, which meant Wally had to meet with the Stanley County state's attorney to discuss the two desperadoes' crimes.

Once Wally was gone, Skye started in on the housecleaning. While she worked, she pondered the identity of Quentin Neal's lover. Where would he have met her? Most places he'd go, he'd be accompanied by his wife and children, and the woman Jenny Vanda had described didn't sound like someone who would hang out at the local gin joints.

So where else would Quentin and his girlfriend

have had the opportunity to meet and form an intimate relationship?

Skye was putting away the vacuum cleaner when it struck her. The most obvious places were school and the church choir. Could his lover be Noreen Iverson? No. The music teacher was neither blond nor sophisticated.

Furthermore, Skye seriously doubted an affair conducted at the high school could have been hidden from Pru Cormorant. That woman was better at sniffing out scandal than Bingo was at inhaling cat treats.

That left the church choir, which had practiced every Wednesday night for as long as Skye could remember. And since Paulette didn't participate, it was the perfect place for Quentin to make a love connection.

Skye finished the housework by ten thirty, and after showering and dressing in jeans and a long-sleeved T-shirt, she settled in to make some calls. Several of her aunts and cousins currently sang in the choir, so she just had to find a relative who had been a member twenty-seven years ago and remembered an elegant blonde who drove a Caddy. Easy peasy, right?

Although Aunt Minnie hadn't been able to think of any sophisticated fair-haired women in the choir around 1978, she had promised to keep trying. Skye had just said good-bye to her aunt when the phone rang again, and hoping Minnie had thought of a name, she scooped up the receiver without checking the caller ID.

"Skye," Simon's voice surprised her. "I may have figured out why Suzette looked familiar. Who she reminded me of."

"Great." Skye reached for her pen and a legal pad. "Who is it?"

"I'd rather not say until I'm certain." Simon's tone was cautious.

"So why did you call me?" Skye tried not to sound impatient.

"I want to see if you agree that this person resembles Suzette."

"Then I need to know who we're talking about." What was up? Simon wasn't usually this unsure of himself.

Simon paused for a couple of seconds, then said, "Here's what we'll do. I'll pick you up and we'll go over to the Brown Bag. You look at everyone there and tell me if any of them reminds you of Suzette."

"You want me to go to a bar with you? At noon on a Saturday? Here in Scumble River?" Skye's voice grew more incredulous with each question. This excursion sounded suspiciously like a date, albeit not a typical one for Simon to plan, but still a date. Wally would have a fit if word got back to him. "I can't do that. Just tell me who you think it is."

"No," Simon argued. "I'm sure this person

will be there. And I want to see if you can pick him or her out."

"I don't have anyone to watch Toby." Which was true, but also a good excuse.

"It's a nice day. We can leave him in the car. We'll roll down the window a little, make sure he has water, and give him a rawhide chew." Simon's voice was firm. "He'll be okay for the ten or so minutes we'll be inside the bar."

Skye felt backed into a corner. Simon was right—the weather had warmed up since yesterday, and a high of seventy was predicted. Toby would be fine. Not to mention that Simon was incredibly stubborn and would never give her a name unless he was sure of what he was saying.

"Okay." Skye hoped that as long as she told Wally beforehand, it would be all right.

"Good. I'll be over in ten minutes."

As soon as Simon disconnected, Skye punched in the number of Wally's cell. When she got his voice mail, she hesitated, wondering if she should try his house or his private line at the police station, then realized that leaving a message was the perfect solution. She could inform Wally of what she was about to do, thus not keeping secrets from him, but he couldn't tell her not to accompany Simon. Skye told herself that getting a lead on Suzette's killer was too important to allow petty jealousy to get in her way.

After all, Wally had no reason to be upset. She was just doing her job.

When Skye and Simon arrived at the Brown Bag, half a dozen guys were lined up on barstools watching a football game. The enormous wall-mounted flat-screen TV showed every grain of dirt and drop of sweat in full high-definition detail, and the men at the bar cheered when blood shot out of a tight end's nose.

The tavern's only other occupants were a group of women wearing elaborate hats. They were seated across the room around two tables that had been pushed together. Half-empty pitchers of margaritas and strawberry daiquiris were within easy reach, and the ladies were sipping from brimming glasses.

The guys' attention was glued to the screen, but the women began whispering the moment Skye and Simon entered. Skye knew most of the ladies, and almost all of them were friends of her mother and aunts. *Yikes!* If she didn't do something fast, they'd be on the phone to May before their next drink was poured.

After telling Simon to go ahead and sit down, Skye stopped at the women's table and said, "Good afternoon, ladies." She needed to do damage control right now, before the gossip grapevine was harvested. "Are you having a meeting?"

"Why, yes," answered Hilda Quinn, wearing what looked like a birdcage on the top of her head. "The Mad Hatters come here once a month."

"Right." Skye tilted her head. "I remember Aunt Minnie mentioning your club."

"I'm trying to get her and your mom to join, but both of them say they're too busy." Hilda *tsk*ed. "The women in your family seem to be always working. Is that true of you, too, dear?" She darted a glance at Simon, who had taken a seat at the far end of the bar.

"Actually, it is." Skye met the eyes of each club member sitting around the table, making sure they understood her message. "Simon and I are here on official police business, and I'd really appreciate it if you kept that info under your wonderful chapeaus."

"Of course, dear." Hilda pantomimed zipping her lips and the others followed suit. "We won't tell a soul."

"Thank you." Skye didn't believe any of them for a minute, but she hoped she had at least postponed the rumorfest until she could present Wally with a solid lead on Suzette's murder. "Have fun, ladies."

When Skye joined Simon, he slanted an unreadable look at her, and asked, "Everything okay?"

"Peachy."

He ignored Skye's sarcasm and asked, "So, do you see anyone who reminds you of Suzette?"

Skye scanned the bar's occupants, then shook her head. "Nope."

"Take a look at this." He took the photo of Suzette from his pocket and placed it on the bar. "Does this help?" He had kept the picture as Skye had left it, with the paper frame blocking all but the facial features.

Skye was studying the image when Jess Larson, the owner of the Brown Bag, walked over and said, "Can I get you two something to drink?"

"Diet Coke, slice of lime," Skye ordered, barely looking up.

There was a moment of dead silence; then Jess tapped the altered photo and asked in a puzzled tone, "Why do you have my picture? And how did you get that makeup on my face?"

Skye lifted her head and stared at him. Now she understood. The resemblance between Jess and the dead singer was uncanny. After assuring the bar owner that he would get an explanation, Skye dragged Simon outside. She immediately called Wally and sketched out the situation.

Wally's cruiser pulled into the parking lot less than two minutes later. He dismissed Simon, who had agreed to keep Toby until Skye was free, told Skye to wait in the squad car, and went inside.

A quarter of an hour later, Wally and Skye sat across from Jess Larson in the PD's interrogation-coffee room.

"Thanks for coming down here." Wally smiled easily at Jess. "As I said back at the Brown Bag, we have a few questions that we hope you can help us answer."

"I'm always glad to cooperate with the police, and since Abe was available to take over behind the bar for me, it's no problem." Jess leaned back in his chair. "But I can't imagine what I can help you with."

Skye glanced at Wally, and when he gave her a slight nod, she said, "Jess, I believe when I first met you, you told me you were from Los Angeles. Is that correct?"

"Yes."

"But you said your father was in the military and you moved around a lot."

"That's right." Jess gave Skye a crooked grin. "Why are you and the chief suddenly so interested in my background?"

"I promise we'll explain," Skye reassured him. "Just a couple more questions. I also recall that you said you bought the Brown Bag from its previous owner, Fayanne Emerick, and that Fayanne was your cousin."

"Yep. Cousin Fayanne's letters made Scumble River seem like a cross between *Mayberry R.F.D.* and *Leave It to Beaver.* It sounded like the kind of place I had been trying to find for a long time. And then when I came to check out the business, I almost felt like I had lived here in some other life."

Wally and Skye exchanged looks, and he said, "Well, see, that's the thing. We think it's possible you *did* live here before, back when you were three years old, but that doesn't jibe with your story of growing up."

"Oh?" Jess wrinkled his brow. "Would it help to know that I was adopted shortly before I turned four?"

"That would certainly make things a little clearer," Skye said, half to herself. "And your adoptive parents were named Larson?"

"Yes." Jess's voice was low and sad. "I never knew my real last name."

"Do you remember a sister?" Suzette had told Skye that she had been raised by an elderly aunt in California. Had the twins been separated?

"I used to pretend I had a sister called Suzie." Jess scratched his head. "But the couple who adopted me didn't have any other children."

"Were you told why you were put up for adoption?" Skye asked gently.

"My parents were killed in an accident. My biological father had been in the same army unit as my adoptive father." Jess leaned forward, his eyes fierce. "Are you saying that's not true?"

Skye started to answer, but Wally beat her to it. "We don't know. We suspect that may not have been entirely factual."

"Because of that photo of me with the makeup on?" Jess guessed.

"Yes." Wally spoke slowly, choosing his words carefully. "Did you ever meet Suzette Neal, the singer from the Country Roads theater?"

"No." Jess shook his head. "I didn't go to the concert because I couldn't get anyone to tend bar that night. I thought about closing since they were serving free booze, but I knew a few of my regulars would show up, so I didn't."

Skye murmured to Wally, "Her picture wasn't on the flyer and Jess wasn't at the Sunday morning meeting at the mayor's office."

Wally took a head shot out of the folder he had in front of him and passed it to Jess. "This is Suzette."

"Suzie!" Jess stared at the image, his face ashen. "I kept telling my adoptive parents that I dreamed of having a sister named Suzie, but they told me I was an only child."

"If Suzette was indeed your sister, you were twins," Skye explained. "She was raised by an elderly aunt after her mother died in an accident and her father joined the military." Skye mused, "I'm presuming she was told she was an only child as well."

"But why would my adoptive parents lie to me and Suzette's aunt lie to her?" Jess was so upset he was nearly crying.

"They probably thought a clean break would be easier for everyone concerned," Skye soothed. "My guess is the aunt could handle only one child, and you were too energetic for her, so you were the one put up for adoption."

"I was nearly kicked out of kindergarten for my behavior." Jess gave a ragged laugh. "That's when my mom decided to call me Jess instead of Jesse. The psychologist suggested I might be trying to live up to the Jesse James image."

Ah, Skye thought to herself. *That's what Pru was trying to remember. Jesse James was an outlaw—or hellion, as Pru had so quaintly put it.* Aloud, Skye asked, "When's your birthday?"

"September first, 1974."

"That means that even if we eventually searched the birth records in all fifty states, we would have never found your birth certificate." Wally tapped his chin with his index finger. "Suzette's DOB was August thirty-first, 1974. You must have been born shortly after midnight."

"That's right—at twelve oh two a.m. So I did have a sister." Jess's tone was bitter. "All those years that we could have known each other were stolen from us, and now it's too late."

"The only way to be certain that you were Suzette's twin is to compare your DNA to hers," Wally cautioned.

"Sure," Jess agreed. He slumped in his chair. "Whatever you need."

After Jess left to get his cheek swabbed, Skye and Wally went upstairs to his office. Once they were behind closed doors, Wally said, "You agree he had no idea that Suzette was his sister?"

"Absolutely." Skye pursed her lips. "Unless he's a sociopath—and I've never seen any indication of that—then he was telling the complete truth."

"That's my feeling, too."

"My only question is, how did he end up in Scumble River?" Skye furrowed her brow. "How did he end up with an adoptive mom who was related to someone in town? How did he and Suzette end up back here together?"

"Maybe"—Wally crossed his arms—"Quentin Neal was friendly with Fayanne when he lived here. And after his wife died, he confided in her when he decided to put the twins up for adoption. Fayanne might then have put him in touch with her cousin, who she knew wanted children but couldn't have them."

"That could be it." Skye nodded. "Come to think of it, I have one more question." Skye looked sideways at Wally.

"What?"

"Are you upset with me for going to the Brown Bag with Simon?"

"Are you kidding?" Wally hesitated, obviously searching for the right words. "All I ask is that you tell me what you're doing and why. Which you did. The only time I'd get mad is if you try to hide anything from me."

"Thank you." Skye wiped imaginary sweat from her brow. "That's a relief."

"Besides, you two found an answer to one of the bigger mysteries surrounding Suzette."

"We did, didn't we?" Skye grinned. "Still, I'm relieved you're okay with what I did."

Wally was showing Skye how okay he was when the intercom buzzed. He gave her one last lingering kiss, then pushed the button. "Yes?"

"It's the Dooziers, Chief." The dispatcher's voice was resigned. "You better get over there right away. You won't believe what they're up to this time."

Chapter 23

"Crazy"

When the dispatcher reported that the Dooziers had opened fire on their neighbors, Skye volunteered to accompany Wally to the scene of the crime. After five years of working at school with the endless supply of Doozier offspring, she had a friendly relationship with the eccentric family —unlike the other law enforcement employees in Scumble River and Stanley County.

Because of that rapport, she was hoping to act

as a goodwill ambassador between the cops and the crackpots. But with the Dooziers, a breed unto themselves, there were no guarantees.

They lived by their wits, which should not be mistaken for smarts, and by their own set of rules, which should not be mistaken for what society calls *laws*. The latter was generally what got them into hot water. The former was generally how they got out without being scalded.

As Wally and Skye drove toward the Doozier property, she recalled a program she had attended her senior year in high school about the history of the town. The speaker had explained that the community had initially been confined to a fork between the two branches of the Scumble River but had eventually spread along both banks and beyond. That overflow was where they were heading now.

Skye remembered the historian talking about the two groups of people currently occupying the acreage along the south bank of the river. The newcomers had moved there from Chicago in the 1980s, and built summer cottages or retirement homes along a forested stretch of land. While these outsiders helped line the pockets of some Scumble Riverites and were welcomed by those town folks, they invaded the privacy of others. The others, who believed a good neighbor was one who lived far enough away to never be seen, were the original settlers known as the Red

Raggers—of which the Dooziers were the ruling clan.

For the first couple of years, the interlopers and the Red Raggers had tested each other's mettle, and eventually an uneasy alliance had been formed. Apparently, since shots had now been fired, that peace treaty must have been breached. Skye hoped it could be renegotiated without bloodshed.

Wally turned the squad car onto Cattail Path. They were entering Red Ragger country, and the first property they came to belonged to the Dooziers. It was shaped roughly like a right triangle, with the hypotenuse resting along the riverbank and the house situated at the smallest point. From the road, Wally and Skye could see only this tip, and from that limited vantage point there was no evidence of any disturbance.

But Skye wasn't reassured. She was fairly certain the real action was taking place in the woods to the side of the house, as this was the land where the shortest leg of the triangle formed the boundary between the Dooziers and their nearest neighbor.

Wally parked and said to Skye, "Keep behind me until we know what's going on."

"Definitely." The Dooziers might be her friends, but there was always the danger of getting shot by accident. And Wally was the one wearing the Kevlar vest.

He got out of the cruiser and Skye followed

suit. The uneven ground in front of the run-down shack was covered with weeds and rocks. The carcasses of junked pickups, shells of old appliances, and a recently acquired troop of garden gnomes added to the obstacle course and forced them to pick their way gingerly toward the backyard.

At the gate, a crooked sign painted on a flattened carton read:

Paintball Advenchore!
Gauranteed Fun! Fun! Fun!
Yer very own rifle, shotgun, or uzi!
$5.00 fur haf hour/$25.00 fur haf day.

Skye was not surprised that the names of the weapons were among the few words the Dooziers had spelled correctly.

She and Wally peered over the fence. Several feet back, where the yard merged into the wooded area, a folding table with a pyramid of guns piled in the center teetered on crooked legs. Sitting with his cowboy boots propped up on the table's surface was a skinny, densely tattooed man wearing a pair of jeans and several ammo belts criss-crossed over his bare chest. A camo bandanna tied around his head had slipped down over the upper third of his face, and empty beer cans were strewn next to his lawn chair like shiny red and silver leaves surrounding a scrawny maple tree.

Skye closed her eyes, praying it was all a

hallucination. She could think of no positive outcome in a scenario that included a drunken Earl Doozier pretending to be Rambo.

Skye glanced at Wally and whispered, "What now?" It was never a good idea to startle an armed Doozier, especially an inebriated one.

Wally tried the gate; it was unlocked. Clearing his throat, he stepped over the metal threshold and said, "Earl, are you awake?"

A snore that sounded like a backfiring leaf blower erupted from Earl's open mouth, and he screwed up his face, then turned away from them.

"Earl?" Wally inched closer and raised his voice. "Wake up, Earl."

There was no reaction from the sleeping man, but the dogs penned nearby jumped against the steel mesh of their cage, bouncing off it while barking and baring their teeth at Skye and Wally.

Skye spotted a bamboo fishing rod leaning against a dilapidated shed. She whispered her idea to Wally, who shook his head no, but she ignored his instructions and squeezed past him. Giving the furious animals a wide berth, she grabbed the pole and inched her way toward Earl.

Once within reach, she used the rod to tap the sleeping Doozier on the shoulder, saying in her outdoor voice, "Earl, wake up."

He leaped from his chair, wrestling with the bandanna that was blinding him, and yelped, "I wuz jes' restin' my eyes, honey pie."

"It's Skye, Earl." Skye took a step closer but then quickly moved downwind. The excessive use of cologne could delay the need to bathe for only so many days, and Earl was way overdue. "Chief Boyd and I are here to talk to you about some complaints from your neighbors."

Earl finally tore off the bandanna and scowled. "You sceered me half to death, Miz Skye." A confused look stole over his face. "Hey, what happens if you gets sceered half to death twice?"

Having no good answer, Skye ignored his question and settled for apologizing. "Sorry for startling you, Earl."

"That's okay, Miz Skye." His wide smile revealed several stumps and missing teeth. "What're you doin' here? I heared yew and yer intended were hot on the trail of a murderer." He loped toward her.

"We are, but one of your neighbors called the police station and said you were shooting at them, so we came to check it out." Skye allowed herself to be hugged, trying not to make contact with any of his many tattoos. Tattoos usually felt smooth, but Earl's were as odd as he was and they radiated a heat that Skye figured explained his penchant for going shirtless even in the coldest weather.

"They's lyin'." Earl let Skye go and scratched the bowling ball–size potbelly that hung over his waistband. "Ain't nobody shootin' at 'em.

We was jes' settin' up our new Paintball Advenchore bizness. You know, gettin' ready for the zillions of payin' customers that that Country Roads guy promised to bring in."

"Rex Taylor talked to you?" Skye was surprised that the entrepreneur had enlisted the Dooziers in his schemes. "When was that?"

"I cain't rightly say." He tugged at his greasy brown ponytail. "A couple or three days afore that free concert he put on." The sunshine highighted the cereal bowl–size bald spot on Earl's head. "He invited the whole part and parcel of us along the river here to a shindig at the country club. He tol' us that iffen we come up with stuff for the tourists to do or somethin' for them to buy, we'd all get rich."

Skye turned to Wally, who had joined her, but before she could speak she spotted an elderly woman wearing a flowered neon green muumuu and red high-top sneakers teetering across the dead grass toward them. She looked old enough to have had dinosaurs for pets and meaner than a soccer mom whose son didn't make the team.

The infamous MeMa was on the prowl. She was the clan matriarch and Earl's grandmother, or maybe great-grandmother; Skye had never quite untangled the Dooziers' twisted family tree.

MeMa walked up to Skye, squinted, and said in a thin quaver, "I heared you were nosin' around askin' questions about the Neals."

"Yes." Skye paused to consider the best way to respond. Mentioning her connection with the police would be a mistake. "I'm trying to help find out who murdered that poor girl."

"Ain't nobody cared who killed her ma." MeMa glared at Skye. "And she was a mighty fine lady." The old woman's tone was defiant. "I cleaned for her once a week back then and she always treated me real nice. Made me a hot lunch. She even poured the beer into a glass."

"Paulette's death was an accident," Skye said cautiously. "Wasn't it?"

"Maybe, maybe not." MeMa shrugged. "But considerin' her husband was playin' around on her, I sure wouldn'a taken his word for what happened."

"Do you know who his lover was?"

"Yeah." MeMa's smile was like a bear trap, her faded brown eyes disappearing into the wrinkles around them. "Theys thought they was so la-di-da smart, but I seed them a-kissin' and a-huggin' in her fancy car."

Skye's heart was pounding. "Who was it?"

"You sure you want to know?" A crafty expression stole over MeMa's face.

"Yes." What did the old woman mean by that? Skye hoped the can of worms she was about to open wouldn't be too slimy.

"Your aunt." MeMa turned and tottered back toward the house.

"Which one?" Skye called after her.

"The mayor's wife." The screen door slammed shut behind MeMa, cutting off anything else she might have added.

Holy smokes! Skye was stunned. Did Uncle Dante know that Aunt Olive had had an affair with Quentin Neal? More importantly, had Olive been involved in his wife's death? And if she had, was she also involved in Suzette's?

Wally, who had been silent, stepped forward, allowing Skye time to recover from MeMa's shocking news. "Earl, you said that Rex Taylor encouraged you to start a paintball attraction?"

"Not eggsacly." Earl reached into a cooler, fished out a dripping can of beer, and popped the top. "Axtually, we was gonna do another pettin' zoo, like the one we done for the Route 66 Hundred Mile Yard Sale, but instead of a lion, this time we were gonna get more tamish kindsa animals." Earl chugged some beer, then continued. "So we goed to the llama and emu ranch over near Kankakee. But we seed Owen Frayne workin' there and we figured he already took that idea."

Skye frowned. Trixie hadn't mentioned Owen was working at—But before her thought could fully form, she heard a high-pitched laugh that reminded her of a deranged birthday clown.

Emerging from the wooded area behind them, and carrying a submachine gun, was Glenda Doozier. From her purple-stiletto-clad feet to her dyed blond hair, she was the embodiment of an ideal Red Ragger woman, but all Skye could think of was—how in the heck had Glenda been able to navigate the woods in four-inch heels?

"Ain't she somethin'?" Earl thrust out his bony chest. "I knew she was my one and only since the day I read that stuff about her on the bathroom wall in the boys' locker room. I asked her to go frog giggin' that very night."

"That's so . . ." Skye searched for the right word and gave up. "Well, it's always good to strike while the—"

"Bug is close," Earl finished for her, then rushed over to his wife. "Baby doll, look who's here. Miz Skye and her future hubby."

Glenda ignored Skye and Wally, and poked Earl with the shotgun. "What do they want?"

"One a our highfalutin' neighbors claimed we was a-shootin' at 'em." Earl rubbed the spot on his shoulder where she had jabbed him.

"We ain't done nothin' wrong." Glenda crossed her arms, the gun shoving her considerable bosom nearly out of the iridescent purple tank top she wore.

"I already explained that, dumplin'," Earl whined. "Yew got paint in yer ears?"

She turned on her husband. "If brains were water, you wouldn't have enough to baptize a flea."

"Now, Glenda." Wally stepped forward. "There's no need to get upset."

"Yer right." Glenda narrowed her rabbitlike

eyes. " 'Cause we got a right to do what we want on our own land. And those nosy Parkers next door can jes' shove it where the sun don't shine."

"That's true, but you have to make sure none of the paint pellets land on your neighbors' property." Wally's tone was firm.

Skye recoiled, then scooted behind Wally. Telling Glenda something she didn't want to hear was dangerous. Not to mention she held grudges long past their expiration date, and she and Skye had gotten off on the wrong foot when they'd first met five years ago.

When Glenda didn't respond, Wally added, "And if you're going to run a business, you need to check out the zoning laws and get a license."

As quick as a mongoose attacking a cobra, Glenda leveled the shotgun. Wally dove to one side and Skye turned to run. But it was too late. Glenda had already squeezed the trigger.

Chapter 24
"I'm So Lonesome I Could Cry"

"You believe me about not knowing you had moved behind me?" Wally called through the glass shower door in Skye's newly renovated bathroom.

"Certainly," Skye shouted back over the sound of running water.

"I never would have jumped out of the way if I knew you were there."

"Of course. You've proven time and again you'd take a bullet for me, so I'm sure you wouldn't duck a paintball."

"Anytime, darlin'." Wally's voice was husky. "For a minute there, before I realized the gun fired paint pellets, I . . . I almost lost it and shot Glenda for real."

"I know, sweetie." Skye scrubbed her neck, feeling Wally's love wrapping around her. "Except for a little cosmetic damage, I'm fine."

"It's a good thing, or I'd round up every one of the Doozier clan and use 'em for target practice."

"Uh-huh." Skye showered in silence for a while, then said, "So do you agree that Owen's job at the llama and emu ranch has something to do with where he was last Saturday and why he won't give you his alibi for that time?"

"Yes." Wally stood at the sink, wiping away stray paint spatters from his clothing. "Do you think MeMa was telling the truth about Olive?"

"Olive does fit the description, and she and Dante have always driven Cadillacs." Skye poured more shampoo into her hand and started washing her hair for the fifth time. Fishy-smelling orange lather ran down the drain. "I hate to say this, but if I were married to someone who treated me as heartlessly as Dante treats her, I'd sure be having an affair."

"I'll keep that in mind." Wally's tone was wry as he patted dry his wet pants leg. "I'm thinking we should tackle Owen first, since we need to talk to Olive when the mayor isn't around."

"Plus Owen will be a lot less complicated." Skye scoured orange flecks from her wrists and hands. She had taken the paintball hit between the shoulder blades, so her shirt had received the worst of the damage, but the paint had splashed outward like a gelatinous water balloon, drenching every exposed patch of skin.

"Interrogating Aunt Olive will be mighty tricky," Skye said.

"That's for sure."

"We should try to speak to Owen alone, too." Skye stepped out of the shower and Wally handed her a towel. "What time is it?"

He looked at his watch. "Three thirty."

"Let's check the llama and emu ranch for Owen first." Skye wrapped the towel around herself and picked up a wide-toothed comb. "This is around the time Owen was missing last Saturday. Maybe it's his regular shift there."

Wally and Skye pulled into the Kankakee Exotic Animal Ranch at four twenty-nine. The lane wound through pastures of llamas and emus, dead-ending at a huge barn and corral. Owen was carrying a bale of hay when they approached him.

As soon as he spotted Skye and Wally, his usually impassive expression was replaced by one of defeat, and he hurled the hay bale to the ground. "I should have known keeping a secret in these parts would be impossible."

"Sorry, Owen." Wally stepped forward and clapped the unhappy man on the shoulder. "If it's any consolation, we'll keep this information completely confidential."

"How did you find out?" Owen took off his work gloves and stuck them in his back pocket.

"The Dooziers saw you here," Wally explained. "They mentioned it when we were out at their place investigating a complaint."

"So what do you want?" Owen wiped his face with a red handkerchief.

"Is this where you were last Saturday when you claimed to be having a drink with a friend?" Wally asked.

Wally and Skye had decided that Wally'd be the best one to question Owen, so Skye leaned against a stall and tried to blend into the background.

"Yes. This is where I am whenever I'm not home." Owen stared at his work boots. "The owner can vouch for me."

"Why didn't you just tell me all this when I asked?" Wally wrinkled his brow.

"Trixie doesn't know that in order to buy the llama and emu herds, I agreed to work off the debt." Owen's face crumpled. "She complains I don't spend enough time with her. If she found out I took on another job, it would have set her off something fierce."

"So you weren't having an affair with Suzette Neal?" Wally asked.

"An affair?" Owen's eyes bulged. "Hell, no." He shot Wally a dark look, then said, "So that's what this was all about. You thought I was sleeping with that singer who got killed, and then for some reason I murdered her?"

"She was seen getting out of a truck similar to yours last Saturday night." Wally's tone was unapologetic. "We had to check out the possibility. We've been talking to all the locals who own black pickups. If you had just cooperated, we could have crossed you off our list long ago."

"I've never even looked twice at another woman. I love my wife." Owen shook his head. "That's why I work so hard. I want her to have nice things."

"She'd rather have you," Skye murmured.

Owen stuck out his chin. "Just because someone doesn't love you the way you want them to doesn't mean they don't love you with all they've got."

But was that enough? Skye was afraid this

might be Trixie's breaking point. Trixie loved Owen, but he kept using all his energy to make money, then had no time left for her. Some rifts in a marriage couldn't be healed.

Sunday morning, despite Father Burns's wonderful sermon, Skye didn't experience the serenity she usually felt when she attended Mass— probably because she and Wally planned to approach Olive after church. It would be the perfect time, because Dante always ate breakfast with his cronies while his wife went home to start Sunday dinner. If Skye and Wally arrived at the Leofantis' shortly after Olive got back from the nine o'clock service, they'd likely find her alone.

Skye had gone to the same Mass as her aunt and uncle to make sure neither of them varied their usual routine. Now she drove over to pick up Wally. They had agreed Olive might talk more freely if they went together in her car and Wally wasn't in uniform.

After exchanging greetings with Wally, Skye was silent for the five-minute ride to her aunt and uncle's farm. She was discouraged by their lack of progress in the murder investigation. Even with all the information they'd gathered in the past six days, they still seemed no closer to solving Suzette's murder.

Just before the lane leading to Dante and

Olive's house, Skye spotted something new. She nudged Wally. "Take a look."

A series of four small signs read:

If you want peace
Prepare for war.
For safety at home
Guns even the score.

"Yep." Wally shrugged. "That sounds like Dante all right."

"Surprising he wants to open the town up to so many strangers," Skye mused. "You'd think the last thing he'd want was a bunch of outsiders invading his kingdom."

"Money talks."

"True, and to Dante it sings a sweet siren song."

As Skye parked the Bel Air, Wally said, "I think it would be best if you questioned your aunt."

"I agree."

"I'll step in when the time is right." Wally exited the car, walked around the hood, and held out his hand to Skye.

The mayor and his wife lived in a rambling trilevel perched on the southern edge of their acreage, surrounded by a large yard studded with mature trees. Clearly someone had recently raked the lawn, because there wasn't a leaf in sight, and Skye would bet a year's salary that that someone was her aunt, not her uncle.

Olive opened the door within seconds of Skye's ringing the bell. "Skye, Chief, what a surprise. Were you looking for the mayor?"

Brandy, the Leofantis' golden retriever, stood by Olive's side. The canine's shiny fur lay in perfect silken order.

"No, Aunt Olive. We wanted to see you." Skye reached down and stroked Brandy's head. "Sorry for dropping in, but it was important to speak to you when Uncle Dante wasn't here."

"Why is that?" Olive's expression was uncertain, but she motioned them inside. "Well, no matter—you're always welcome to come by."

"Thank you." Skye felt terrible that they were about to accuse this sweet woman of adultery, but they had to check out anyone who had a motive to kill Suzette.

As Olive led them toward the kitchen, she said, "I hope you don't mind if we sit in here. I'm in the middle of making dinner."

"Great." Wally's smile was charming. "I always say the heart of a home is the kitchen."

Brandy followed them, and when Skye took a seat at the table, the dog lay at her feet. She felt comforted by the animal's presence. While Olive bustled around pouring them coffee, Skye gazed at the decor. Unlike the rest of the house, which was done in brocade and velvet, with stunning floral arrangements and beautifully framed art, the sunny yellow kitchen was cozy rather than elegant. Chintz curtains, an obviously well-used oak table and chairs, and whimsical prints on the wall all added to the warmth.

Olive placed a tray of cookies between Skye and Wally and sat down. The three of them chatted about the weather and the family for a while.

Finally, Olive glanced at the wall clock and said, "Dante will be home in twenty minutes. What did you need to talk to me about?"

Skye took a deep breath. "I'm sorry to have to bring this up, but we recently learned that many, many years ago you knew Suzette Neal's father." Skye paused, then said as gently as she could, "In fact, we understand that you and he were very close."

"We were friends." Olive stared down at her cup.

"From what we've been told, you were much more than friends." Skye bit her lip. This was even harder than she'd thought it would be. "You had an affair with him. Didn't you?"

"No. That's ridiculous." Olive's fair skin became nearly translucent. "Who told you that?"

"The Neals' cleaning lady saw you and Quentin in your car." Skye covered her aunt's hand with her own. "We aren't here to judge you, but we need to know what happened back then and if it has anything to do with Suzette's murder."

"I was probably just giving him a ride home from choir practice." Olive tried to smile, but her lips were trembling. "As I recall, they only had one car, and he often walked to the church so his wife could use it."

"The cleaning lady saw you kissing him, and not on the cheek." Skye tightened her grip on Olive's fingers.

"She must have been mistaken." Olive shook her head. "It was so long ago, maybe she misremembered."

"The neighbor across the street saw you as well." Skye knew she couldn't let her aunt pretend the affair had never happened. "We don't intend to share this information with Dante, or anyone else, unless it's pertinent to Suzette's murder."

The ticking of the grandfather clock in the living room marked off the seconds until Olive spoke, tears in her eyes. "I loved him so much." This time her smile was sincere and tremulous. "He was such a wonderful man. He made me feel beautiful and smart and happy."

"Unlike Dante?" Skye murmured.

Olive nodded. "I knew what we were doing was wrong, and I never asked him to leave his family for me, but I just wanted something sweet in my life." Olive wiped a tear from her cheek. "Even if it was only for a little while."

"I understand. And I wouldn't bring this up except that the neighbor who saw you kissing Quentin in the car also saw you at his house the day his wife died. In fact, just before the ambulance arrived."

If possible, Olive's face paled even more. She opened her mouth, but at first no words came out. After a few seconds, she said, "It really was an accident."

"Yes," Skye encouraged. "Tell us what happened."

"Paulette called me and asked me to come over." Olive gazed over Skye's head as if looking into the past. "She said it was about a committee we were both on, but as soon as I got there she started yelling at me about the affair."

"Then what?" Skye asked softly.

"I told her I would end it and I never meant to hurt her or her family, but she didn't believe me." Olive's voice was barely audible. "I tried to explain that I was sorry, that I had just wanted a little bit of kindness and warmth, but she lunged at me. I leaped aside—I'd trained to be a ballet dancer before I married Dante—but Paulette couldn't stop her momentum. She fell and hit her head on the corner of a marble-topped table. I couldn't get her to wake up and there was so much blood."

"Can you show us where all this happened?" Skye pulled the flyer with the house plan out of her tote and laid it in front of her aunt.

Olive pointed to a tiny foyer.

"Did you call an ambulance?" Skye asked.

"I was looking for the phone—you know, back then there were no cells, and most people only had one telephone in the whole house." Olive shook her head. "But Quentin walked in the door before I found it, saw what had happened, and ordered me to leave."

"So he took over?" Skye asked.

"Yes." Olive put her hands over her face. "Up until then, I had no idea the twins were in the house, but he told me they were there and he'd handle everything."

"Was Paulette alive when you left?"

"No." Olive shook her head. "Quentin checked and said she didn't have a pulse. He said he'd clean up the blood and put her in the bathroom so it would look as if she'd slipped in the tub."

While Wally asked several additional questions, Skye considered what her aunt had told her and whether she believed Olive's story. Olive had had no warning that Skye and Wally would be confronting her, and once she'd admitted to the affair, she had given her account of Paulette's death with no hesitation.

Yes. Skye nodded to herself. She did believe her aunt. Olive had never been a good liar, and Skye was sure she would have been able to tell if her aunt hadn't been telling the truth. What a relief that Paulette's death was truly an accident —but what a waste of a life.

"Quentin blamed himself, you know." Olive's

voice broke into Skye's musings. She sounded as if she were saying aloud something she'd thought about for years. "He wasn't the same man after that. And then, one day, he and the children were just gone."

"One more question, Olive," Wally said. "Did Suzette Neal contact you when she came to town?"

"No." Olive looked surprised. "I didn't put together who she was until after her death. Quentin always called her Suzie, and Neal is a fairly common name."

"But you were the one who stole the contents of the police file on Paulette Neal's accident, weren't you?" Wally raised a brow.

Olive looked Wally in the eye. "Yes. I over-heard you talking to Dante on his cell phone. You said you were going to look for it that afternoon. I was afraid something in it might connect me to Quentin, so I borrowed Dante's key to the storage facility and took it. Do you want it back?"

"Yes."

Olive pushed away from the table, rose, and crossed over to a cupboard. She took out a box of spaghetti, opened the flap, and pulled out the rolled-up pages. "Here."

Wally got to his feet. "Okay." He, Skye, and Olive moved to the foyer. "We won't mention any of this to Dante unless it turns out to have something to do with Suzette's murder."

Olive blew out a breath. "Thank you."

Once they were in the car, Skye said to Wally, "I believe Olive. How about you?"

"I believe her, too. Your aunt didn't kill Suzette, and Paulette's death was accidental."

As Wally flipped through the pages of the police report, Skye put the Bel Air in reverse and drove away.

Several minutes passed while Wally read. Finally he said, "As I predicted, the accident report is short—only three pages—and contains minimal information about the incident. Nothing we didn't already know." He replaced the paper clip and threw the pages in the backseat. "We're back to square one."

Chapter 25

"STAND BY YOUR MAN"

Since Skye had persuaded the superintendant to let her skip the district's Teacher Institute meetings, she had Monday off. Few if any of the institute's programs would have any relevance for her, and in exchange she would attend the Illinois School Psychologists Association's conference in January, where she could earn the continuing-education credits she needed to renew her certificate.

Celebrating having the day to herself, Skye slept until ten; then, after feeding Bingo—Toby was still with Simon—she decided to treat herself to an early lunch and a good book.

As Skye drove toward McDonald's, traffic was heavier than usual on Water Street. With the kids out of school, Scumble River's main drag was bustling. While she was stopped to wait for a gaggle of pedestrians to cross the street—including all five members of Flint James's backup band—she scanned the parking spaces along the road. Ever since Suzette's murder, she'd been looking for the black truck she'd seen the singer getting out of at the park.

Nothing on the left side. On the right, red Jeep, green Jag, and blue Avalanche by the dry cleaner. Black pickup in front of Stybr's Florist. Yel—

Skye's gaze swung back to the truck. Now that she saw it, she remembered the unusual tow-hitch cover and the metallic bumper sticker. That was the pickup Suzette had gotten out of Saturday night before the concert! *Holy moly!* How could she have forgotten those details? If she hadn't been an idiot, Owen would have never been a suspect.

Abruptly, Skye spun the Bel Air's steering wheel to the right and pulled in behind the truck. Since the florist was bracketed by empty buildings, the driver was probably in the flower shop. Jumping out of her car, she ran across the sidewalk and pushed open the door.

Cool carnation-scented air washed over her face, and Skye took a minute to look around. Only one customer was present, a man in his early thirties wearing jeans and a Pink Floyd T-shirt. She tilted her head. It was Rod Yager. She knew him from his brief stint as a guitarist in her brother's rock band.

After assuring the clerk she didn't need any help, Skye turned to the musician and said, "Hi, Rod. Can I talk to you for a minute?"

"Sure." He smiled. "How's Vince doing?"

"He's doing great." Skye tugged at Rod's sleeve, pulling him away from the counter. "He and Loretta are house hunting."

"I heard he got married. That was sure a shocker." Rod shook his head. "I would have sworn he'd be on the prowl until the day he died."

"Yep. People are full of surprises." Skye took a breath, then said, "Speaking of surprises, did you know Suzette Neal?"

"Sort of." He transferred the bouquet of daisies and mums he was holding to his left hand and hitched up his pants. "I met her when I auditioned for Mr. Taylor."

"You were with her just before the concert last Saturday night, weren't you? Did you tell her about my sleuthing?"

"Yeah. She asked me for a ride to Joliet so she could do some shopping at the mall." Rod rubbed the back of his neck. "But the funny thing was she didn't buy anything. Just talked to an old guy who she said lived next door to her when she was a baby."

"Did she mention this man's name or where he lives now?" Skye wondered if Suzette had found out anything from her chat.

"No, but he works at the bookstore in the mall." Rod was looking at Skye funny. "If you're thinking I had anything to do with Suzette's murder, I can prove I didn't. I left for a gig on a cruise ship the next day, and I just got back in town this morning. I only found out she was killed a couple of hours ago when I saw it in the newspaper."

"I see." That explained why neither the cops nor Skye had spotted his truck around town the past week. "The police will probably want to talk to you and verify your alibi."

"That's fine by me." He snuck a peek at his watch. "Is that it?"

"Yes—No. One more thing." Skye thought of what the singer had said that night when she had finally shown up for the concert. "Do you know why Suzette would lie to her boss about where she'd been and who she was with?"

"Well . . ." Rod looked distinctly uncomfortable. "She did mention that the guy she worked for was really possessive of her, so it was better if he thought we were cousins."

"Anything else?" Skye asked.

"She said he was always hitting on her." Rod sounded angry. "I told her she had talent, and she didn't have to put up with that kind of shit to be a star. She said it had been okay until recently, because she'd made it clear she'd never sleep with him. But lately he'd been more and more persistent, and just recently he'd started claiming he loved her. She was a little worried about that."

"Interesting," Skye said, starting to get a glimmer of an idea.

"I gotta go." Rod glanced at his watch again. "It's my mom's birthday and I'm taking her to lunch."

"Okay. Thanks for talking to me."

Skye got her lunch to go at McDonald's, added a combo for Wally, then drove to the police station. The reporters hadn't come back, but the PD was full of activity, so she used her key to let herself in through the garage entrance. As she walked down the narrow corridor, she saw Flint James in the interrogation-coffee room.

Wally was standing in the room's open door-way, and Skye heard him say to Flint, "I'll be back when your attorney gets here."

"What's going on?" Skye asked once Wally had closed and locked the door.

"The DNA results came in an hour ago. The semen the ME found in Suzette belonged to Flint James."

"Why did he agree to be swabbed if he was guilty?" Skye answered herself: "Either he didn't think we could recover enough evidence because she was crushed, or he had consensual sex with her and didn't kill her."

"Those are both good ideas, and I'd be asking James about them if he hadn't lawyered up as soon as we arrested him."

"Shoot!"

"I just spoke with the Nashville police and asked them to see if they can find a witness who saw James entering or leaving Suzette's apartment there."

"So you're free for a while?" Skye brightened. "That means you have time for lunch, right?" She held out the McDonald's bag.

"Yep." Wally took her hand. "Let's go up to my office. I could use a break."

Before they reached the stairs, shouting erupted from the front of the station. A nanosecond later, Thea, the daytime dispatcher, yelled, "Chief, you'd best get in here—fast!"

Wally rushed toward the reception area with Skye on his heels. As they reached the lobby, they found Rex and Kallista Taylor standing nose to nose. Kallista had her hands on her hips and Rex's face was so red, Skye worried he was about to have a stroke.

"I told you to wait in the car!" Rex bellowed at his wife. "I'll handle this."

"All you care about is your precious theater!" Kallista screeched. "Flint's being framed and all you're worried about is the media impact."

"Woman, I don't know how you can be so stupid and so beautiful at the same time."

" 'Cause God made me beautiful so you'd be attracted to me. And He made me stupid so I'd be attracted to you."

"Folks, let's all calm down." Wally stepped between the arguing couple. "We'll go up to my office and discuss this quietly."

"This has nothing to do with her." Rex pointed to his wife. "I don't know why she insisted on coming."

"We'll get everything figured out, Mr. Taylor." Skye took Rex's elbow and fluttered her lashes while gently pulling him after her. "Just come with me."

Wally followed suit and offered Kallista his arm. "Right this way, Mrs. Taylor."

Once they were all seated in Wally's office, Rex said, "I demand to know why in the hell you arrested Flint James."

"His semen was found in Ms. Neal's body." Wally folded his hands on the desktop.

"That's not possible," Rex stated. "Your lab made some sort of mistake. It must have mixed up Flint's sample with one of the boys in the band."

Skye, sitting slightly behind and to the side of the couple, saw Kallista stiffen and turn pale. *Aha!* Skye replayed the conversation she had overheard between Kallista and Flint James Thursday night. Kallista had said she had thrown her husband off the scent of their affair by letting him think she was messing around with one of the musicians.

As Wally reassured Rex that the DNA samples had not been mixed up, Skye's mind raced. She needed to talk to Wally while Rex, Kallista, and Flint were all in the police station. But how could she get him alone without raising anyone's suspicions?

She eased the legal pad from her tote and wrote in large letters: *TALK/HALLWAY!!!* When Wally glanced her way, she held up the tablet. He nodded slightly and she stuffed it back into her bag.

Wally waited for a lull, then made a show of looking at his watch. "Sorry, folks. Ms. Denison and I have to take a conference call. Please excuse us. It won't take more than five minutes."

As soon as they were out of the office and the door was shut, Wally said, "Rex Taylor is hiding something."

"Exactly," Skye agreed. "And not just his charms."

"What's up?" Wally walked her to the far end of the hall.

Skye explained what Rod had told her, then reminded Wally of what Kallista had said to Flint about Rex's temper and diverting her husband's suspicions toward a member of the band. She concluded with, "So I wonder if somehow Rex is behind all of this. He still doesn't have an alibi."

"Even though Taylor's DNA wasn't the one found inside Suzette, I agree something doesn't smell right about James as the murderer. I suppose he could have been two-timing Kallista and killed Suzette to keep her quiet. Still, the whole thing feels wrong." Wally shook his head. "But we don't have anything on Taylor beyond a rumor of a bad temper and the fact that he flirts with women. Any ideas?"

"Divide and conquer." Skye leaned forward and said quietly, "Let me take Kallista and make sure she gets to talk to Flint. I think she knows more than she's saying."

"Okay." Wally nodded. "We might as well give it a try. But remember spousal privilege. She *can't* tell you anything her husband said to her in confidence."

"But if she overheard something or saw something, that's fair game, right?"

"Right." He walked back to his office and opened the door. "Mrs. Taylor, could I see you for a moment?"

Once Kallista was in the hallway, Wally turned her over to Skye and then returned to Rex.

Skye took the other woman's arm and said in a sympathetic voice, "I thought you might want a chance to talk to Mr. James alone."

Kallista hesitated. Her expression held both suspicion and longing. Longing won, and she said, "Thank you. That would be wonderful."

"You're very welcome." Skye led her down the steps, unlocked the interrogation room door, and ushered the blonde inside. "I can only give you a few minutes." Skye adjusted the blinds so that it appeared no one could see in through the interior window, then exited, leaving the door slightly ajar.

Skye stepped to the side, angling her body so she could both peer through the opening in the blinds and hear through the door.

Kallista wasted no time berating Flint. "How could you sleep with that skanky whore?"

"I didn't!" Flint protested, trying to embrace Kallista. "Think about it for a minute. We were together that afternoon from two o'clock to nearly four thirty."

"Oh, yeah." Kallista giggled. "How could I have forgotten that? First we did it in the RV, then around three or so we went and got some food from Mickey D's and brought it to your cabin at the motor court."

"Exactly." Flint took Kallista in his arms.

"Remember how cute you looked with the pickle slice bra and hamburger bun bikini?"

Ew! Skye suppressed a groan.

"So how come they said your baby makers were inside that slut?" Kallista demanded.

"I have no idea." Flint kissed her. "The only thing my love juice has been inside lately is a rubber."

An idea skittered through Skye's mind, but she needed to think about it. Was what she was considering even possible?

"So you'll tell the cops we were together?" Flint asked, nibbling Kallista's neck.

"I guess I have to." Kallista hugged him.

"Are you afraid of Rex?"

"I don't think so."

Skye could see the calculating look on the woman's face even though Flint couldn't.

"I'm sorry you won't be able to get as much of his money as we originally thought." Flint wrinkled his brow.

"Oh." Kallista's expression conveyed satisfaction. "I think I'll do all right."

After another minute or so, Skye stepped back into the interrogation room. "Sorry, guys. We need to wrap this up."

While Skye escorted Kallista back to Wally's office, she asked the other woman, "Did Flint flush the condom he used last Monday afternoon at the RV?"

304

"You eavesdropped on us?" Kallista's tone was outraged. "That's not fair!"

"I don't enjoy intruding in your personal life," Skye said, hoping to soothe the other woman's indignation. She was used to teenagers who thought everything done to them was unfair. "But this is important. You want Flint to go free, don't you?"

"Yes, but when I say he was with me, that will do it."

"Not with the DNA evidence hanging over his head," Skye reminded her. "So, about that condom?"

Kallista was silent, a pout marring her beautiful face.

"I'm ready to help," Skye said. "Are you ready to be smart?"

"He didn't flush it," Kallista muttered. "The plumbing in the Airstream can't take stuff like that. He usually just wraps them in toilet paper and tosses them in the trash."

"Does Rex know how to drive a steamroller?"

"*Uh-huh.*" Kallista nodded. "He worked construction during the summers when he was in college."

"I wonder why the police didn't find that out when they did the background check."

"He was paid off the books."

"Oh. Okay." Skye stopped halfway up the stairs. "Wait. One more question. What do you have on your husband? Why will you still get money from him even after admitting your affair with Flint?"

"That's two questions."

"Look, I can help Flint or not." Skye raised an eyebrow. "Your call."

"Fine." Kallista tossed back her hair. "Last Monday afternoon, when I got back to the RV, I noticed the bathroom was a mess, with garbage from the wastebasket scattered all over the floor."

"And?"

"And I was cleaning it up when Rex got home. He didn't realize I was there because the bathroom door was shut nearly all the way, but I saw him change clothes from the skin out and bundle what he'd been wearing in a paper grocery sack—we like to recycle, so we don't use the plastic ones." Kallista twisted her glossy lips into a thoughtful frown. "Him putting his clothes in the bag seemed weird to me, so I followed him, and I saw him toss the sack into the Dumpster by the bandstand."

"Damn!" Skye swore. "I bet that trash was picked up already and the bag is long gone."

"Nope." Kallista's smile was triumphant. "I took it out after he left and hid it in the trunk of my car for safe keeping."

"That was smart." Skye guessed that Kallista's motive was leverage when she sued for divorce. The blonde probably figured she'd get more from Rex through blackmail than if she did the right thing and turned the evidence over to the police. And she'd made no secret of her hatred for Suzette, so she wouldn't care if Suzette's killer was ever brought to justice.

"I only pretend to be dumb so guys will like me," Kallista confided.

Skye cringed at the idea that women still thought they had to hide their intelligence to be popular with men, but she didn't comment. Instead she asked, "Did you look inside the bag?"

"Yep. His clothes were covered in blood."

After requesting that the dispatcher keep an eye on Kallista, Skye asked Wally to step out of his office and filled him in on what Kallista had revealed.

"Didn't she realize she could be arrested if she withheld evidence in a murder investigation?" Wally fumed.

"I don't think it even occurred to her." Skye shrugged. "Is Kallista in trouble?"

"No." Wally sighed. "If she testifies against Taylor, she won't be charged."

"Anyway," Skye said, "I think after Rex killed Suzette, but before he ran the steamroller over her, he went back to the RV, retrieved the used condom from the trash can, and somehow inserted the semen into Suzette."

"And he did that because he didn't know it was Flint's semen." Understanding dawned in Wally's eyes. "He would never have implicated his star attraction. He thought Kallista was sleeping with one of the musicians."

"Exactly."

"But why did he kill Suzette?" Wally asked.

"My guess is she rejected him one too many times," Skye answered. "And remember, Rod told me that Suzette was getting worried because Rex had started to say he loved her."

"Hmm." Wally nodded. "I see."

"If there's one thing I've learned," Skye explained, "under everyone's hard shell is someone who wants to be loved. Obviously, Kallista and Rex didn't have that kind of marriage; maybe he thought he could have it with Suzette. And when she rejected not only his sexual advances, but also his love, he couldn't stand it."

When Wally arrested Rex an hour later, he protested long and loud, but when the paper bag full of his bloody clothes was produced, he snapped his mouth shut so hard Skye thought she heard a tooth crack.

After a moment, Rex said, "It was an accident."

Skye shot Wally a look. Where had they heard that before?

"I was just trying to kiss her. She jerked away, tripped, and struck the back of her head on the corner of the desk. It must have hit just right, because by the time I got back with the first aid kit she was already dead."

"Why didn't you call the police?" Wally asked.

"A scandal like that would ruin me and the music theater." Rex looked at Wally as if he were crazy. "Country music fans want wholesome entertainment."

"So steamrolling her body was better?" Skye blurted out.

"I gambled they'd get over that faster than me killing my assistant while trying to fu—make love to her," Rex explained. "And I figured the steamroller was the only way I could make sure that no trace of me on her body would be discovered."

"Why go to all the trouble with the semen?" Wally asked.

"I figured it was a twofer." Rex shrugged. "I'd seen the used rubbers in the garbage on other occasions, and I thought, what the heck, if there's one there today, I can use the stuff inside to implicate my wife's lover and point any interest away from me." He glowered. "I didn't realize my dumb bunny of a wife was getting it on with my star. I thought she was shacking up with some nobody from the band."

"That was your fatal mistake." Skye stared Rex in the eye. "Never underestimate a woman."

Epilogue

"I Hope You Dance"

"Any idea why we've been summoned?" Wally asked as Skye turned her Bel Air into the crowded parking lot of an empty building near the Better Than New used-car lot and the Tales and Treats Bookstore.

"Nope." Skye shut off the motor. "Aunt Olive asked us to come and said she'd explain when we got here." She gazed up and down the dark street, thinking how the town would have changed if Rex Taylor had had his way.

It was a month since Rex had been arrested for the murder of Suzette Neal, and Scumble Riverites were still reeling from the news. Some of the citizens were happy that their community would remain as it was, but others mourned the loss of the music theater project and the revenue it would have generated.

With Rex in jail awaiting trial, Kallista and the rest of the Country Roads staff had left the area without a backward glance. Other than the big FOR SALE sign on the Hutton dairy property, there were no indications that Rex or his crew had ever planned to turn Scumble River into the Branson of Illinois.

Kallista had immediately begun divorce proceedings, and was back in Nashville building a mansion modeled after Tara. Rumor had it that her and Flint's duet album was scheduled for release next summer.

Wally broke into Skye's thoughts. "It seems out of character for Olive to take this kind of initiative." His expression was quizzical. "In my experience, directives come from Dante, not his wife."

"Mine, too." Skye got out of the car. "Which is exactly why I said we'd be here. Something's up."

"Then let's go see what it is." Wally tucked her hand into the crook of his arm.

The door to the building was open, and Skye and Wally walked inside. The foyer was dark, but lights and conversation to their left beckoned them.

"This is a little creepy," Skye said, tugging on Wally's sleeve. "Do you think Aunt Olive might still be afraid we'll tell Dante about her affair? Is she setting a trap to get rid of us?"

"Not with a room full of witnesses."

"Maybe the voices are recorded and the vehicles in the lot are from Hugo's used-car dealership."

"I'll protect you." Wally steered Skye toward the brightness. "We made it out of Doozierville alive—I'm sure we can handle your sixty-three-year-old aunt."

"We *barely* made it out alive," Skye reminded

him. "And you weren't the one who ended up painted as orange as an Oompa-Loompa." She reluctantly allowed herself to be led forward.

When they turned the corner, the area they entered was one big space with polished wood floors and mirrored walls. A long table holding plates of snacks and an assortment of drinks was set off to one side. Soft music came from a CD player, and people in groups of three or four stood around talking softly.

Skye scanned the crowd, spotting her parents chatting with the Leofanti aunts and their spouses. Another cluster contained her Leofanti cousins and their families. A third group contained Trixie and Owen. Skye was relieved to see that the couple must have patched up their differences, because Owen had his arm around his wife's waist and Trixie was smiling up at him with love shining from her eyes.

Among the nonrelatives, two guests caught Skye's eye—Simon and Jess from the Brown Bag. The men appeared deep in conversation, and Skye wondered what Suzette's twin was discussing so earnestly with Simon.

Her curiosity was satisfied when she overheard Jess saying, "I intend to be at Rex Taylor's trial every day, and once he's found guilty, I'm asking the prosecutor to let me speak before the court, during the time family members are allowed to address the judge."

Simon murmured something Skye didn't catch; then Jess continued, "I'm planning a trip to California and Nashville to find out more about Suzette and my biological family."

Skye and Wally joined a group of business owners, but when the others began discussing how disappointed they were that Branson of Illinois wasn't coming to Scumble River, Skye subtly pulled Wally away and asked, "Do you see Olive or Dante?"

"No." Wally examined the assemblage. "That's odd. The mayor usually makes sure he's the center of attention."

Skye frowned. Where were the party's hostess and her husband?

As she opened her mouth to make another comment about her aunt's absence, she heard a querulous male voice. "Why the hell are we here?" There was an indistinct murmur; then the same voice complained, "What's gotten into you, woman? You're not going through that mental pause again, are you?"

Dante waddled through the arch leading into the party room, followed closely by Olive, who was wearing a purple velvet cape that covered her from her neck to her feet. Once they appeared, everyone swarmed toward them.

Skye blinked in surprise as Olive spoke over her husband. "Thank you all for coming on such short notice. I guess it's a good thing there's not much to do in Scumble River on a Tuesday night."

Several people chuckled and Olive continued, "I'll explain everything in a few minutes. In the meantime, please help yourself to the refreshments."

Dante made a grab for her arm, but Olive eluded him, walked toward a door at the rear of the room, and disappeared.

Once everyone had a beverage and a plate of munchies, conversations continued and Skye said to Wally, "So, how did it go with Darleen today?"

"About as you'd expect." He shrugged. "She was happy her boyfriend took a plea deal so she didn't have to testify against him, but she still claims she doesn't need to be in rehab and begged me to change my mind."

"But you didn't?" Skye's green eyes were sympathetic.

"No." Wally's jaw firmed. "I told her if she didn't complete the program, you would press charges."

"Good." Skye paused, then asked, "Did she give you the truthful annulment letter, or is she still threatening to write a fictional account that would hold up the process?"

"She gave me the honest version, but only after trying to wheedle money from me for it." Wally put an arm around Skye. "I dropped the envelope off at the church, and Father Burns said that by spring he'd be able to give us an idea of the timeline."

"And once we get that, I can start planning our wedding."

"What in blue blazes are you wearing?" Dante's bellow interrupted Wally and Skye's kiss, and she looked in the direction of her uncle's ire. Olive had removed her cape to reveal a leotard and wrap skirt. She'd replaced her boots with ballet slippers. She pirouetted gracefully into the center of the floor and curtsied with a sweep of her arm.

After a brief hesitation, the guests applauded, although most looked bewildered.

Olive brought her hands together at chest level, then said, "Welcome to the Scumble River School of Adult Dance. I will be teaching the joy of ballet and my partner will be teaching the pleasure of modern dance. She is sorry she can't be with us tonight, but she will be here when we open our doors January second."

Everyone crowded around Olive, asking questions and congratulating her, but Dante roared, "Wait just a cotton-pickin' minute! I didn't say you could open a dance school. Of all the dadgum fool ideas of yours, this takes the cake."

Olive's face paled, but she straightened her spine and said, "I don't need your permission, Dante, and this isn't a stupid idea. None of my ideas, which you refuse to listen to, are stupid."

Silence ensued as the guests watched the couple.

"You need my say-so to spend my money." Dante's face was stained with an ugly flush.

315

"I didn't use your money." She paused and took a gulp of wine from the glass someone had handed her. This moment was clearly a difficult one for her. "I used the money my mother left me."

"But . . . but . . ." Dante sputtered. "We agreed that would go for a new combine."

"I never agreed." Olive held her ground. "In recent days I've realized that although life isn't always tied with a bow, it's still always a gift."

"But you're my wife," Dante protested. "You promised to love, honor, and obey."

"Well, from now on all you're getting is two out of three." Olive's gaze was unbending and rebellious. "Take it or leave it."

At Dante's look of astounded disbelief, Skye buried her head in Wally's shoulders and shook with laughter. When she glanced up, her uncle was gone. She switched her gaze to Olive, who seemed unfazed by her husband's departure. She was flitting from group to group, talking excitedly.

People stayed for hours, drinking, eating, and socializing, and when Skye whispered to Wally that she needed to find the bathroom, no one else seemed to notice. However, when she emerged from the ladies' room, Simon was waiting for her in the tiny hallway.

"Hi." He pushed off from the wall he'd been leaning against. "Got a minute?"

"Of course," Skye answered cautiously. He'd

made no more outrageous attempts to win her back, but she still wasn't sure that Simon had accepted the fact that she was marrying Wally.

"I just spoke to Jess Larson and he's allergic to his sister's dog, so if it's okay with you, I'd like to adopt Toby."

"That would be wonderful." Skye would miss the little white pup, but it would be better for all concerned if Simon took him. "I'm just not home enough to care for him. When I drop him off tomorrow morning, I'll bring all his things with me."

"Good." Simon started to walk away, but turned and said, "I wish we were adopting Toby together. I still miss you every day, Skye. There are times I'm sorry we ever met."

"Please, don't be." Skye swallowed a lump in her throat. "I can't remember who said it, but I think it's true that we should never cry because something is over. Instead we should smile because it happened."

As Skye and Wally drove home later that night, she told him about Simon adopting the dog; then she said, "You never did tell me why you were so against my keeping Toby."

Wally didn't answer right away. Eventually he said, "When I was thirteen, I begged my dad for a dog and he bought me a collie I named Rags."

"Oh?" Skye was afraid of where this was going.

"The next year I made the high school football team and I had to spend a lot of time practicing and doing homework. Dad told me I was neglecting Rags, but I didn't listen. One day I came home and Rags was gone. I thought he'd run away, but my dad had given him to one of his employees' sons. He said a dog had the right to an owner who spent time and attention on him."

"I see." Skye wanted to hate Wally's father for taking away his dog, but it was hard to fault the man for making sure that an animal he was responsible for was treated well. "I'm sorry you had to go through that."

"Me, too." Wally crossed his arms. "But it was a lesson well learned."

They sat silently for a few minutes; then Skye said, "I still feel so bad for Suzette. I can't get her out of my mind. She never got to know what really happened to her mother or to meet her brother or to be a star."

"That's the worse thing about murder," Wally agreed. "The victims never get a chance to reach their full potential."

"Exactly." Skye chewed her lip.

"Suzette *did* get to sing at the concert." Wally stroked Skye's cheek.

"That's true." Skye brightened. "So many people go to their graves with the music still inside them. At least Suzette got to let hers out."